Restoration's Journey

An Unseen Dominion Novel
by
Robert Roush

Hearts of Compassion Publishing

Holland, Michigan

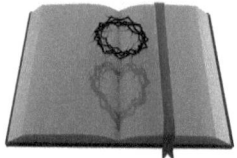

Stories for Compassion is a program that directs net proceeds from book sales to fulfilling Jesus' call in Matthew 25:40 to provide clean water, food, clothing, and compassion to those who are in need.

This program provides a win-win opportunity: God-honoring stories for readers to enjoy and be challenged in their walk with God, all while investing in the welfare of children around the globe.

Special thanks to the many teachers, professors, and instructors throughout the years who shaped my skills and passion for science, writing, theology, and most importantly, my love for the Creator and the true source of creativity.

PROLOGUE

Saturday, May 9, 2020

Ophois released a blood-thirsty howl and leapt from the roof of the building. His ears rang from the crack of the rifle. He longed for the days of chariots and swords, instead of Humvees and armor-piercing ammunition.

He darted down the side of the castle-like building, known as CeSiR Tech.

"You best hurry," Mael said. "Your prey shall soon be floating down the river."

Ophois ignored the jab, or at least he tried to.

As the ground approached, he crouched into the power of his hind legs and sprang from the white-stone wall. His front claws sliced through the rain-soaked grass and propelled him onward.

Above him, Mael bellowed something about a battle. Losing battles held little attraction for Ophois. How many times had he battled the heavenly host? Too many to remember and too many scars not to realize a head-on attack seldom brought anything but pain. Better to hide in the shadows, and then strike with bitter ferocity.

"Prepare for war!" Mael's proclamation thundered from atop the building. "Soon the banks of the Lamine will run red with the blood of humans, and the sky will turn dark with shreds of the heavenly host."

Unlikely, yet the blood on the banks of the Lamine—that he intended to bring to pass.

As powerful paws drew him forward ever faster, he caught the scent of his prey.

Fear, and blood.

Unlike so many of his fellow demons, Ophois savored taking physical form. The thrill of his senses. The feel of flesh tearing between his claws.

Soon, very soon.

A dense unseasonable fog rolled past the river's edge and into the lawn. As much as he despised the heavenly interference, the fog proved a gift. How unfortunate it would have been, to have lost his prey to a sniper's bullet. Now, the hunt was on.

Moments later the fog enveloped him. The scent of the old man's blood grew strong—fast.

Too fast.

He dropped to his hind quarters and extended his front legs. At first his razor sharp nails slid through the damp soil.

Just before reaching the river, his grip found a layer of rock. His forelegs jerked to a stop. His body did not. He flipped over his front paws and landed on his back. A whimper escaped his throat. Hundreds of demons echoing Mael's war cry overshadowed his pathetic expression.

It was close. He nearly charged right into the river. The surging storm-fed currents of water. Nothing in the physical realm posed a threat. But he despised water.

A river—there had to be a river.

He rose to his hind legs and attempted to peer through the fog. The smell of death hid any scent of the girl.

The last they saw from the top of the building was the bullet ripping through the old man and the inflatable raft. With the recent rains, the current would surely have swept Ophois' prey down the river—if not sucking her under.

With luck, she would survive the currents and the rocks downstream. Many months had passed since he last had a good hunt.

~~~~~~~~~~

"You need to get up child," Eitan said. He set his silver shield against a tree and approached the girl.

Plastered against her head, the young girl's blond hair looked almost auburn. Shivers roiled through her body.

Only a hundred yards away sat the River of Life Church. A short walk to safety. Yet he sensed the Spirit had other plans for this helpless lamb.

Determination kindled within her bright blue eyes. She climbed to her feet and picked up two backpacks.

He longed to accompany her on this journey. So young, so innocent. A lump rose within Eitan's throat. How much would she have to learn in the next months, perhaps even hours?

The two backpacks dwarfed her small frame. Yet she threw one on each shoulder.

From across the river, another howl pierced the humid air. The enemy was restless.

The girl took a few steps away from the river, barely able to walk under the weight. Not of the backpacks, but of a heavy heart.

She stumbled when her foot caught a tree root.

Eitan shot to her side, grabbed her elbow, and she stabilized.

She paused and glanced from side to side.

Such awareness would serve her well.

When she started north along the river, Eitan turned and retrieved his shield. War was coming to Arrow Springs and he was needed.

But if the girl were to survive, she would need someone to go with her.

~~~~~~~~~~

CHAPTER ONE

Saturday, May 9, 2020

Despite the cold wind blowing across her river-dampened clothes, Ima felt a warmth permeate her left arm. It reminded her of sitting next to the heat register, alone in her room at CeSiR.

Alone.

She knew what it was like to be alone. She had no friends, except Uncle M.

Was he dead?

Why would someone at CeSiR shoot him? He was CeSiR Tech. He founded the company. He'd told her so.

It had to be Maiya's doing. The cold-hearted woman always sought to keep Ima away from Uncle M. He said they needed to leave. To get away from CeSiR—from Maiya. He said he would save her from them.

Now, he'd been shot.

It was Ima's fault. Realization of the truth chased away the last vestige of warmth she had felt. They'd shot Uncle M because of her. Cold tears streaked down her cheeks.

No matter what happens to me, ya must flee. The words had gurgled out of Uncle M's labored breaths. Her heart wouldn't accept it, but her mind knew the truth—her friend was gone. *Cross the river*, he'd said, before he disappeared into the water.

She'd barely made it across. The deflating raft had plunged her into the water. The raging currents pulled her downstream until somehow the raft seemed to defy the water and floated upstream, like an invisible hand had pulled her to shore.

Follow the tracks west. Uncle M's sputtering words bobbed through her mind.

The tracks.

Which way were the tracks? She had never left CeSiR. But she had seen them. Railroad tracks ran away from Arrow Springs to the north. Which way was north? She closed her eyes. Remember. Where had she seen the tracks?

From his office. Uncle M's office at the top of the building overlooked the river.

Her mind drifted back to her discussion with him, only days earlier. She'd stared out his large window, as she sipped on one of the few sodas she'd ever been permitted to drink. The view out the window had not included train tracks, only green grass, lush trees, and the river. But she remembered the tracks.

Yes. Months earlier she had visited his office. The trees had no leaves that time. Uncle M brought her to his office saying something about a white Christmas. He laughed and swirled her around in his arms. Seldom did she see such joy in his face. As he pointed to the white-powdered lawn, she could see the tracks through the trees.

Which way?

She stood on the other side of the river now, staring into the fog. The tracks were north of the river. Right. She needed to follow the river to the right.

She turned and began jogging under the weight of the two water-sogged backpacks. Through the fog, a warm glow reached out to her from a window.

Speak to no one. Trust no one. They were Uncle M's last pain-filled words.

This time warm tears crept down her cheeks.

She began to run. Away from CeSiR. Away from the window with the light, from which someone might see her. Away from everyone and everything she'd ever known.

Once again, she was alone.

~~~~~~~~~~

Ophois followed the scent of blood along the bank of the river to his right. The fog made it impossible to see the body. His only option was to assume the girl would stick with the body of her beloved doctor.

The scent of death slowed its movement downstream. With the direction of the currents they had to be closer to this bank than the other. Though the river didn't run deep, it had a significant breadth. Any moment she would step from the river.

Saliva dripped from green fangs, as he thought about slicing the girl to shreds. Ever since Mael introduced him to her, she had refused to submit to his control. The other demons called him a coward. They suggested it was because her body was made of water.

Ridiculous.

In his homeland he had acquired great respect and even the worship of the locals. They thought he was a god. He gave great power to those who followed him. They painted images of him—even on their crypts.

Now he was reduced to chasing a measly child like some kind of rabbit. Cursed Creator and that bumbling traitor Moses. Even the wind-swirled fog reminded Ophois of the tempestuous currents of the crashing walls of water in the Red Sea. The fog was God's attempt to protect the girl. More interference with *His* creations. The thought rekindled Ophois' desire to rip the rag doll to shreds.

He let out another howl.

Water sloshed no more than ten feet from where he stood. He swept his teeth with his tongue. He could leave physical form and float out over the water to have his prey. Even the thought of hovering above the flowing water brought flashes of his past defeats.

Always water!

No, he could wait. If she drowned in the river, he would be disappointed, but the end would still be accomplished. Though, he would prefer to torment her before killing her.

The scent of death began to move once again, down the river. Perhaps she would try to get the body all the way to town before coming ashore. That made no sense. To his knowledge, the girl had never been allowed to leave CeSiR Tech. Mael was intent on using her as a surrogate. After dealing with her insolence for the past few days, Ophois understood this desire. But that was not his style. Fear, torment, and death were more to his liking.

He followed the movement to an old bridge embankment. Once again something sloshed in the water. He climbed onto the embankment and prepared to attack, as soon as the girl emerged.

~~~~~~~~~~~

Ima dodged trees, as she ran along the river's edge. Her labored breathing accompanied strange noises in the fog. Low guttural croaks taunted her. Overhead, some kind of insect buzzed its displeasure at her presence. At least she assumed it came from an insect. Though the rain had stopped, someone forgot to tell the trees. Giant droplets of water splattered off her nose blending with equal sized tears.

To her left something moved in the rotting leaves from the previous year's fall. She didn't wait to see if it was a friend or foe.

Who was she kidding?

There were no friends, only foes.

Never friends.

Growing up at CeSiR, each childhood friend turned on her. Accused her of being different. Broken. An outcast.

Her feet sloshed against wet leaves and mud. Veiled silhouettes writhed in the dusky fog. She left CeSiR sometime after five o'clock. It shouldn't be this dark. Clouds, tree cover, and dense fog limited her vision to no more than a few feet.

Ignoring the weight of the backpacks, she picked up speed. She had to flee. But from what? In a sense, she fled from everything, at least all she knew.

She sidestepped a tree.

Wham!

Another tree awaited her just past the first.

Face first, she plowed into the rough bark and bounced to the ground.

Pain pierced her forehead. She was no stranger to pain—physical or emotional. She wiped a hand across her face. The large raindrops had turned red. She wiped her hand on her blouse and then checked her forehead. Less blood than before. Apparently, it wasn't as bad as it felt.

She struggled to her feet and breathed a sigh of relief. At least nothing was broken.

Her right shoulder felt lighter.

Where was Uncle M's backpack?

She searched the ground and found the pack on the other side of the tree, which had her face engraved in it. She walked to the pack and slung it over her shoulder. It fell back to the ground. Again, she picked up the pack.

Great.

The strap had broken. No wonder the pack landed past the tree. She set her own pack on the ground and put Uncle M's on her left shoulder. Then she hefted her own pack to her right shoulder. Shaking off the stiffness in her neck, she began to jog. Once again she followed the edge of the river.

Pain, despair, loss, and fear fought for control of her mind. She couldn't let herself go there, at least not yet. She needed to get as far away from whatever pursued her as possible.

Up ahead the river turned. If her memory of the view from CeSiR served her, she was nearing the railroad tracks.

~~~~~~~~~~~

At the turn of the river, Ophois sat crouched, ready to spring at the movement on the river's edge. Water splashed higher and higher against the banks of the river. The rains were swelling the river.

Then he saw it.

A body.

Not the girl, but the doctor. Surely the girl would not be far behind.

The water spit the man's body onto the gravel of the riverbank. It lay face down. Though the girl could not see Ophois, unless he so chose, she always seemed to sense his presence. So he waited. Waited on his perch overlooking the body. The girl would soon emerge.

~~~~~~~~~~~

The trees around Ima swayed in the dusky fog—monsters waiting to reach down and grab her as she ran past. Silence surrounded her. No, not silence. She still heard the buzzing above her and the occasional croak. But something had changed.

She slowed to a stop. What was it?

The water. She no longer heard the rushing of the water. She hadn't changed direction. The river had. She expected the bend in the river to come gradually. She turned in circles. Which way was which? Had she run past the tracks? She'd never seen a railroad up close, at least not in real life. But she loved to read. Surely something referred to as an iron-horse needed a more substantial path to drive on than the roads for cars.

She bent down to the ground to see if she could tell which direction her footprints came from. All she saw were leaves and grass. Hopelessness invaded her mind. How could she possibly get away? She couldn't even find the railroad tracks. She'd already failed Uncle M's dying instructions.

She fought to listen, to hear the river. As her breathing slowed, the faint sound of water returned. But which way? It seemed to come from everywhere. The trees reflected the sound all around her. She wanted to collapse, to give up.

Small beams of sunlight drilled into the fog, but she still couldn't see the river.

Gradually, her eyes adjusted to the brighter lighting. Once more, she turned in a complete circle. She stopped. There. A brighter patch of light shone through the fog. If breaks in the trees let small streams of light through, it made sense that the river would be more illuminated.

She walked toward the brightness.

No river.

Instead, she saw four straight dark lines on the ground. The lines disappeared into the fog in both directions. She walked up to the tracks. A giggle rose to her throat. How would she have run past these? She reached down and touched the cold rounded steel. She'd found the tracks. Uncle M would have been so proud.

She missed him already.

She turned left and began to walk between the first two tracks. She walked in relief for a few minutes. But the tracks weren't her destination. They were the beginning of her journey.

Where would she go? How long could she follow the tracks? Her accomplishment felt so short lived.

She began to jog, but nearly tripped on the wood slats that separated the metal rails. She jumped to her right, between the sets of rails. The gravel proved much easier terrain.

Ima jogged for what seemed like half the day, though she knew it was probably less than an hour.

The fog had thinned as she continued, though to her left, where she assumed the river ran, a cloud seemed to hug the ground.

The angst within her began to ebb. But as it withdrew, her legs began to scream at her. How long could she keep this up? Ahead, a small grass clearing sat beside the tracks. Surely she could rest for a few minutes. She couldn't continue to carry two backpacks. She needed to consolidate them.

~~~~~~~~~~~

Eitan stood in the yard at Marilyn's house, as her white sedan pulled into the drive. The corners of his lips pulled up at the sight of two mighty warriors crammed into the back seat of the car. Alex and Adiya both wore huge smiles as they exited the car.

"My, you look joyous," Eitan said. "I take it the discussion between Sarah and Marilyn proved productive?"

"Years of broken relationships being restored," Alex said, "with both God and man."

"Very good," Eitan said.

Adiya approached and knelt on one knee. "Captain Eitan, it is always good to see you, sir. Though from your look, your experience this evening has brought more pain than restoration."

"Ever perceptive, Adiya. That is precisely why I have come." He went on to tell them of the events by the river and who he feared tracked the girl.

"Ophois can be ruthless," Adiya said. "She needs someone to protect her."

"I fear this assignment will require diligent attention to the Spirit's guidance. I believe this child holds great significance. And yet she is coming of age and will need to make her own decisions." Eitan put his hand on Adiya's shoulder. "This will not be an easy assignment. I know not when you will again receive the Spirit's regeneration. Protect her life, but beyond that, remain unnoticed."

"Understood." Adiya rose and turned to Alex. "Take care of Marilyn, my friend. She is finally finding the strength of forgiveness."

Alex embraced Adiya. "I will, my friend. Go in the strength and peace of God."

~~~~~~~~~~

Ima set the two backpacks in the grass. Already the sun worked to dry the grass. She stared for a couple minutes at the backpacks Uncle M had packed. This was supposed to be a joyous occasion. He'd said they were going out for the evening. Then the car wouldn't start. If only the car had started, perhaps he'd still be alive. Why did he insist on using the raft? What had he said?

His words ground into her mind. *Ima ya hafta trust me! We've gotta leave this place. It's no longer safe here—for me, and more importantly for you. Do ya trust me?*

She had.

And it got him killed.

She got him killed.

She unfastened her backpack and flipped it open. He'd packed them both, but somehow going through his seemed disrespectful. As she pulled open the largest compartment, she wept. It contained clothes. The prettiest things she'd ever seen.

At the facility everyone wore the same thing, at least as children. Dark-blue cotton pants and white tops. One time, she'd asked one of the nurses about having something more colorful. The nurse scolded her for her pride. "Do you think you are something special? What is good enough for everyone else is not good enough for you?"

Ima pulled bright red, green, and blue tops out of the backpack. Some even had flowers on them. Seven total. She had enough tops to wear a different one each day for a whole week. Excitement wrestled with her recent loss for control of her body. Her legs wiggled. She pulled out two pair of blue jeans and a pair of tan slacks. She carefully set the clothes on top of Uncle M's backpack so they wouldn't get dirty or stained by the grass. In the bottom of the compartment, she saw the necessary undergarments to go with a week's worth of outfits. Uncle M had intended more than an evening out.

The front compartment of the backpack proved much less exciting. Toothbrush, toothpaste, soap, and something called antiperspirant. At least they all smelled pretty.

She carefully put the clothes back in her pack. No one was as nice as Uncle M. She lifted her gaze to the trees that surrounded her small place of solace. Leaves rustled in the wind. A hypnotic lullaby. Warmth from the sun called her to lay back in the grass and give in to her fatigue.

No. The danger lurked too close.

She had to press on.

She shook her head and looked at uncle M's pack. Should she just leave it? She couldn't bring herself to open it. It didn't belong to her.

She stood and picked up her pack. She had all the clothes she would need. As she reached the tracks, her stomach let out a loud growl. They hadn't eaten. That is where they were headed. She looked back at the large backpack, still sitting in the opening.

Had he packed anything to eat? If she left his pack there with food in it, an animal would rip it to shreds. She couldn't let that happen.

She walked back to his pack and sat down. She unzipped the front pouch. More toiletries. His bag had more compartments than hers, including a zipper inside the front pouch. She unzipped it and a wad of money pushed the compartment open.

She knew about money from her classes at CeSiR. She'd never had a need for it, so she had no clue whether this was a lot or a little. She grabbed what was there and stuffed it into her front pouch. Money would be good for food at some point, but she was hungry now.

She unzipped the main compartment of his bag and stopped cold. She buried her face in her hands.

~~~~~~~~~~

The doctor's body had lain on the rocky riverbank for at least half an hour. The water's edge retreated a few feet from the body, leaving bloody trails in the gravel. Ophois remained perched, waiting for any sign of the girl.

The fog hung over the river, but he sensed he had made a dire mistake, unless the girl had drowned in the torrent of water. A fitting end for the obstinate mim. CeSiR's other creations were so easy to control. Mael told him that this one would be a challenge, and Ophois savored the opportunity. Hopefully, she had not drowned in the river. That would be quite disappointing.

He approached the body of Doctor M'Gregor. It lay face down in the river stone. He sniffed the body and found only a trace of the girl's scent. The raft was missing. Had she floated down stream? Could she have plugged the hole quick enough to keep it from sinking? Doubtful.

He had lost her. At least for the moment.

He looked at the bridge a quarter mile downstream. Had she made it to town?

Wait.

He could see the bridge. How fortunate. The fog was thinning. With keen sight and an even better sense of smell, he would find her.

He rose to his hind feet and unfurled his black wings. Now that he could see across the river, the search would progress quicker from the air. He followed the river downstream. In a little over an hour, she could not be far. If his search downstream proved unproductive, he would circle back and hunt upstream.

~~~~~~~~~~~

Ima sat frozen. She stared at an envelope in Uncle M's backpack. *Happy Birthday, Ima!*

It was supposed to be a day of celebration. Her first trip outside CeSiR, for her twelfth birthday. She cautiously reached toward the envelope, as if expecting it to bite her, or maybe disappear. She'd never received a birthday card. She picked up the envelope and examined it. The flap was sealed with some kind of glue. There was a slight opening in the corner. She slid her shaking finger into the slit and carefully separated the flap from the rest of the envelope. About half way through, it did bite her. Just a paper cut. She grabbed the flap with one hand and the rest of the envelope with the other and pulled.

The card fell into her lap.

She picked up the card. An animated squirrel smiled at her under the words, *It's Your Birthday.* She had watched squirrels playing in the yard at CeSiR.

She opened the card.

18

The inside had the same squirrel pointing at her. *Go Nuts!*

She giggled and then drew in a quivering breath.

She closed the card and slid it back into the envelope. She stuffed the card into her backpack.

She returned to Uncle M's backpack and found water bottles and a bag full of peanuts, raisins, chocolate chips, pretzels, and almonds. She stuffed some other snacks into her bag along with a couple bottles of water. She kept out the mix and one bottle of water for the walk. She looked through his clothes, but didn't have any room in her bag. She did decide to keep a sweater that might prove useful if she got cold.

One item remained in the bottom of his pack—a box with shiny paper wrapped around it. A present? She pulled off the paper and stared at a white dress with blue flowers and a cute pair of white shoes. Sobs racked her chest. She'd never had anything so beautiful. She removed the sweater and pressed these last two items into her pack. Hopefully, the zipper would hold.

She quickly stuffed the rest of the items, including the sweater, back into Uncle M's backpack. She tossed it into the brush, so no one would find it.

Once again, she started down the tracks. Joy and sorrow swirled through her at the thoughtfulness of her now deceased friend.

Her only friend.

~~~~~~~~~~

Adiya sat in the clearing north of the river and watched as the young girl started her journey down the railroad tracks. According to the birthday card from Doctor M'Gregor, the girl's name was Ima. Such a sweet name, and such a vulnerable child.

Where could she possibly hope to run?

Eitan appeared correct in his assessment that whoever tracked her from the enemy camp headed downstream. Of course, Adiya could probably count on one hand the number of times the captain had been incorrect. This would give them a head start, but a head start to where. If Ophois tracked the girl, it would not matter how much of a lead she possessed. He would find her.

After glancing around the clearing to ensure there were no prying eyes, Adiya walked to the large backpack, which Ima had thrown into the brush. Perhaps it held some insight to the precarious predicament in which this child found herself.

Ima had pulled several items from the bag, but Adiya noticed a side pouch that Ima never checked. Opening the zipper, it became clear that Ima's flight down the railroad was an improvisation.

Two airline tickets stared out from the zippered pouch. Adiya removed the first ticket—Ima Fredericks. The second ticket was the doctor's. The original plan had been to fly to LAX in Los Angeles. Was the girl trying to make her way to Los Angeles on foot? It would take her weeks. She would never survive that long, whether Ophois found her or not.

Whatever her plans, Adiya needed to give her more time. Time to create more distance between her and Ophois.

Perhaps the ticket could help. Adiya left Ima's ticket in the bag, but pulled out the doctor's.

If someone found the backpack they would know she had come this way. There was no time to walk the pack somewhere else. And though angels could fly unseen in the physical realm, a flying backpack might raise suspicion. Instead, Adiya grabbed two large rocks from the railway and stuffed them into the pack. The center of the river would do nicely.

The bag sank toward the bottom, as large bubbles of air floated to the surface. Even if someone found the pack, they might assume Ima had crossed back to the other side of the river, instead of following the tracks.

Now for the ticket.

Adiya flew between buildings across the north side of town, careful to stay out of sight of the enemy. This plan would only work if unseen. At the east edge of town, Adiya spotted Ophois flying along the eastern bank of the river.

Time was short.

Adiya turned toward the tracks and managed to stay out of sight for a few more minutes. Near the bend where the river turned east, another grass clearing came into view. Adiya quickly patted down the grass and set the doctor's ticket in a strategic spot on the downwind edge of the clearing.

Now to test the astuteness of the demon tracking Ima.

~~~~~~~~~~~

CHAPTER TWO

For the last twenty minutes, Ima could see the structure looming up ahead. Now in the dim of twilight, it towered overhead, taunting her to enter. The surface of the river before her ran calm, almost glassy. If only it were glass, then she could slide down the hill and walk across its surface. A surface that bore the deep gray shadow of the structure some thirty feet above it.

She returned to the center of the tracks. The steel skeleton before her groaned in expectation.

As far as she could see, there were no other options. But was this really an option?

Twenty yards before the massive bridge, the tracks merged into a single pair. No walking on the more stable gravel here. She could walk between the two rails and hope not to stumble on the wood slats, or she could walk beside the tracks, with nothing but sixteen inches of slats between the metal track and a straight-down thirty-foot drop to the river below.

She stood and stared.

Unless her fear deceived her, the slats became harder to see by the minute. Twilight would soon fade to blackness.

The sky contained no moon. She didn't even know if there would be one. She'd read about solar eclipses. Sometimes the moon was out during the day, and not at night.

She couldn't wait for the moon.

But she could wait for the sun—lay down beside the track, put her head on the backpack, and sleep until morning. Her clothes were dry. It probably wouldn't get much colder than it was already. She could handle the temperature. If only she had Uncle M's sweater.

Ima, ya must flee. The words of Uncle M bounced in her brain, as if echoing off all the steel beams supporting the bridge.

No. She wasn't far enough from CeSiR. Maiya's minions would find her. What if a train passed by during the night and spotted her? They'd tell the authorities. Maiya controlled the authorities. The nurses constantly reminded Ima of that.

She had to cross.

She had to cross now, before blackness completely engulfed the bridge.

What if a train came while she was *on* the bridge? Chills shuddered through her body. Tears formed in the corner of her eyes. Why? Why did Uncle M have to leave her?

Did trains even use these tracks anymore?

He'd know. If they didn't why was the bridge still there? Why would the tracks still be clear? So many questions. And no one to ask.

Ya must flee!

She took her first step out onto the bridge. The wooden crossbeams didn't seem to notice her. What once appeared thin and weak, she could now see were several inches thick.

She could do this. She took a few more steps, before turning to see that she now stood several feet from the gravel-edged embankment. Thick wood beams supported her without motion.

Quick steps carried her ten, twenty, thirty yards toward the center of the bridge. The smell of oil and rust rode a slight breeze.

She paused and looked at the thick beams supporting the track. Beneath them sat—nothing. Nothing but air. With more light, would she see the water sweeping beneath her?

The tracks began to creak and groan. Surely, her weight wasn't enough to cause the motion.

She pressed forward.

Steps became more difficult.

She stopped and steadied herself. This was a bad idea. She never should have walked onto the bridge. A roaring whir drowned out the increased groans and creaks.

She should go back. She turned. She was more than half way across the seventy-five yard span.

The secure wooden slats, so thick and unmovable only moments before, now swayed and lurched.

She had to get across, now.

~~~~~~~~~~~

Ophois finished scanning the river to the northeast of town. It seemed impossible that the raft had survived this far. Ima had to be traveling on foot, but where? He could double back to the point where the doctor was shot. If he picked up her scent, he could pursue her wherever she chose to go—or hide. He banked to his left and headed toward the west side of town.

A flash of whitish-gray flickered beneath him. Probably just trash. Humanity took no pride in the incredible creation that surrounded them. Then again, most rejected the existence of their own Creator. Which suited Ophois just fine. With the exception of his prey, the one called Ima, the mims were a perfect creation. Manufactured in the image of man. Certainly superior to *His* creations.

Perhaps Ophois had been hasty when he accepted Mael's challenge to control this spirited little one.

No. The others could have their blind obedience. Ophois savored forcing himself on the will of others.

He banked and moved in closer to the item in the clearing below. Just a piece of paper. Like he thought—someone's trash. Yet he felt compelled to investigate. He landed in the opening and looked around him. Was someone watching him? He saw no one. He bent down and took the paper in his claws.

Yes. He knew to trust his instincts. He held an airline ticket for one Wilhelm M'Gregor for a flight from COU, Columbia Regional Airport, to LAX. The flight time listed was nine o'clock. It would be impossible for her to catch that flight on foot. Unless—she had help. At least he knew where she was headed. He would need to hurry to reach the airport before the flight left. If she showed, he would kill her there. If not, then he would backtrack and find her.

Either way, he *would* have his prey.

~~~~~~~~~~~

Ima heard no whistle and saw no light.

Did trains even use their whistle unless they approached a road? She hadn't seen any roads since leaving Arrow Springs.

She ran for the end of the steel death-trap.

As she drew closer, the surface under her feet seemed to stabilize. She glanced over her shoulder. Nothing. No train.

The wind gusted and the bridge swayed.

Of course, the wind. She had panicked for nothing.

If only that were true.

Uncle M was gone. She was on her own, in an unknown world.

Her footsteps slowed and she leapt to her left, anything to get off the bridge. The backpack dragged her to the ground. Rough gravel from the embankment dug into her hands. She'd made it across. Still no train in sight.

After a few minutes rest, she pushed herself up off the gravel and continued down the tracks. The occasional animal scurrying from the tracks caused her pounding heart to screech to a stop.

For the next hour, she pressed on with a new determination. Uncle M always told her she was special—that she could accomplish anything she put her mind to. This journey, wherever it took her, would need to prove him correct.

Ahead she saw lights in the darkness. It was the first town she'd encountered since leaving Arrow Springs. The tracks skirted the edge of town. With luck, no one would see her. She jogged past a building built right next to the tracks. Big round storage buildings lined the far side of the building. Probably, some form of granary. It made sense that the local farmers would bring their grain to the tracks to be shipped off to other parts of the country.

Past the granary, she approached an intersection with a road. She stepped onto the pavement of the road. Walking on the solid ground soothed her throbbing calves. She stood for a moment. Should she continue down the tracks? The road was smooth and easier to walk on than the gravel.

No. Uncle M told her to follow the tracks. She needed to do what he said. He'd never given her a reason to mistrust him. He was the only one. Everyone else she'd ever met seemed to hate her.

Brakes squealed behind her and a loud horn snapped her out of her ponderings.

She turned and two bright headlights blinded her. She put her hand up to protect her eyes from the intense bluish light.

"Hey, get out of the road!" A man's voice yelled at her. With her eyes shielded from the blaring light, she saw the driver's door open. "Are you deaf? What are you doing out here?" A foot appeared beneath the car door and his shoulder popped out of the car. "Hey, I'm talking to you, stupid."

No, walking along the road was not a good idea.

Ima ran. As fast as her feet would carry her, she sprinted down the tracks.

"Hey, get back here! Where do you think you're going?" The man's speech slurred slightly.

She didn't turn to see, but crunching gravel told her he was jogging after her.

A loud deep horn cut through the night air. Definitely *not* a car horn. Apparently, the tracks were used after all.

"Oh . . ." The man swore a couple times, before the sound of a door slamming cut off the barrage.

Tires squawked against pavement.

She turned to see the car shoot forward from the intersection.

None too soon.

A bright yellowish beam illuminated the tracks beside her. She jogged to some trees at the side of the tracks.

Her stomach vibrated in resonance with the rumble of the train as it roared past her. The sharp smell of burnt diesel assailed her.

Bright red lights flashed against the train from the road. In the flashing light, she watched the steel of the railroad tracks bounce up and down. She could hardly fathom anything bending the metal beams she had spent so much of the past hours walking on.

Apparently, everything gives, at least a little, when submitted to enough pressure. Is that what Uncle M meant when he said they had to leave? Perhaps, even the founder of a company like CeSiR Tech had to give when under enough pressure.

After the train passed, she gradually made her way back to the tracks. She needed to get as much distance between herself and CeSiR as she could before morning.

Twenty minutes later, she approached a large clearing with another intersection. She pulled up at the edge of the tree line. The moon she had wished for earlier, now hung big and bright behind her. It illuminated the intersection ahead. A car sat beside the road, perhaps thirty feet from a red light. The light faced the tracks. It wasn't telling the car to stop. More likely, it was a caution for other trains.

It was dark, but the car looked a lot like the one she had stared down only a little earlier.

She sat down next to a large tree and waited.

~~~~~~~~~~

Adiya stood next to Ima as she crouched in the underbrush next to the tree. So unfair. The poor child knew so little of the real world. How would she ever survive on her own? Yet she seemed responsive, even to the slightest of suggestions. She needed a place to stay. Somewhere she would be cared for. But Eitan was clear. Ima needed to make her own choices.

On ahead, the man from the intersection leaned against the fender of his car. His arms rested across his chest with his hands curled into fists. His tongue swiped his upper lip. He waited—for Ima.

Adiya scanned the car and then the surrounding fields. No sign of the enemy. That meant nothing. Since their fall from grace, they craved the night. Sometimes they took the form of people, other times they chose some malformed image of animals or creatures of myth and fear. But more than all, they chose darkness.

"Holy Spirit, help me see the evil ones," whispered Adiya. "Father, give me strength to protect this young one."

My grace is sufficient.

Adiya knelt to one knee for a moment then stood and approached the man. Even from five feet away, the scent of alcohol radiated from him.

"Ah-deeee-yah." The screechy voice came from the right, near the back bumper of the car. "How nice of you to join the party." A demon of lust stood and approached.

"It would appear you have me at a disadvantage," Adiya said. "You obviously know of me, but you, I do not recall."

"My friend," the demon said, "you do not remember me? I am hurt. Truly." The lizard-like face flashed to that of a brown haired angel and then back.

So many millennia had passed, yet Adiya did remember. They had worshiped together at the throne of the Creator, before the great rebellion.

The demon smiled. "Ah yes, you remember." The demon took a couple steps toward Adiya and then rested his hand gently on the hilt of his saber. "For old times' sake, we will let you leave now. Without messing up that pretty little face of yours."

Though neither angels nor demons possess gender as humans do, it always fell to the demons of lust to draw attention to Adiya's feminine form. "For too long you have hung out with this human, if you believe my appearance makes me any less of a warrior." More memories of worshiping next to this former angel of heaven flooded her mind. How could anyone who experienced the loving presence of the Creator ever rebel against Him?

The demon slowly circled Adiya drawing her gaze away from the car. As if answering her unspoken question, the one every angel had asked a thousand times, he said, "Did I abandon Him? Or did He abandon me?"

Adiya knew the arguments. She had even struggled to reconcile them herself. But she never doubted the Creator's love—even for those He cast out of Heaven. "You followed the deceiver. He desired to elevate himself to a place of equality with his own Creator and you followed him in his arrogance." This was a useless distraction.

Yes, he had said, "*we* will let you leave." There were others. This *was* a distraction. She reached for her sword. "You know you cannot best me."

"Are we not having a friendly conversation for old times' sake?" the demon asked. "Calm yourself Ah-deeee-yah. There is no need for violence. Sweetheart, I am a lover, not a fighter."

Adiya unsheathed her sword. She was no sweetheart. She was a warrior. "Leave now, snake, and take your drunken pervert with you or I will remove *your* sweet heart." Her instincts were correct. Motion flickered in the corner of her vision. The demon had not drawn her attention as much as he intended.

Adiya dropped to one knee and raised her shield over her neck.

Strength equal to her own crashed down on the shield. Without the shield, that single blow would have returned her to the throne room. As much as she always longed to sit at His feet, she demonstrated her love for Him through obedience, not selfishness.

She spun with the impact on the shield and struck her sword against a sinewy black leg.

The stench of sulfur swirled about her.

The attacker cursed and toppled to the ground. Not destroyed, but injured. He rolled, cursed again, and rose to a knee to glare at her.

She looked down the blade of her sword at the assailant. The bull-like face of a demon of rage stared at her. The strike had him thinking twice about his next move.

"Hey, hey, come on. She is not worth it." This voice came from a third demon somewhere near the car.

The demon of lust stared at her and shook his head. "Ah-deeee-yah, how long will you blindly follow Him?" He tapped the bull and motioned toward the car. The demon snorted, cursed, and limped to the car. "He does not care about you, Adiya. He only cares about His precious humans. They reject Him at every turn." He pointed in the direction of the trees where Ima hid. "Yet he still offers them hope. Such forgiveness—He will never show you."

Adiya drilled the demon with a stare. He was correct. She worshiped at the throne of the Creator. She would never turn her loyalty, and thus would never need His forgiveness.

"It is you who are blind," Adiya said. "Now, leave!"

He smiled, as if he had proved his point. "Until next time, Ah-deeeee-yah."

The car drove off.

~~~~~~~~~~~

Ima shivered as she huddled next to a large tree. The man, who'd sat against the hood of his car, tossed a glowing red ember to the ground and stepped on it. He opened the door of his car and climbed in. Cussing streamed from his open window as he spun the car around in the middle of the road. As headlights swept toward her, Ima pulled close to the tree. The headlights continued back to the road and the car squawked as it accelerated down the road back toward town.

After waiting several minutes, Ima stood and headed down the lonely tracks.

The remainder of the night proved relatively uneventful. An occasional animal would move in the weeds or shriek some unearthly noise. Despite crossing several more intersections, she hadn't encountered another person.

Exhausted from hours of hiking with senses on ultra-high alert, reality began to settle in. She couldn't keep up this pace all day. She needed a place to rest. The risk of being spotted would rise with the morning sun. Better to travel during the night and rest during the day.

Still well before sunrise, the sky already began to brighten. Everything became easier to see, including her.

She came to a Y in the tracks.

Follow the tracks west.

The words of Uncle M echoed through her memory. The horrific gurgling of his voice wrapped her mind in ice. A shiver passed from her neck to her toes. She stopped and stared at the decision before her. Which way was west?

Her science books told her the sun would rise in the east. But she couldn't see the sun. How long would she need to wait? Every minute she waited, someone might see her. She needed to make a decision. The sky to her right glowed brighter. That had to be east. She took the tracks to the left.

After following the tracks a couple minutes, another pair of tracks merged into the ones she followed. They formed a single path, which she continued to tread. Perhaps it was the security she'd found in the wooded slats on the bridge or the way the looser gravel next to the track made her legs scream, but she preferred walking between the metal tracks. Before darkness set in, she had even tried walking on the smooth metal rails. Though fun at first, the slippery surface and the onset of darkness made it too risky.

As she walked, something tickled her ankles. In the growing onset of the morning sky, she saw weeds reaching up from between the wooden slats.

She walked for another half hour before the tracks suddenly ended, giving way to grass-laden gravel.

Trains couldn't drive without tracks. Could they? The fork in the tracks—she'd made a wrong turn. Apparently the tracks she'd taken were no longer used.

Should she go back?

Uncle M was very clear that she should follow the tracks.

Something told her to keep going.

Morning would be on her soon and with it many prying eyes.

She pressed onward.

~~~~~~~~~~~

"That a girl," Adiya said. She placed her wing over the shoulder of the exhausted child. She had just returned from scouting out the area ahead. It was still early enough to avoid being seen, but soon someone would see the girl. Adiya needed to be sure that person would help Ima and not inflict harm.

When Adiya returned and found Ima had wandered off the primary tracks, she was pleased. The girl's instincts had led her to the best option. It would not be without challenge. She would pass through a populated area before getting back into the cover of the tracks. Thankfully, Adiya knew many faithful warriors in the small town ahead. And most of the enemy's charges would still be in bed, after a late Saturday night of partying.

"Just keep on the straight and narrow, dear one."

~~~~~~~~~~~

CHAPTER THREE

Sunday, May 10, 2020

The light of early morning chased darkness from Patricia Sherwood's bedroom. Her knees ached, though not from the hour she had spent in prayer. No, at eighty years of age, she knew better than to get down on her knees. She might not get back up. She prayed seated in her white rocking chair. Charles had painted it a year before the Alzheimer's set in.

She glanced at Charles sleeping peacefully in bed. It seemed the only time he was peaceful anymore. A *blessing*, everyone told her, given his advanced state. She loved him. Loved his presence, even if he typically didn't know who she was. Yet she had to wonder, was it selfish to want for him to stay with her? She couldn't help feeling that his anxiousness resulted from a desire deep within his soul to be somewhere else. Somewhere so many of their friends, loved ones, and even one of their children had already gone. She would never be able to bring herself to ask God to take him home. But when the day came, she knew it would be for the best.

She closed her eyes and listened to the nasally breathing of the dearest person she'd ever met. It was Sunday. Soon she would begin preparing him for the arduous trip to church. Charles seldom created a scene at church. He had gone there his entire life. No matter what stage of life his brain found itself in, the church was the one constant—the one thing that always belonged.

Patricia laid her head back against the floral padding and began to pray one-by-one for each person ministering at their church. Then she moved on to her three remaining children, eight grandchildren, and twenty-three great-grandchildren. Though she prayed every morning, it never became a ritual. In fact, it didn't even come easy. She simply understood the need.

Devote yourselves to prayer with an alert mind and a thankful heart. The passage from Colossians chapter four had become her daily call to prayer. Until Charles' illness, she had never fully appreciated the concept of an alert mind and how thankful that alone made her heart. But this morning, the alertness of her mind concerned her. Something hung just beyond her perception—a feeling. Good or bad, she couldn't quite tell.

She wrapped up her time with the Lord and made her way to the kitchen. She needed to tidy up the house before Charles awoke, more a force of habit than necessity. No one ever came to the house. Most of the family had moved away and those that remained in central Missouri had their own lives. Lives that seldom included old people—except for Sylvia. She was quite faithful about visiting, until the dementia. Sylvia loved her grandpa. It shredded her heart every time she visited and Charles didn't know her.

Though Patricia moved slowly, the cleanup didn't take long. The house never really got dirty. Dusty perhaps, but the invention of the Swiffer made good old fashioned dusting a thing of the past.

A noise came from the bedroom. She needed to get to Charles before he got himself worked up.

~~~~~~~~~~

Ophois prowled the foyer of Columbia Regional airport. He had waited at the gate until the flight departed—with at least two empty seats. His prey never arrived. Though it left him with a myriad of options that Ima could have taken, he drooled at the expectation of a full-on hunt. Humans often proved so impatient in their manhunts. Not him. Ophois had hunted a single prey for years, even decades. Barring the unexpected

34

fulfillment of the long proclaimed second coming of the enemy, Ophois had all the time in the world. He rather enjoyed the fact that the girl did not show for the flight.

Half a day had passed since the shooting of the doctor. If the girl had been intent on reaching the airport, she should have arrived by now, even on foot. Time to backtrack, to exercise his tracking brilliance and zero in on his prey.

He paused to cause a harried young woman to drop her keys into the trunk of her car. The key-fob landed as she slammed the trunk shut. Two beeps announced the locking of the car. He grinned. He could only guess whether she carried a spare.

"Ma'am, you can't leave your car there," a security guard warned. "That is a restricted loading and unloading zone only."

The woman's face flushed pink. "But my keys. I just locked them in the trunk."

Ophois snickered. He would love to stick around to watch her scramble to recover the keys and still make her flight. But he had a flight of his own.

He spread his wings and gave a howl, as he soared into the morning air. Minutes later, he descended on the Katy Trail, west of the airport. If the girl had tried to walk to the airport, she would have crossed at Boonville. From there the Katy Trail was the only good choice for walking to Columbia.

They had never let Ima out of CeSiR, but she was well studied. She had to have seen maps and heard of the historic trail. He flew along the treetops that lined the trail. He watched for movement. More important, he sniffed the pine scented air for the familiar scent of Ima—of fear.

~~~~~~~~~~

Ima found herself walking down the sandy remains of an old railroad passageway. She felt compelled to press on. So she did. Ahead, houses sat closer to the walkway.

Somewhere to her right a dog barked and growled. She picked up her pace.

Light continued to seep into the morning sky.

More barking.

"Shut up!" The half-awake scream came from somewhere inside a yellow rectangular home, which appeared to be made of metal. It reminded Ima of photos she'd seen of railroad cars, only bigger.

She moved beyond the odd looking home. To her left sat a redbrick building with a fenced yard. The fence extended almost to the path where the tracks used to be. A sign at the front of the building indicated that it was an elementary school. Quite a difference from the bland rooms where she'd received her education. As she approached the school, a whole set of play equipment came into view.

How many children must play there to have such fancy equipment? Slides, swings, arrays of bars to swing on, and a black rubbery looking surface beneath them. What would it be like to have so many friends to play with? Then again, all the children she knew treated her like trash. They would drive her to tears and then laugh at her for crying. She'd never met a child with emotions like hers.

Even those thoughts brought tears to her eyes. And that made her mad. She smacked at the water on her face and pulled her gaze from the children's playground. That would never be for her. She marched on, determined, exhausted.

Up ahead Ima saw more round storage buildings for holding grain. Several semi-trucks surrounded the building. Did they use trucks because the train tracks were gone? She approached the building and found her answer. More tracks. She hadn't messed up after all. She was back at the tracks. She could still follow Uncle M's instructions. Follow the tracks west. West to where? How could she possibly know?

He left her.

He died—because of her.

For another hour she followed this new set of tracks. She'd seen a few people in cars. None of them seemed to pay her much attention.

The morning sun now fully illuminated the fields around her. The temperature began to rise. Her legs throbbed and she couldn't even feel her shoulders. The straps of the backpack had become one with her skin. Her damp shirt clung to her body in the morning humidity. Bloody stains splotched her white blouse. Despite a slight breeze, the smell of iron and sweat hovered about her.

She needed a place to rest. Soon.

She found a clump of trees near the tracks. It provided some shade and hid her from sight as long as no one was looking for her. With Uncle M gone, Maiya would be unchallenged. Yes, they were surely looking for her. She sat down for a few minutes rest. She couldn't stay long, but she had to rest.

Ima's eyelashes pulled on her eyelids like shades on a summer day. A few minutes sleep couldn't hurt.

She floated on a raft into the deep waters of sleep. A deep guttural moan reached out of the waters. Uncle M! He was dying.

No. That wasn't quite the sound. She heard it again. The waters of sleep receded and she heard the sound once again. As reality resurfaced, she recognized the sound.

Somewhere in front of her a cow mooed.

Despite the trees, she was too visible. She needed to find a more secluded place to hide until dark. If someone spotted her, Maiya would know. She always knew. She knew everything. Ima couldn't let them find her. If they did, they would probably kill her—just like Uncle M—or worse.

He had told her she needed to leave CeSiR. They wanted to use her as one of the surrogates. She had always pitied the surrogates. So unhappy. So alone.

Once again, she started down the tracks.

~~~~~~~~~~

Patricia smiled at Charles. He stared out the window, as they drove home. His usual absence had returned about a mile from church. Today, more than usual, she had prayed his awareness would continue. He had even hummed along as the band beat out what the pastor had called a brilliant reminder of God's creative blessing on their church. It wasn't the music she would prefer, but she loved to see young people the age of her grandchildren praising and worshiping God. On occasion the music unsettled Charles. Last week, she could have died when he stuck his fingers in his ears when the music started. Thankfully, he hadn't fought with her when she scolded him for such rudeness.

She glanced in her rearview mirror and dug her fingers into the steering wheel of their Chevy Impala. A bright blue pickup roared past them like she had the car in park. Young people felt such a need to get everywhere fast.

If she was honest with herself, she had been no different, back when she actually had something to warrant hurry. Now in her late age, she simply enjoyed the freedoms she still possessed. How many times had her children fought with her about the need to stop driving? As if an occasional dented garbage can, or scratch on the car, meant she was no longer fit to exercise her right to freedom.

"Did you enjoy the message?" she asked Charles.

He responded with a grunt.

He didn't argue with her—didn't claim they hadn't been to church. That was a positive.

The gravel crunched under their tires as she pulled next to the side door of their house. Even before she had the car door open, Goldie barked out a greeting.

She helped Charles settle into the porch chair, where he now spent his best days. She unlocked the house and opened the door.

Goldie practically ran her over in an urgency to empty her bladder. "You silly dog," Patricia said. "You could at least let me get out of the way. I'm not sure how many falls these hips can take."

Next to her, Charles chuckled at the dog.

It warmed her heart to hear him laugh. Even if it came at her expense.

Goldie barked twice. It seemed the dog barked more and more as she got older. After years of training, it only took a little bit of slack on the part of Charles and Patricia to see the dog revert to her old ways.

Another two barks, and a growl.

That was new. She usually reserved her attempts at ferociousness for coyotes or raccoons.

Patricia set her purse down on the dining room table and returned to the porch.

"Goldie, get in here you silly dog." She clapped her hands twice. Their universal symbol for this-time-you-better-listen-to-me. "Goldie! Let's go."

"She's probably just playing with Danny," Charles said. "They'll come in for lunch."

Danny was their youngest daughter's dog—forty years ago, long before Julia's death. Though the years had dulled the pain, it still hurt to be reminded, especially when accompanied by a reminder that she was losing Charles.

Three more barks and a whine, got Patricia's attention. She walked to the end of the porch to see why the dog threw such a fit.

Oh great.

Goldie stood barking at the barn door. If she hadn't stirred up every animal yet, it would only be a matter of time. Everyone that visited expressed surprise that they still kept some of the animals. It helped her feel young. To feel that something still needed her, even if her family had long since moved past that point.

The last time Goldie got this worked up, they lost six chickens to a coyote. The dog continued to bark at the narrow gap between the two barn doors. While she barked, the dog dug at the dirt beneath the doors. It wouldn't take long at that rate for her to get into the barn.

Patricia returned to the dining room and grabbed the barn key. She also picked up two twelve-gauge shotgun shells. Behind the hutch she grabbed the shotgun and loaded a shell.

As she approached the barn, Goldie finally made it under the doors. Two more barks came from inside the barn. Then silence.

She picked up her pace and in moments the padlock swung open.

Patricia slid the right door open about three feet. She coughed twice as a wall of straw dust met her. She stepped in.

"Goldie?" She leveled the gun. "Come here, girl." Her voice was dry and raspy.

The only response was a soft whimper. Had a coyote gotten into the barn? Even then she would have heard a tussle. Perhaps something worse, a badger? They were pretty uncommon these days. The whimper came from one of the uninhabited horse stalls on the left.

The closer she got to the stall the darker the barn grew. She hadn't thought to turn on the lights when she entered. Near the door the sunlight outside provided plenty of light.

She rounded the corner of the last horse stall.

An ear-piercing scream echoed through the barn.

Goldie growled and snarled—at her.

From the corner of the stall, two round ice-blue eyes stared at Patricia. A young girl huddled into the fetal position. "Please don't kill me too." The girl begged through deep sobs.

"Patty! Put that gun down before you hurt someone."

She spun to see Charles standing in the doorway of the barn. His silhouette appeared twenty years younger leaning against the barn door. How many times had she seen him standing there with an ear-to-ear mischievous grin? Her face blushed at the memories of their time in that barn.

"Well don't point it at me either."

She raised the barrel of the gun to her shoulder, just like he'd taught her so many years ago.

Charles joined her to examine their guest in the horse stall. "Well hi there," he said. "What's your name?"

"I—I—" The girl paused apparently waiting for her heart beat to stop rapping and return to a slow dance. "Ima," she managed.

"Ima. That's a pretty name," Charles said. "Don't worry about her." Charles pointed to Patricia. "I don't even remember the last time she shot that thing." He stepped into the stall. Goldie returned to the girl's side and she put her arm around the dog's neck.

Charles held out a hand to the young girl. "What do you say we take Goldie here inside? I'm hungry. Are you?"

The girl nodded, her eyes still large as saucers. She reached out and took his hand and they walked out of the stall.

"Why don't you give me that before someone gets hurt," Charles said, pointing to the shotgun.

The last few minutes of normalcy nearly tricked Patricia into complying. Ten minutes earlier, she never would have considered handing her dementia plagued husband a shotgun. That was why she had changed its hiding place. "No, I got it."

The girl looked to be not much over ten. Still, she made Patricia nervous. Her skin crawled with caution at the recent turn of events. She relished the sudden awareness Charles exhibited, but she feared it would only set her emotions up for yet another betrayal.

~~~~~~~~~~~

Adiya sat on an old hewn rafter surrounded by straw. Eitan's instructions were clear—observe, keep her safe, but do not interfere. Devoted to her mission, she wrapped herself in her cloak. Hidden in the shadows, but with sword drawn. The elderly couple would not see her, but were there others?

A white haired figure approached the couple. If she had chosen a place for Ima to hide, she could not have done better. Though she had never met the elderly couple, she definitely recognized this angelic warrior.

She had always admired Eldwyn. His flowing hair seemed to generate its own light. Though angels did not age, Eldwyn possessed an appearance of age and wisdom. Time and again he had lived up to his appearance in the demonstration of godly wisdom, beyond any other she had met. Rather than the typical sword of a warrior, Eldwyn carried a gnarled wooden staff. Humans would likely mistake him for a prototypical wizard from their movies.

Despite his appearance, Eldwyn was a capable warrior. True power came not from size or skill but from the Holy Spirit. And, based on the brilliant white glow of his hair, wings, and face, Adiya had no doubt that at least one of this dear couple was a prayer warrior.

Eldwyn stepped through the barn door, as the couple led Ima toward the farmhouse. He paused. "Well Adiya, are you going to remain perched on that rafter like a barn-pigeon, or will you be joining us?" Though he faced away from the doors, his slow-deep voice echoed throughout the barn.

She shook her head, how did he do that? He had never even looked in her direction.

She floated down from her perch and trotted to catch up with the wise warrior. They walked in silence until they reached the house.

"A unique one this is," Eldwyn said. "What can you tell me about her?"

Eitan had also spoken of Ima's significance. As of yet Adiya could not see it. Perhaps, the wisdom of Eldwyn would shed some light.

"Why do you say she is unique?" Adiya asked.

The wise angel said nothing. He simply pointed to Charles.

Charles offered Ima a seat at the table. "Ima, would you like something to drink? Water, iced tea, we might even have a soda?"

The girl smiled and nodded at the mention of a soda.

Eldwyn looked at Adiya. "For most of the past year," he said, "even Patricia's name he has not remembered. Let alone some random child he just met. And the glow of his spirit, I've not seen it this bright for years." Eldwyn put his fingers to his chin and nodded. "For this one, God has plans."

Charles set a soda in front of Ima. Adiya glanced at Eldwyn. "Almost two weeks ago, Eitan accompanied an Arrow Springs detective into the enemy stronghold. A place called CeSiR Technologies. They have created human clones, which they call mims, short for Manufactured Images of Men."

At the mention of these creations, Eldwyn fell to his knees. "Will they never learn?" His white cloak now covered his wings. He bowed his head. "For how long? How many?"

"It would appear for twenty-five years. There are at least sixty adults and another sixty children. But there is more." Adiya knelt to one knee. It felt wrong to converse with this great warrior while standing over him. "It would appear the Creator has chosen not to endow these creations with souls and the enemy is using this to their advantage."

Eldwyn kissed the golden cross emblazoned on the front of his cloak. "From Arrow Springs, I have heard rumors. More than rumors it would appear. I had not heard Captain Eitan had come. Most encouraging."

"He is the one who sent me to accompany this child," Adiya said.

Eldwyn stood and walked to Ima. "She is one of these mims. Is she not?"

"Yes, straight from the facility. They have sent Ophois to hunt her."

"Hmm." Eldwyn knelt in front of the little girl. He stared directly into her eyes. "Most interesting." He rose and leaned on his staff. "There is much pain and confusion in this one. I fear the enemy will be most intent on her return. Or perhaps, her elimination."

Patricia placed a hand on Ima's shoulder. She held the girl's backpack in her other hand. "Come on, Ima. Let's go get you cleaned up."

The girl stood and followed Patricia to the bathroom.

Eldwyn tapped his staff on the floor. "Ophois is a formidable foe. Long it has been, since I last faced him. He will not come alone. He prefers to work in a pack. We need to be vigilant."

~~~~~~~~~~

Ima wore a red shirt—as bright as the smile on her face, and so soft. Goldie licked her on the face and she giggled. They rolled around on the floor of the farmhouse. This had been the best day of her young life. After washing Ima's face and hands with a soap that actually smelled like cookies, the kind lady had insisted that Ima eat as much as she desired. Never in her life had she been shown such kindness. Nor had she been so full. So much yummy food.

For the past half an hour, Patty, as she had insisted on being called, clanked away in the kitchen. She told Ima that she had a surprise for her when she finished playing with Goldie. Charles told Ima they called the dog Goldie, because she was a golden retriever.

From the kitchen an incredible aroma wafted into the living room. The food at the facility was minimal both in quantity and taste. None of the other mim children complained. Ima was informed that they were provided all that was necessary for survival. But here with Charles and Patty, the food tasted delectable. "What is that smell?" It was a sort of spicy mixed with sweetness.

"Smells like cinnamon," Charles said. He continued to stare at the television.

Goldie dropped a red ball next to Ima and gave a whimper. The ball jingled as it bounced. Something on the TV caught Ima's attention. The lady said something about a shooting and the Lamine River. By the time she looked up, Charles held a remote control in his hand and a man on the television was talking about the Kansas City Royals.

"Here we go," Patty said. She handed Ima a bowl with apple slices, ice cream, some golden brown crust, and a deep red sauce drizzled over the entire thing. "Now you keep an eye on Goldie. She might try to snatch a bite of your dumplings."

Ima held the bowl up to her nose and inhaled. Even before taking a taste it was the most delightful food she had ever been offered. She put a spoonful to her mouth and the crust practically melted. Her next bite contained a large scoop of ice cream. Something she soon regretted. The center of her head felt like it would explode. Such intense pain had never tasted so sweet.

44

"Ima dear," Patty said, "are you sure there's not someone we should call to let them know where you are?"

Only Uncle M. If he somehow survived. Her brain chided her for holding to such crazy hope, but her heart just couldn't let him go. Couldn't believe that he was gone for good. Besides, she didn't know for sure. He fell into the river. Maybe the coolness of the water kept him alive.

Tears filled her eyes. Why did this dear couple insist on asking? It was the second time they had asked since they found her.

"I'm sorry, sweetie. How about we just get you some rest tonight. We can deal with that tomorrow."

After they all finished their desserts, Patty invited Ima to follow her to the second floor to check out her room for the night.

Tears burst from Ima's eyes when Patty showed her the room. The bed was nearly half as tall as Ima, with plush blankets. Purple and green flowers were scattered across both the blankets and the sheets. Seated on the bed between two pillows was a pink stuffed bear. She stood staring in disbelief. Surely, something so special wasn't really for her. More tears streamed down her cheeks.

"What's the matter, dear?" Patty asked. "Do you miss your home?"

Fear flooded back into her brain. She shook her head. She couldn't possibly let this couple know she came from CeSiR. They would send her back. *Trust no one.* Uncle M's words were burned into her heart. She stuck to her story that she didn't have a home. That her parents were dead. To the degree that she had parents, it was the truth. As a mim, she had a surrogate and she was dead, but no parents.

"Well you are welcome to stay here as long as you need, Ima." Patty pulled her into a warm, compassion-filled hug. The woman smelled like some of the flowering bushes Ima had run past the previous night.

Heaving sobs wracked her chest at the unfamiliar, yet glorious feeling.

"This was originally our daughter's room, but most recently it has been used by our granddaughter Sylvia. Sylvia would adore you. She's a bit older than you, but I think you would like her too. I put your backpack over there in the corner. Feel free to put your clothes in the dresser so they are less wrinkled. Make yourself to home." Patty stepped back from the room and pointed to a door at the end of the hall. "The bathroom is down there. It's all yours. Feel free to wash up in there."

Ima couldn't even fathom the concept of having an entire bathroom to herself. This was too good to be true. At the thought of having her own comfortable bed, fatigue began a full-on assault.

Patty clearly could tell. "Well, I'll leave you alone now. You should have everything you need. You can take a bath tonight or if you're too tired, you can wait until tomorrow morning." Patty kissed her on the forehead. "Goodnight, sweetie. Would you like me to pray with you?"

Ima had no idea what Patty was asking, but the woman had already done so much for her. "No, that's okay. Goodnight."

~~~~~~~~~~~

Fury surged through Ophois, as he reentered Arrow Springs. No sign of the girl. Not even the slightest trace of a scent. How was it possible?

It was not.

The enemy had duped him. Clearly the girl had not traveled to the airport. The ticket was a diversion. He sniffed around the clearing where he found the ticket. He had been careless— charged ahead in pursuit of his prey. Rage mounted as he scolded himself for his haste. Why could he not learn? How many times must he charge ahead and not stop to assess the situation. The clearing was absent of any residual scent of the girl. No, she had not come this way.

He allowed his rage to explode from him in a wind-piercing howl.

He would not return to Mael and the facility, but he needed assistance. He did his best work in a pack. No, as the leader of

46

a pack. He knew just the demon. They had opposed the enemy on many occasions, dating back to their glory days among the Egyptians. They were viewed as god and goddess. Unlike Ima, he knew where he would find Anput.

With one mighty sweep of his wings and a long haunting howl, he shot into the clouds like a Saturn-missile on the Fourth of July. It may take a day to reach her and convince her to return, but together they would find the little mim and make her wish she had died with the doctor.

~~~~~~~~~~~

Adiya sat next to Eldwyn in the living room of Charles and Patricia. "Such a sweet couple," she said. "How long have you accompanied them?"

"Charles was born to a war widow," Eldwyn said. "His father was a pilot in London. Shot down eight Luftwaffe bombers, before being shot down himself. When she received word of his father's death, Charles' mother went into premature labor."

Adiya remembered the horrible loss of life in Europe. She hated the pain caused by The Fall. So many wars. So much hatred. People could not see just how much they held in common.

Eldwyn continued, "At that time, I was assigned to keep Charles alive and have been with him ever since."

A lifetime assignment? This must have been a special individual for Eldwyn the wise to guide him for a lifetime.

Surely the Spirt had guided Ima to this couple. So much care and compassion for a fragile stranger. Would they be so caring, if they knew? When so many were judged by where they were born, their gender, shade of skin, or affluence, how would the world respond to mims?

"You mentioned that Charles seems different. How so?" Adiya asked. "Does it happen often?"

Eldwyn rubbed his white beard and shook his head. "Since the disease began to take his mind, this is not something I have observed. He seems as if the Alzheimer's never happened. For many months, Patricia has not been more joyful."

The elderly couple sat next to their fireplace chatting about family. Memories they had believed gone forever. Patricia laughed at one of Charles' jokes.

"Oh my," Patricia said, her gaze affixed to the top of the stairs.

Adiya turned and saw a pair of pale cheeks streak into Ima's bedroom. She giggled, before she could consider the coming response from the elderly couple. They had no way to understand the girl's background. Seemingly normal actions from Ima's former life would not be well received in this home.

A hearty belly laugh rolled from beside her.

She turned to the couple. Patricia sat with pursed lips and a scolding finger pointed at Charles.

His shoulders continued to bounce, though he managed to contain the sound of his amusement.

"Well, that's certainly not appropriate for a young lady," Patricia said. She stood and headed for the stairway, which led up to the semi-open second floor.

"Oh, calm down, Patty. She's just a child," Charles said.

"She's not a child. She's a young lady, and she needs to understand appropriate public behavior."

Adiya turned to Eldwyn. He possessed a grin to rival Charles. "It would appear your charge is going to get a bit of a talking to," Eldwyn said.

"A valuable lesson that I am certain she never received at CeSiR Tech," Adiya said. How many common courtesies had this poor child not been taught? If she could avoid giving them a heart attack, this dear couple would be just what Ima needed. Lessons to survive in the cruel world ahead of her. "I suppose I should go check on them." She stood, nodded to Eldwyn, and floated to the second floor.

She entered the girl's room and found Ima sitting on the bed wearing a pair of pajamas. She sniffled. "I'm sorry, Mrs. Patty. I didn't know."

"It's okay, child." Patricia pulled the young girl into an embrace. "Perhaps that's why the good Lord brought you here. Every young lady needs someone to explain what it means to move from being a girl to being a woman."

Adiya listened with joy, as the woman talked to Ima for the next half an hour. She had to wonder, how many mothers shared so much wisdom with their daughters in ten years as Patricia had shared in only a few minutes.

Soon, Ima pattered down the stairs and up to Charles. "I'm sorry for being, um, inappropriate, Papa Charles" Her hands were folded behind her. "Will you please forgive me?"

"There is nothing to forgive, hon," Charles said. "We all make mistakes. Yes, there are more appropriate ways to act as a young lady, but I'm sure you will learn."

A smile sprang from ear to ear across Ima's face.

Had she ever received such forgiveness and grace? Adiya could only wonder. From what she had learned from Eitan, Doctor M'Gregor was the only kind person in the child's life. Now he was dead. This child was so blessed to have hidden in Charles and Patricia's barn.

"Good night, Papa Charles." Ima gave the elderly man a quick peck on the left cheek, giggled, and ran back up the stairs.

"Good night, hon." Charles called after her. "Sleep tight, don't let the bedbugs bite."

The girl spun with a worried look. As soon as she saw his grin, she ran into the bedroom and jumped into the big fluffy bed.

Patricia pulled the sheets over the girl's shoulders and kissed her on the forehead.

~~~~~~~~~~

CHAPTER FOUR

Monday, May 11, 2020

Ophois dove toward the city. Lights spread across the desert. Even from thousands of feet in the air, his destination was easy to spot. A bluish beam called to him from a giant square below. He approached at break-neck speed. He shot through the point of the pyramid, matching the slope of the black glass wall.

He slowed his approach. Floors and walls streaked past. He decelerated more as the sound of arguing approached. One more floor passed.

"You lost everything we had!" A woman leaned over her husband, who stared at the room's television. "That money was supposed to send Christie to college." The man grunted and leaned to see around her.

Ophois descended through carpet, concrete, steel, and drywall.

"You were so wasted," a man said.

"I had fun." A woman lay on top of the bedspread, her eyes glazed.

"At my expense," he said. "How many men did you flirt with last night?" He waved a finger at her. "You may as well have put out a tip jar. As least you'd have earned some cash."

Carpet, concrete, steel, and drywall.

"She's never gonna forgive me," a middle-aged man said. His voice was barely discernible with his head buried in his hands.

A slender twenty-something came out of the bathroom. She cast an empty glance at the middle-aged man. When he ignored her presence, she gathered her clothes from the floor and got dressed. Quietly, she slipped out the door.

A snakelike demon of insecurity smiled at Ophois and then followed the young girl.

Ophois veered into the open center of the pyramid. Anput was doing well for herself. He only hoped he could convince her to help him.

He swept past robot-like individuals feeding the slot monsters. They reminded him of a primeval civilization attempting to appease some ancient god with their sacrifices.

He arrived at the back offices and found Anput overseeing a discussion about an expansion plan.

"Ophois," Anput said. "How long has it been?" She wrapped her arms across her chest and stared at him.

"Too long, if I had my say," he said. "You have built quite an empire here." He approached and lifted her golden hand to his lips.

"Flattery always was your strong suit, Ophois." Anput smiled and patted his cheek. "But thank you. Things are proceeding quite well."

Several other demons in the room paid them little attention. They discussed objectives, and prompted their charges accordingly.

Anput motioned Ophois to an adjacent room. "We can talk in here. I can only guess that your long-overdue visit is not arbitrary."

She looked as beautiful as ever. Unlike most demons, she chose not to appear black as night. Perhaps, because she operated in a city that never slept—a city where neon and millions of LEDs drove away the blackness of night. Or maybe, she chose the rich golden color to reflect the greed that she preyed on daily among her guests.

In their glory days in Egypt, Ophois too had chosen the golden appearance of a god. But, since his epic failure with the

Israelites, like so many demons, he found it easier to remain black—the true color of his heart.

"Rumors spread of an army of the host, forming in the west to march on Arrow Springs," Anput said. "You are still stationed in Arrow Springs, yes? Is that why you have come?"

"The rumors are true. War is coming. However, that is not why I have come. There are enough forces in Arrow Springs to thwart any effort the enemy may throw at us." Should he tell of his inept handling of such a simple assignment? Of his certain demise, if Mael found out? It would play on her past loyalty, but it would also highlight his weakness.

"Mael has given me a more important mission." His ego won out. "There is a young girl, a mim." He went on to tell her about their work at the facility.

Her eyes flickered at the prospect of fully controllable human-likeness with no will-power with which to contend. Green saliva seeped from her lips. She swiped it with a golden tongue.

"Two nights ago," Ophois continued. "Mael ordered the execution of the doctor who created the mims, but a young female escaped the attack."

Anput hung on his every word, like the days of old. He would again be respected and revered.

"Mael called on me to find her." Okay, not exactly how it happened, but close enough. "I immediately thought of you. I would love for you to accompany me on this mission. I do understand, if your empire here cannot survive without you." The truest test of leadership was the ability to step away without everything falling apart.

"I would love to join you," she said. "It would be fun to work with you once again." She stroked the underside of her canine chin. "One thing I do not understand. What is so special about this female?"

How many times had Ophois asked himself that same question? So weak and fragile, yet so strong and willful. What was the Creator up to with this one? The very thought raised the hair on the nape of his neck. "I fear we have not yet discovered what it is that makes her so special, but the enemy is intent on protecting her."

"Give me a day here to see what I can find regarding her whereabouts." Networking for information was Anput's specialty. "I will join you in Arrow Springs tomorrow." She cast a playful, almost mischievous, glance at Ophois. "Should I meet you at the facility?"

"No." He scrambled for words. "I mean, there is so much going on there. I do not wish to concern Mael with this matter. Let us meet at the railroad tracks northwest of town."

Anput nodded, as if Ophois had just said the most sensible thing possible. He missed working with her.

"I have reason to believe she headed west along the river, or perhaps the tracks," Ophois said. "We can start there, unless you uncover something about her whereabouts."

"I will see you tomorrow," Anput said. "I have so missed our hunts." Anput began to giggle. "This girl, she was not wearing a red hood?"

They each let out a howl.

~~~~~~~~~~~

Ima set down her fork on the plate. After a horrendous weekend, she had slept most of the morning. When she finally awoke, she marveled at the sun streaming through pink flowered curtains. The Sherwoods had told her she could stay as long as she desired. Such a dear couple. She'd never met anyone so kind and caring—with one exception. The one individual who treated her like a person and not some lab rat.

She picked up a rugged yellow drinking glass and downed the rest of her morning orange juice. The food at CeSiR was meant to provide sustenance, not enjoyment. On occasion they let the mims drink milk, mostly the surrogates. They gave Ima water and some pills that were supposed to be better than real food. One more thing for which she was ridiculed, when she voiced her dissatisfaction.

Mama Patty took food to a whole new level. This meal, which she had referred to as a late brunch, was unlike anything

Ima had ever tasted. The sweetness of maple syrup made her want to bounce around the kitchen. When Mama Patty told her it came from the trunk of the big tree out front, Ima had wrinkled her nose. Then she tasted it. How could something so fantastic come from wood?

She carried her plate and glass to the counter.

"Did you enjoy your pancakes?" Mama Patty asked. She stirred something on the stove. She was always cooking something that made Ima's mouth water.

Ima nodded. "Where's Papa Charles?"

"Oh, I'm sure he's in the living room." A sadness seemed to flit behind Mama Patty's hazel eyes before her normal smile returned. "He never misses the news."

Ima hadn't tried to upset Mama Patty, but she always rubbed people the wrong way. The other children at CeSiR never wanted her around and they weren't shy to let her know.

She slipped into the living room. Just as Mama Patty said, Papa Charles sat watching the television.

"Whatcha watching, Papa Charles?"

The kind old man turned and smiled at Ima. "Hey there, kiddo. I'm just watching the news. It's important to know what's going on in the world you know."

"Why?"

He cocked his head like a puppy trying to understand its owner. "Why what?"

"Why is it important?" She plopped down on the couch and bounced twice, before grabbing a white-laced pillow and hugging it.

"To be prepared, of course." He passed his hand through half a head of white hair. "The world's a pretty messed up place. Every day there are new wars or threats. Don't eat such and such because it contains E. coli. And that's not to mention the threat the Tigers present to Kansas City."

Ima's breathing quickened as he described a world full of woes and worries. She thought she knew the worst. The facility at CeSiR represented pain, violence, dishonesty, and even death—that she knew. But now she was free. Uncle M had died to get her to freedom. But, if the world outside contained this much pain and sorrow, why did she leave? Was all of humanity as discontented as the other mims? "Are we safe—here?"

"Don't you worry your baby-blues," Papa Charles said. "The news comes from all over the country or further. I don't recall the last time something significant happened around here. Our news is more like, someone drove off from Stan's without paying for their gas."

A woman appeared on the television screen. "This is WKXV TV reporter Alison Cronheim." In the corner of the screen was a picture of a black police officer. "Yesterday, we were on scene of what we were told was Arrow Spring's second murder in a month. The body washed up from the Lamine River, sometime yesterday morning."

The Lamine River? Ima dug into the lace pillow with her shaking hands. It couldn't be. Papa Charles said this was from all over the country. She tried to convince herself she wasn't seeing what she knew she was seeing.

"This was the statement from Arrow Spring's own Sergeant Chris Davis." The screen now contained a live shot of the officer, as the camera panned out to include the scene from the river.

She'd never seen that part of the river. Maybe it wasn't him.

"We're here with Chris Davis, Arrow Spring's very own hero. Thursday night he saved a young woman from an arson fire at her home. Today he's investigating this gruesome discovery. Sergeant Davis, what can you tell us about the body?"

They had found a body. Ima's mind fought to maintain her belief that Uncle M might still be alive. She wanted to run—to flee from the reality crashing in on her from the television.

"I'm afraid I can't tell you much," the officer said. "It does appear to be a homicide. However, we don't believe the victim was shot at this location. We'll tell you what we can as the investigation unfolds."

"Can you tell us who the victim was?"

Please no. Ima's chest began to shake at what would come next.

"No," the officer said.

The blood thumping in her ears began to ease. He wasn't going to tell her.

The officer continued. "We still need to locate the next of kin. And I don't think any of us want them to hear about it from their daily news."

"Oh dear," Papa Charles said. "Hey, Patty! You might want to see this. Someone was shot in Arrow Springs. Down by the river."

"Probably a drug deal went bad down at the River's Edge Bar," Mama Patty said, from the kitchen.

"No, this was upstream from there," Papa Charles said.

Ima's fingers began to release the pillow. They could be talking about someone else. Mama Patty said so.

The woman's voice returned to the television.

Ima turned to see a picture of Uncle M fill the screen. Her fingers clenched the lace of the pillow.

"WKXV has since learned the identity of the victim to be none other than Dr. Wilhelm M'Gregor, founder of CeSiR Tech, one of Arrow Spring's most successful companies."

Sobs wracked Ima's body. She fought to hide her brokenness at the finality of the statement. Fought, and lost.

She had known.

She saw it happen. Yet somehow, the truth descended to her soul like the Titanic. Hope vanished like the final ripples on the surface of the ocean.

"No!" She buried her head in the pillow. "Uncle M."

Her shoulders shuddered and convulsed.

"Shh," A strong hand settled on her shoulder. "It's okay to cry, sweetheart," Papa Charles said. "You knew Wilhelm?"

~~~~~~~~~~

Adiya wrapped her wings around the sobbing child. Death was always hard, but to see her beloved and only friend on the daily news—only once had Adiya experienced that kind of pain. The day her Creator hung from a tree and willingly gave His life for those who most despised Him. The Spirit had stayed her hand when she reached for her sword to cut Him free from that wretched chunk of wood.

She could still see Mary Magdalene. She had become Adiya's charge after Jesus cast seven fallen angels out of the woman. Tears streaked through the dust on Mary's face. Her chest heaved as their Lord spoke the words, *it is finished!*

Adiya hated death. Hated the enemy for their role in leading humanity toward the inevitable end. And hated the pain it caused those left behind.

She held Ima tight for several minutes. Charles and Patricia sat with the child in silence, incapable of comprehending all that the girl had experienced in the past couple days.

Gradually a peace settled over Ima. The doctor's death wasn't new information, but this announcement surely left her feeling alone. Praise God that she was not alone. Only He could have led her to this couple, if only for this very moment.

Finally, Charles broke the silence. "I used to know him."

Ima turned puffy-red cheeks to him. "You knew Unc—, Doctor M'Gregor?" Her crystalline eyes rounded to saucers and her lips pursed.

"I didn't know him well," Charles said. "But I met him on several occasions at the store."

Adiya turned an inquisitive look to Eldwyn.

"Before the onset of the disease," he said. "Charles ran the local hardware store. He knew nearly everyone in the area, even in Arrow Springs. All the homeowners eventually found themselves in need of his wares or expertise." Eldwyn smiled and nodded. "Both were nearly unlimited it seemed."

As Charles went on to lighten the weight of Ima's despair with stories of his interactions with the spunky Scotsman, Adiya walked through the front door of the home.

She needed some time alone. Time to meditate on the truths she knew so well. She walked to a maple tree that shaded the entire front yard, and sat at its base. She unhooked her shield from her right shoulder. Tears of love and anger dripped onto the shield as she held it with the embossed image of the cross facing her.

So much pain. Pain that the enemy brought against humanity—the after-throes of their own rejection of their Creator. Pain that humanity brought against itself. But what hurt most was the pain that so many of His creations brought to their Creator.

Apart from pain the greatest expressions of love cannot exist. The words were spoken into the core of her being.

She traced the edges of the golden cross. The symbol of perfect pain expressing perfect love.

Her understanding was so limited. She had served Him without hesitation or question for millennia. She observed His actions, His wisdom, His creation, and yet she possessed only a minute fraction of His knowledge. How could the enemy claim plans and power to thwart the infinite? She would never understand. Even their worst, He planned to somehow use for the ultimate, eternal good.

"I see you have found my favorite thinking spot." Eldwyn had approached without notice. "After so many years of warring, this assignment provides much reprieve."

Adiya nodded and returned her shield to its holder. Her current assignment would not provide such a respite.

Eldwyn sat next to her. "The death of the doctor gives indication that the enemy is prepared to act, I fear." He patted the flap of armor covering Adiya's shoulder. "We should get inside." His voice bore an urgency.

She followed Eldwyn's gaze to the south-east. The sky seemed to darken as they spoke. "The enemy is on the move," she said. "They cannot know Ima is here."

Eldwyn pushed himself up with his staff and then reached out an arm to help Adiya stand.

Though angels had no limitation to movement in the physical world, she accepted the offer of camaraderie. She pulled herself up and followed Eldwyn to the house.

~~~~~~~~~~~

58

Eldwyn sat atop the Sherwood farmhouse. Like a plague of flies, the sky darkened inch-by-inch, mile-by-mile. The blackness of the enemy blotted out the blue skies of the east. On occasion, dozens of black beings broke formation to attack a home or business. This was a full blown battalion. The enemy never pulled such a force together in one location without the express intent of war. If their destination was the farmhouse, nothing he or Adiya could do would protect the young girl or the dear couple that offered her respite.

Their movement gave indication of a different destination. Somewhere well west of the farm. Excelsior Springs, perhaps. For what evil purpose? He could not speculate.

The afternoon sun still shone brightly on Eldwyn. Given the battalion's numbers, his only hope of protecting the people under his care, including the mim called Ima, was to convince them that a diversion to attack this particular farmhouse would prove most costly. Deep in his being, warmth began to well up. He closed his eyes and basked in the glory of God.

God bless Patricia. The woman spent so much time in prayer. Now, she readily sensed the Spirit's calling. Over Eldwyn's many years, he met many valiant prayer warriors, but he respected none more than Patricia.

Even before his disease, Charles was not a prayer warrior. But he was a man who loved God and His Word. Charles was more of a front line leader and communicator, rather than the behind-the-scenes warrior to whom he was married. That made them a powerful couple for many years. Their reputation alone might keep the enemy from exerting the necessary effort.

"I thought you were going to stay inside?" Eldwyn asked Adiya, his eyes remained closed.

"You need to teach me sometime how you do that," Adiya said. "I will remain out of sight and ensure that any enemy who enters the home regrets it."

Eldwyn held no doubt of Adiya's ability to protect Ima and the Sherwoods, unless the enemy chose a full-on attack. He turned to look at the warrior. "They will be safest on the lower level of the home."

Adiya grinned and nodded. "Ima got too warm in the living room—with a bit of help. Charles and Patricia took her to the basement to play some billiards in the game room."

"Nicely done," Eldwyn said. "I am amazed they could find the billiard balls. Many years have passed since they were last used."

The blackness had nearly reached the farm. "Please stay out of sight," Eldwyn said. "Your presence will raise unneeded suspicion."

~~~~~~~~~~

Adiya nestled into the home's large chimney, removing a brick so she could see Eldwyn seated on the roof. Most of the black mass passed well overhead. The farm was not their destination, nor would she expect such a vast army to be sent for a single mim, no matter how special the child might be.

An imposing demon barked out a halt order. A dozen lesser demons joined him as he descended toward Eldwyn.

"Quite an army, is it not?" the demon commander asked. He stopped fifty feet from Eldwyn. His head appeared as that of a bull, much like the mythical Minotaur. "I am Prince Cadfael." He spun a large battle-axe in his hand as he spoke.

"I know who you are, Cadfael," Eldwyn said. "Though I have to wonder of what you would consider yourself prince."

Cadfael snorted and green sulfurous smoke rose from his nostrils. "It would seem you have me at a disadvantage." He grunted. "I have no idea who you are old one."

Eldwyn remained seated. His legs were crossed and he held his staff across his lap. "It makes no difference who I am, only whom I serve." Eldwyn finally looked up at Cadfael. "What concern do you have with this little farm? Why do you bother this *old one?*"

Adiya rested her hand on her sword. She had met Cadfael before. He was a formidable warrior.

Cadfael's muscular form rippled. "I have no concern for this little farm. Only that you would sit defiantly on this roof and challenge our passing."

"I do not challenge your passing," Eldwyn said. "Only your stopping."

Four of the twelve demons, accompanying Cadfael, where archers. The demon prince held up his axe. "Teach this old angel a lesson." He pointed his axe at Eldwyn.

The archers released a volley of black arrows.

The arrows sailed toward Adiya's friend.

Every muscle in her body pushed to drive Adiya to the angel's assistance. But she waited, trusting his wisdom.

As the arrows reached the angel, he swept his staff in a fiery arc.

The staff connected with the arrows, but they did not break.

Instead, they reversed their direction, striking four warriors hovering next to the archers. In a puff of green smoke the four vanished.

"Take him!" Cadfael's voice roared with irritation. The remaining four warriors charged Eldwyn.

He rose to meet the attackers. He took a step backward with his right leg to add power to his stance. Again he swung the staff in a sweeping red arc. Three of the four attackers flew from the roof.

Adiya marveled at the power Eldwyn possessed. The three attackers landed hundreds of feet from the house, where green puffs of smoke appeared.

The remaining attacker ducked to avoid the blow. His momentum carried him through the roof and into the house.

Adiya dropped down the chimney wielding her sword.

The demon grinned, apparently happy to face the feminine warrior instead of the sage old angel on the roof.

His joy was short lived, when she severed the grinning head from its shoulders with a single swing of her sword. The demon vanished into the abyss to await judgment.

Adiya returned to the chimney in time to hear Cadfael say something about wishing he had time to deal properly with Eldwyn. "I'll return when my business in Excelsior Springs is complete."

"Your choice," Eldwyn said.

As Cadfael returned to the mass of demons, Adiya noticed the absence of the four archers that had flanked him. Eldwyn's work no doubt.

The horde moved westward blocking out the afternoon sun for several minutes. Finally, the blackness became just another cloud on the horizon.

"I am glad we are on the same team," Adiya said, as she emerged from the chimney.

Eldwyn nodded. "As am I, my friend." A brief look of panic washed across his face and he looked at the point in the roof where the single demon had made it past him.

"Not to fear," she said, "I dealt with him." The house was secure. "They are none the wiser. Ima and the Sherwoods are safe."

"For the time being," Eldwyn said.

For the time being.

~~~~~~~~~~~~

CHAPTER FIVE

Tuesday, May 12, 2020

Anput soared high above the Lamine River. Beneath her, the river wound its way around the facility known as CeSiR Tech. At three o'clock in the morning the facility buzzed with activity like black ants streaming to and from their hill. While the flawless control of the humanlike puppets intrigued her, Anput preferred preying on humanity's own depravity.

Up ahead, people stumbled out of the River's Edge Bar. That was more her style. She banked and dove closer to the bar. Such a small town. Its entire population could fit in her casino. Still, no matter where you travel in the world, the depravity of humanity prevails. Beneath her a woman slapped a man outside the bar. She then proceeded to climb into his truck.

As much as she desired to explore the *exciting* town of Arrow Springs, she needed to bring her intel to Ophois. Nothing thrilled her more than a good old-fashioned manhunt. Or in this case, a mimhunt. She banked left and followed the river north to the railroad.

As she approached the rail, she saw Ophois, seated in a small clearing. No surprise, he chose to sit next to the railroad rather than the river. She had been present for the Red Sea fiasco, but she had not retained his repulsion for water.

He had not seen her. With the moon behind her, she appeared as black as a typical run-of-the-mill demon, rather than her luxurious gold, turquoise, and lapis lazuli. She circled and landed behind a thicket. She crept around the thicket until she could see Ophois.

A mischievous grin swept across her face.

She let out a low growl and pounced on him.

"What the—" Ophois never sensed her approach.

They rolled across the grass knoll in a flurry of fangs, growls, wings, and howls.

She rolled past him and spun to face him. Laughter erupted from within her. "You are losing your edge Ophois."

He shook himself, spread his wings to realign them, and then tucked them back in place. "Anput," Ophois said. "Are you crazy? I could have destroyed you."

She laughed again. "I think you need a good hunt to sharpen your skills."

He began to respond, but she shushed him. She turned back toward town. She had heard or at least sensed motion. "Who is there?"

A humungous fruit-bat of a demon stepped out from behind a house on the edge of town. "I am truly impressed, Anput. Your awareness far exceeds that of your acquaintance." He nodded to Ophois. "I believe Mael would be interested to know that you are still in town, Ophois." The demon approached.

"What do you want, Tudur?" Ophois asked. "Do you not have that puppet the mayor to tend to?"

"I appreciate your concern, Ophois, but my charge does exactly what I tell him to do. And at this time of night, that is sleep." Tudur swept at the dirt with his leathery wings. "So how is that pathetic excuse for a mim with whom you were charged?" He glanced around the tracks in a mock search for her. "Have you lost her already?"

The back of Ophois' lip quivered as a low growl escaped his mouth. "My charge is none of your business."

"Relax," Tudur said. "I wish you no harm. The fact that you have lost the girl is of no concern to me. Besides, Mael grows more dangerous by the day. The last action I intend to take is to bring him bad news."

Anput stepped up to Ophois and turned her shoulder slightly away from Tudur. "We should be going," she whispered. "I came all this way for a hunt." She stepped back and looked at Tudur. "Not some pointless banter."

Tudur drew his wings. With a mighty swipe, he began to rise backward into the sky. "If I can help, send word." He turned his body toward town, but hooked his neck so that he still faced them. "We have a common enemy. Thwarting His plans is all that matters to me. And it would appear that *she*," he spat out the reference to the mim child, "is somehow part of that plan." His wings flapped again. "If I hear anything, I will let you know."

Anput watched the demon fade into the black sky. She doubted their mutual success was all that mattered to Tudur. She knew his kind. Deception was his skill. He would do, or say, whatever best served him. However, at twice the size of either her or Ophois, better an ally than an enemy.

Together, she and Ophois rose into the air and headed west along the railroad in search of their prey.

She cast a glance back to see if Tudur was following them.

~~~~~~~~~~~

The dull light of an overcast morning seeped through blinds and eyelids. Patricia sat in her white rocking chair meeting with God. She thanked Him for the opportunity granted to her and Charles to bless the sweet young Ima. The girl was beyond hesitant to share anything about her past. In fact, at the mere mention of interest in where she grew up, fear assaulted the child like mid-summer winds tossing ripened stalks of wheat.

Lord, please let her trust us. I do not understand the challenges she has faced, but I can only imagine they were significant.

So many lessons, which most young girls learned early in life, seemed unconsidered by this little one. And yet graciousness and gentleness oozed from her very being. It didn't make sense.

"You are so beautiful when you pray."

She opened her eyes and turned to Charles. Life shone from his hazel eyes, like she had not seen in years. Her heart fluttered in her chest. How could she love a man so much for almost sixty years?

It would seem their guest wasn't the only thing that did not make sense. Since the girl's arrival on Sunday, it was as if the Alzheimer's had simply vanished, like the dew on a July morning.

"I don't want to interrupt you and God," he said "But when you wrap up, why don't you come back over here, so I can cuddle my bride?" He patted the bed where she had rolled back the sheet and blanket about an hour ago.

She had planned a surprise for Ima. Hopefully it would help the child open up a bit. Still, she could spend a little time in the arms of the newly revitalized love of her life.

~~~~~~~~~~~

Adiya sat next to the large maple tree, lost in thought. She considered the audacity of the enemy in Arrow Springs. To think they could supplant the true Creator, by creating their own version of humanity.

Why had the Creator remained silent about their defiance? He spoke them into being with just a few words, He could end this all just as quickly. Yet He allowed them to persist. To revel in their affront to His sovereignty.

Paws slapped at the ground. Heavy breathing approached her. The dog barked and ran past her toward the road.

A black Mercedes turned into the Sherwoods' drive. The morning sun reflected off the windshield and dust rolled from the unpaved gravel.

Unable to see the occupant of the vehicle, Adiya pulled her sword from its sheath. Even in the morning sun, the blade shone a bright flaming red. She shot to the house and stood at the entrance. Her wings quivered as she waited for the car to arrive. She held her sword with both hands pulled to her chest and her elbows pointed outward.

From behind her, a hand settled on her shoulder accompanied by a soothing voice. "Peace, my friend." At the ease of Eldwyn, she withdrew her wings and relaxed her stance.

Goldie ran alongside the car barking.

The car rolled to a stop.

Behind Adiya, the door of the house swung open. She had barely moved aside before an excited Patricia stepped from the home.

A twenty-year-old with curly brown hair bounced from the Mercedes. "Grandma!"

"Sylvia, it is so good to see you," Patricia said. "Where's your car?"

"Brakes need some work and dad didn't want me driving it all the way here." She smiled. "So I was forced to drive his car."

Adiya sheathed her sword and relief swept over her. Clearly, this woman was welcome and should pose no threat to her charge.

~~~~~~~~~~

Ima sat at the table in the dining room eating a sweet and fruity cereal Mama Patty brought home from the grocery store. Every morning of her life, Ima had eaten milk and rice. She had not expected the explosion of flavor when she took her first bite of this cereal.

She picked up the small glass of orange juice and took a sip. It tasted like she just bit into a fresh juicy orange. Oranges were a rare occurrence at the facility. But never to drink.

"Ima," Mama Patty said, "I'd like to introduce you to someone."

Ima looked up from her bowl and saw a woman standing next to Mama Patty. A sandy-brown curl hung down in front of the woman's face. She smiled and swiped the curl to the side. "Hi, Ima. I'm Sylvia." The curl flopped right back into place.

"Sylvia is my granddaughter," Mama Patty said.

Trust no one. The words of Uncle M echoed from somewhere deep in her subconscious. Tension gripped Ima's vertebrae.

"Hi Sylvia. Nice to meet you." She didn't ask the question sitting at the tip of her tongue. *What are you doing here?*

Goldie licked Sylvia's hand and whimpered, softening the tension in Ima's spine.

Mama Patty answered Ima's unspoken question. "I asked Sylvia here to meet you, Ima. I figured it would be nice to talk with someone closer to your own age."

Sylvia looked closer to the age of Maiya, or the nurses that had controlled her life at the facility. She wore small hoop earrings that appeared to pass through holes in her ears. Her tall tanned figure was not that of a pre-teen or even a teenager.

Sylvia must have sensed Ima's assessment. "Closer is obviously a relative perspective." She laughed. Her laugh was infectious. It came from deep within, not the surface laugh Ima so often observed, and not at the expense of someone else. "I'm guessing you must be about twelve?" Sylvia asked.

Ima nodded. She started to speak but her voice caught. The image of Uncle M's birthday card passed through her mind.

"That's only six years younger," Mama Patty said.

Sylvia grinned and pursed her lips, but decided to correct her grandma. "Actually, it's eight years difference, Grandma. I'm twenty now."

"Of course you are," Mama Patty said. "My memory isn't bad, just my math." She chuckled. "To someone as old as me, six or eight years, why that's just a rounding error."

Goldie had returned to her spot next to Ima's chair. She cast sad eyes Ima's way, begging her to drop something.

"I see Goldie likes you," Sylvia said. "I remember being your age and sitting in that same chair. Does she still set her wet nose in your lap if you ignore her too long?"

Ima giggled and nodded.

"Well you finish eating, Ima. Mama and I have a few things to discuss. Maybe we can take Goldie for a walk later."

The two women walked into the kitchen.

~~~~~~~~~~~

Patricia had known what was coming before they entered the kitchen.

"Mama, you can't just keep her here like she's some stray cat that wandered into the barn." Sylvia meant well.

Patricia wondered why her children, and even her grandchildren, felt that somewhere between sixty and eighty she had lost her ability to think for herself. "I understand your concern, but you haven't been here. You haven't seen the fear in her eyes at any mention of her past or the authorities."

Wrinkles crept into the corner of Sylvia's eyes. She worried too much. A twenty-year-old woman shouldn't have enough worries to cause wrinkles—even if she was scrunching her face in concern. "Perhaps, her fear of authorities is all the more reason to be cautious," Sylvia said.

"Charles and I have discussed that," Patricia said. "He thinks she's seen more pain than we can fathom for a girl so young."

"Mama—" Sylvia shook her curls from side to side. "You know grandpa isn't in a state of mind to make such a decision. He barely remembers who you are."

Patricia could hardly contain the joy bouncing in her old knees. On the phone, Patricia had told Sylvia that she had a surprise for her. Most likely her granddaughter thought she meant Ima. A grin crept to her face. "I think you should go talk to him."

Sylvia's eyes shimmered. "I—" She took a deep breath.

Before she could finish the thought, Patricia pointed to the doorway. "He's in the living room."

As much as Sylvia disliked seeing her grandfather with the dementia, she obeyed her grandmother. She turned and left the room.

~~~~~~~~~~

Ophois and Anput followed the railway to a metal bridge that crossed the Blackwater River. They dropped to the center of the bridge. Even from twenty feet above the bridge, Ophois smelled the familiar scent of fear.

They landed on the bridge. "Can you smell her?" he asked.

"Yes," Anput said. "She was none too happy about crossing this bridge."

Ophois looked to his left, water. He glanced to the right, water. His legs began to quiver. Through the slats beneath his feet he saw more water. "Let us," he licked his drying lips, "leave this place."

"Relax, Ophois." Anput placed her hand on his shoulder. "The water cannot hurt you."

Yes, he knew. The fear was inexplicable. He tried to redirect his thoughts. "Despite such intense fear, the child still came out here. That can only mean she is intent on sticking to the tracks." When they reached the end of the bridge, the pungent aroma of fear dissipated. Any scent of the mim was soon overwhelmed by the stale smell of diesel. They needed to find a more recent trace to track her.

They soared through the air following the tracks. A small auto salvage yard lay ten miles west of Arrow Springs. As they descended toward the graveyard full of rusted accident remains, three junkyard dogs began barking ferociously. Dogs often seemed to have the strange ability to sense spiritual beings.

"Shut up!" yelled a male voice. It appeared the individual was not too fond of being awoken before his hangover wore off. Several choice profanities followed and the barks became growls.

Ophois let out a loud howl of his own. To his right Anput echoed the howl. Her sources had uncovered an interaction between this man and Ima. Apparently, a feminine angel named Adiya had bested three demons who had desired to ambush Ima.

A lizard-faced demon sat atop the trailer that served as both a home and salvage yard office. "Ophois, nice to see you my friend." The demon of lust turned his leer to Anput. "And even nicer to see your friend here." He sucked green drool back through the corner of his mouth.

They needed to get the necessary info before Anput tired of his boorish actions and eliminated him.

"It is our understanding that you have information about a young girl who passed this way. She travelled along the railroad tracks," Ophois said.

"And what if I do?" the demon of lust asked.

"You could always talk with Mael, about how you allowed her to escape," Ophois said. "Though I should think you would prefer to assist us."

Anput tapped Ophois on the shoulder. She nodded her head toward a stack of cars.

"Perhaps your friend over there saw something and would care to share," Ophois said.

From the stack of cars came a grunt and a bull-faced demon stepped toward them. "Yeah, we saw her. She and that warrior headed northwest along the tracks."

"See," Ophois said, turning to the demon of lust. "That was not so hard." He and Anput began to rise back into the sky. "Send us word, if you hear anything more."

"On one condition," the bull-faced demon said.

"Which is?"

"If you find her, allow us to join you for the attack."

"I am sure that can be arranged," Ophois said.

A good diversion always proved valuable when squaring up against heavenly warriors.

~~~~~~~~~~~

Sylvia slipped into the living room and sat on the sofa. Her grandfather sat in his easy-chair, comatose. Perhaps it was her fault that her grandparents had taken in the stray child. They hadn't even made a call to the police to see if the girl was a runaway. Sylvia had spent nearly every weekend and most of her summers with her grandparents, ever since she could remember.

Her dad and step-mom split up when she was ten, but even the years prior to that held tension and trial. One time when she was too young to know better, she had broken down in tears when it came time for her grandparents to take her home. Charles insisted they drive around the countryside until she composed herself. He had feared she would be in trouble with her step-mom. Actually, her step-mom treated Sylvia like she was her own daughter, and still did, even after the divorce.

Then came the Alzheimer's. As much as Sylvia loved her grandparents, the tears came whenever she headed toward *their* house. Even now, as she sat on the couch watching Papa sleep, the familiar lump slid up her throat like a dead rat through a snake. When the disease first set in, he would mistakenly call her Julia, her deceased mother's name. That wasn't a big deal, her step-mom constantly called her by her half-sister's name. But then he started calling her by his dead sister's name. This unsettled her. Her brilliant Papa had slipped to his childhood, and beyond repair. The last time she came, he had never even acknowledged her presence.

What had gotten into Mama? *Charles and I have discussed that . . . He thinks . . .*

Could it be?

Was the wretched disease finally overtaking Mama, as well? Warm water slid from the corners of her eyes.

She arose and started to tiptoe from the room. She would convince Mama to contact the authorities—or do it herself.

"Hey there, Window Syl."

The rat grew to a raccoon.

She turned glossed eyes to the easy chair where her grandfather sat with an ear-to-ear grin.

The dam burst. Three years of guilt-ridden-sorrow gushed through. She could no longer see Papa through her tears. Sobs wracked her chest as she felt for the sofa.

She sat and buried her soggy face in her hands and tears ran across her wrists.

The cushion moved next to her. "Shhh. It's okay Syl. I've been away for quite a while." Papa's voice spoke warmth into her soul. He pulled her into a strong embrace.

After what seemed like an hour, she finally began to regain her composure. She swiped at her face with tear and snot laden hands. The raccoon had surely moved from her throat to her face. She didn't care. She looked into the sparkling hazel eyes of Papa. Life danced behind them.

"I—I don't understand," she said.

"Neither do I," Papa said. The grin returned to his face. "Then again, I think that's been par for the course for some time now."

Her mind told her it wasn't funny—not to laugh at his condition. But her heart laughed anyway. A laugh that rolled from her heart to her face.

"Have you met Ima?" he asked.

It was one thing for him to remember his granddaughter, with whom he'd spent nearly twenty years. But he even remembered the name of a young girl who wandered into their home only two days ago. Mama always talked about God being capable of miracles. Never had Sylvia dreamed she would experience one firsthand.

"The man told me we should take care of her."

The laughter fled like air from a balloon. "Who told you?" Was he seeing things? Talking to imaginary people? It was one of the stages.

"In my dream." He pointed to his easy-chair. "Right there, Sunday morning."

~~~~~~~~~~

Adiya looked at Eldwyn. "You?"

"Not me," he said. "Must have been a vision direct from God." He walked behind the elderly man and rested his wing on the man's shoulder. "Of this, I have not heard. Until now."

Charles continued, "He said that through her, I would be whole."

Eldwyn locked eyes with Adiya. "Ima, Germanic for *whole*."

Adiya dropped to her knees. The child, Ima, her charge had been used by the Heavenly Father to bring wholeness to Sylvia's grandfather. Yet she could not shake the feeling that her name meant more. The weight of responsibility grew immense as she reflected on the implications.

73

"No wonder the enemy is intent on destroying her," Eldwyn said. "The Creator has chosen her for His good work and it would appear the enemy may be aware, at least in part."

Sylvia seemed to struggle with Charles' story of divine revelation. She stood and paced only feet from Adiya. "So you believe you had a vision or dream or whatever that told you to take care of this Ima?"

"Crazy, huh?" Charles chuckled. "Sylvia, look at me. What proof do you need beyond my own awareness?" The man watched his granddaughter pace and then asked another question. "Do you remember why I called you Window Syl?"

The young woman stopped pacing and stared at the floor. She said nothing.

"You do, don't you?" Charles asked. "It is still true." He waited until Sylvia looked up at him. Tears once again flitted across her eyes. "The window is clear as ever," he said. "I can see straight to your heart, Sylvia. Don't you ever lose that."

The young woman ran to him and wrapped her arms around him. "I love you, Papa."

Sylvia stepped back and rested her hands on her grandfather's shoulders. "And I do believe you."

~~~~~~~~~~~

A black BMW, license plate CT06-F24, pulled off the road and up to a large oak tree. The Sherwood farmhouse sat beyond the intersection. The driver unbuckled his seat belt, but remained behind the wheel.

Perched atop the car, Tudur watched a golden retriever roll around in the Sherwoods' lawn. He dared not get Mayor Richards out of the vehicle with the dog so close. The dog seemed oblivious to the car, but a person wandering near its property would get the wretched beast barking.

The time for action might come, but not yet.

His information indicated that the Sherwoods were harboring the mim, Ima. Information he had not shared with that pathetic excuse for a demon, Ophois. Let them look. Nor did Tudur see the need to inform Mael. With Detective Davis snooping around CeSiR, the demon prince had become exceptionally malevolent.

No, Tudor would not make the self-destructive mistake of Legion. Legion, Leon as he desired to be called, chose to work closely with Mael—to kiss the feet of the prince to win his favor. A great way to live, until one screwed up. As Leon, discovered.

Tudur had rather enjoyed the authority he amassed when Mael eliminated Leon. But now, Detective Davis' investigation was beginning to feel like a louse in a hair salon. The police department in Arrow Springs was under the mayor's control. And Tudur controlled the mayor. No doubt, Prince Mael would see the interference as a failure on Tudur's behalf.

If it came to the point where he needed to bring Mael bad news, he would need an offering of propitiation.

The dog ran to the front porch of the home and a young girl swung the door open and allowed the beast to enter.

His information was correct.

His sacrificial offering stood on the porch watching a cow graze beyond an electric fence. How many cows had died in the glory days of sacrifice? He missed those days. The days when humanity's attempts to appease their gods, and even the True God, came through bloodshed rather than pathetic acts of retribution. He had driven so many to the point of sacrifice throughout the years. He had mastered the cycle of failure and guilt. Acts of rebellion followed by self-justification followed by more acts of rebellion. He could keep a person in the sin-cycle for years, even a lifetime. Anything to keep them away from the only sufficient sacrifice.

The mim turned and walked back into the house, oblivious to Tudur's presence.

He returned to Trenton Richards, still seated behind the steering wheel of the BMW. For now, the location of the girl would remain his little secret. Hopefully, Ophois and Anput would not find her. If they did, he would deal with them.

The tides were turning in Arrow Springs. He would love to deal with Ima in his leisure. But he would soon be pressed to return for the young mim.

"See you soon, little lamb," Mayor Trenton Richards said.

~~~~~~~~~~~

For the first time, since Mama Patty discovered her in the barn, fear washed through Ima. Was it the arrival of Sylvia? She seemed sweet enough.

Sylvia had spent several minutes with Papa Charles in the living room, then they both joined Ima and Mama Patty in the kitchen. Their faces were red from crying, but they bore wide smiles. After a few minutes getting to know each other, Mama Patty had asked Ima to let Goldie out.

Though the weather outside was warm and pleasant, Ima shivered as she closed the front door. She walked back to the kitchen, but stopped beside the entrance.

"Are you sure you shouldn't at least contact the authorities?" Sylvia's voice drifted soft but impassioned from the kitchen.

Ima stepped to the side of the archway. She rested her back against the wall.

"I don't see what that would accomplish," Papa Charles said.

"Look, I like her too," Sylvia said. "She seems sweet. But no twelve-year-old is that naïve. She's playing you."

Ima slid down the wall to the floor. Her lips quivered.

"Sylvia. That is enough." Mama Patty didn't sound mad, just hurt. "We may be old, but we're not foolish."

Were they planning to return her to CeSiR? Had they already contacted the police?

"Mama," Sylvia said. "I would never call you foolish. You are the wisest people I know."

Should she run now, before they turned her over to the people who made her life so miserable? Her knees shook.

"But," Sylvia continued. "You are also the most loving people I know. I just don't want to see you hurt."

76

Ima couldn't imagine wanting to harm Mama Patty or Papa Charles.

"Not because of some dream that you think was from God."

There was a lengthy pause in the kitchen. Ima needed to move. They couldn't come out and find her eavesdropping. They would never trust her again. She commanded her body to move. It wouldn't listen. Any moment someone would walk through the archway.

Mama Patty's voice broke the silence. "What dream?"

"I'm sorry, Papa." A slight tremor ran through Sylvia's voice. "I didn't know you hadn't told her."

Goldie army crawled up to Ima, as if she knew they were spying on those in the kitchen. Ima scratched her behind the ears.

"With the shotgun, a girl in the barn, and my restored faculties," Charles said, "I guess it just slipped my mind."

"Shotgun?" Sylvia's voice rose an octave.

Mama Patty's laughter snorted from the kitchen. Soon, all three appeared to be laughing.

"Granny, get your gun," said Papa Charles with a chuckle.

This seemed like a good time to join them. Ima couldn't run away. Where would she go? She needed to trust the couple. Maybe she could convince Sylvia to trust her. Even before Ima could convince her body to move, Goldie headed toward the laughter in the kitchen. She probably associated laughter with dropped food. The dog scurried into the kitchen.

"Hey there, Goldie," Sylvia said. "Where've you been?"

Ima followed the dog into the kitchen. "What are you all laughing at?" As if she didn't know.

Papa Charles smirked. "We were just telling Sylvia about Annie Oakley here." He pointed to Mama Patty. "When she caught a stowaway in our barn." He winked at Ima.

Mama Patty swatted him on the shoulder.

They laughed again. This time Ima joined them, though she had no idea who Annie Oakley was.

A couple hours later, the three of them stood on the porch waving to Sylvia. She pulled away in her dad's Mercedes.

~~~~~~~~~~~

Ophois and Anput spent several hours scouting the small town of Marshall. They asked several of their associates if they had seen anyone matching Ima's description over the past couple days. An overweight demon of gluttony claimed to have seen her walking along the tracks on the southeast side of town. So Ima had stuck to the tracks since leaving Arrow Springs. It also seemed she had moved on, rather than staying in town.

Several of the heavenly host had made it perfectly clear that their inquiries around town were unwelcome. He and Anput narrowly escaped one encounter.

Now, they soared north of town along the railway. The opposition in Marshall had unsettled him. He needed to compose himself—to refocus on the task at hand. The hunt. A mere child could not evade their skillful hunt for long.

Below them a unique intersection of tracks presented a decision. Which way would she have chosen? They alighted on the top of an old railway overpass. He could hardly imagine the long modern trains of today traveling over this bridge. Its sharp slopes and narrow breadth evidenced a usefulness long since past. The girl would never have climbed up on this bridge, unless needed.

Was there a purpose to her decisions? Did she even know her destination?

When she fled CeSiR, she was accompanied by the doctor. Certainly any plans for travel were made by him, as evidenced by the plane tickets that went unused. No, her decisions were more primal—ease, survival, fear.

They investigated the girl's options. The crossing tracks were decrepit and would have scared off the timid child.

Anput swept back her intense golden wings and shot into the air.

Ophois leapt after her. They soared along the tracks, dodging side-to-side to avoid the occasional tree branch hanging over the tracks. White-concrete crossings flashed beneath them as they picked up speed. Most of the crossings were not roads, nor options to consider, but rather farm-implement crossings. The occasional river, creek, or drainage ditch passed underneath, quick enough to prevent dwelling on the water beneath him.

In mere seconds, a lengthy coal train churned past them. Down he dove, inhaling the rich exhaust.

"They worry so much about this." Anput motioned toward car after car filled with coal. "The damage it will do to the environment, and *His* creation." She laughed. "While they destroy His most precious creations, themselves."

"I have no problem with that." Ophois let out a train-whistle howl.

They continued on their way, occasionally checking a farm, or a town—not much bigger than a farm. No sign of Ima. Nor had any of the demons in the area seen her.

Soon they came to the town of Waverly. The railroad passed uncomfortably close to the Missouri river.

"Let us stop here and see what we can uncover." He surveyed the area. "Why so many demons for such a tiny little town?"

~~~~~~~~~~

CHAPTER SIX

Wednesday, May 13, 2020

Ima laughed at Goldie. The dog ran in place for what seemed like several seconds, trying to get traction on the linoleum flooring. Tags tinkled, as Goldie chased a pink rubber ball across the kitchen. The dog tried to both brake and turn, but proved successful at neither. She smacked into a white cabinet door.

"You two be careful," Mama said. "You make me drop this mixing bowl and there won't be any dessert tonight."

It seemed Ima had just finished helping Mama clean up dinner dishes. Already, the dear woman was hard at work on dessert.

"What ya making?" Ima asked. She spied a box of graham crackers sitting on the counter. Three days ago, the crackers would have been at the top of her all-time food list. Once, Uncle M had smuggled a similar box in to CeSiR. She ate the entire box in one sitting and washed them down with water. To Ima, that was heaven, until she met Mama.

"Well," Mama said. "I don't really know what to call it. I've heard many different names, but never found one I like." She pointed to the bowl in her hand with a rubber spatula. "This here is chocolate pudding. I made it before dinner and put it in the refrigerator to set. I'm going to spread it over top of the graham crackers and cream cheese that are already in that pan there."

She'd just eaten, but Ima began to feel hungry.

Mama kicked the rubber ball out of the kitchen and Goldie bolted after it. "Would you like to help me make it?" she asked.

"Really?" Ima ignored the flash of golden fur flying past her. "Can I?"

"Of course." Mama slid the bowl next to the pan and handed the spatula to Ima. "Use this to spread the pudding evenly over that cream cheese layer."

Ima plopped a big dollop of pudding in the pan and began swiping it around the pan. "Like this?"

"Yep. Be careful not to dig into the cream cheese with the spatula."

Ima continued wiping the pudding toward the edges. Suddenly, the spatula slipped and a large gash of white filling mixed with the brown chocolate. "Oh no." She dropped the spatula in the pan. The bridge of her nose started to burn, as tears crept to her eyes. "I'm sorry. I didn't mean to." She stared at the line in the pan where graham crackers peeked through. "Did I ruin it?"

Mama laughed and put her arm around Ima's shoulder. "Goodness no, child. It's just a dessert. There's nothing to fret about. If something doesn't go quite right, just try again." She picked up the spatula and deftly swept the cream cheese back into place. "See, just like that. Good as new." She lowered her voice to a whisper. "I bet Papa won't even notice." She winked at Ima.

Ima took a deep breath. Her caretakers at the facility never smiled at a mistake. They would have slapped her and accused her of messing up on purpose. She took the spatula from Mama and began again. Soon, all of the pudding was in the pan. "Now what?" she asked.

"Now—" Mama said. "Now the best part." She pointed to the counter by the sink. "Now you take the spatula over there and make sure you've licked all the pudding off it." She glanced in the bowl. "It looks like you might have to do that a few times to get all the yummy crusty pudding from the edges of the bowl."

81

Ima giggled and scurried, with the bowl and spatula, to the counter next to the sink. The pudding was fabulous, even better than it had smelled. When she finished, Mama was shaving pieces of a dark chocolate candy bar onto the top of a layer of whipped cream.

"Now, we put it in the fridge, until its snack time." Mama set her hand on Ima's shoulder. "Wash that chocolate off your face, and then go see what Papa is up to. I'll clean up in here."

Ima splashed warm water from the sink onto her face and then wiped the water, and some leftover chocolate, onto a towel that hung over a cupboard door.

Soon, Ima sat on the couch in the living room and glanced at Papa. Wrinkles furrowed his brow. He had not looked so serious since the news about Uncle M.

"What's the matter, Papa?" The television showed a mug-shot of an ornery looking man. Whoever the man was, Papa looked completely disturbed.

"I can't believe it happened again," Papa said. "I remember my father telling me about an almost identical incident. It occurred nearly a hundred years ago in the same little town of Excelsior Springs." Papa shook his head and looked down at the floor. "We live in a country with the right to a fair trial— until a mass of people think they know better." He stopped talking and stared at the bloody picture of a man who, according to the words on the television screen, was beaten to death by a vigilante crowd.

Ima listened to a woman's voice coming from the TV. "Yesterday, the police apprehended a new suspect in the sexual assault case. Upon interrogation the suspect confessed—not only to the sexual assault, but to the murder last week, which had driven a vigilante crowd to kill the then-primary-suspect." The picture cut to the woman sitting behind a desk. "It would appear the suspect, and riot victim, was innocent of all crimes. Police are reviewing video footage from the beating to determine who will face charges."

"What a zoo," Papa said. "Excelsior Springs is one of the nicest towns I know." He shook his head. "It's like the whole town went nuts."

"Why do you call it a zoo?" Ima asked. "I thought there were only animals in a zoo?" Though she had never even seen a zoo. Did they keep people in zoos? She envisioned her tiny room at CeSiR, but with bars and people gawking at her.

"It's a figure of speech, child." Mama laid her hand on Ima's shoulder—apparently done with her chores in the kitchen.

Papa pointed a remote at the television and the image disappeared. "Enough bad news. Have you ever been to a zoo?" he asked Ima.

"No." She pushed the words through tight lips. "Sounds scary."

Papa laughed—from his belly. "No, child. Zoos are lots of fun. We should take you."

"That's a great idea," Mama said. "I don't remember the last time I went to the K.C. zoo."

~~~~~~~~~~

Ophois and Anput spent most of the day in Waverly. Within the first hour, it became clear they would not find Ima there. Instead they joined in the freeing revelry of demonic activity. None of the gathered demons paid Ophois much mind. Anput, on the other hand, gathered quite a crowd, and with it significant information on the horde's mission.

It seemed Cadfael, one of the commanders stationed at CeSiR Tech, had led an army to Excelsior Springs to await a wave of reinforcements being sent by the angelic host. Though Ophois had no desire to reunite with Cadfael, it seemed the demons that remained in Waverly were simply stragglers, buying time and unleashing havoc.

After a night of arrests, adultery, drunkenness, and brawls, the time had come to continue their search.

They proceeded along the railroad. Ophois stayed to the left of the tracks, while Anput flew to his right, between him and the Missouri River.

The tang of tar scented railroad ties approached. They shot past wooden planks, readied to replace older ties, bleached and rotted by years of sun and weather. From above, the new ties looked like ebony sharps and flats on a massive grand piano.

Soon, the railroad widened to dual tracks. They had neither heard nor sensed any sign of their prey for a couple days. Still, he could not help feeling that they had headed in the right direction. Perhaps, a night of debauchery had simply improved his outlook.

At times, the path they followed wound inland, a comfortable distance from the rushing waters of the Missouri. Then inexplicably, it wound back and ran mere feet from the dreaded water.

They came up empty in the towns of Lexington, Wellington, and finally the town of Buckner passed. No scent or indication of the young mim. Anput cast him a concerned look. "You realize we will soon reach the town of Independence, and then the train yards in Kansas City."

The same thoughts had run through his mind for the past hour. Two great dilemmas sat before them. Once the young mim reached the train yard, it would be impossible to predict her actions. To this point, the tracks would have led her here. But, in the train yard, there were many options. They still had no indication of her purpose or destination.

The second concern brought more fear than losing the girl for good. Once they entered Independence, only minutes away, they would no longer be in Mael's territory. Garnoc, prince of the Kansas City region, would learn of their presence. Ophois and Garnoc often butted heads—never to Ophois' advantage. To wander into his territory uninvited would raise his treacherous ire.

"Should we turn back?" Anput asked. "We have no solid evidence that she came this way, or this far." She pulled up and landed on a tree next to the tracks. "Do we risk his wrath without reason?"

Ophois alighted next to her. "I wished I could be certain. Instinct tells me to push on, into Kansas City." He swallowed hard. "Besides, I am uncertain that facing Garnoc would be worse than—"

"Returning and facing Mael?"

Ophois simply nodded, unwilling to admit his fear of returning to his prince.

Ophois breathed deeply. He and Anput soared into the sky, and then sped along the tracks toward Independence.

~~~~~~~~~~~

Garnoc sat high in his city stronghold. Many of the heavenly host had responded to the unrest in Excelsior Springs. Criminals were being bussed in to the Kansas City jails from the small town to the northeast. With the enemy so preoccupied, the effectiveness of Garnoc's forces had never been better. Each day, people drifted to their own desires; power, lust, money, accomplishment. He cared not what turned their hearts, so long as they turned from *Him*.

Sure he relished the days when their deceptions were more overt. Witchcraft, sorcery, outright worship of the sun, moon, stars, and his favorite, the waters. But the covert proved just as effective. Save the planet, but deny its Creator. Rescue abused animals, but turn a blind eye to the children being trafficked into the cities. Decry the hypocrisy of religion, while making right and wrong a matter of personal opinion.

Yes, the battle progressed nicely, though the ultimate war seemed impossibly hopeless. "Force *His* hand," Lucifer had once cried. The one way to claim at least a minute equality to the Sovereign was to force Him to intervene. Cause enough dissension and destruction, and He would have no choice but to step in. Only in such an act of desperation by the Almighty could their victory emerge—the usurping of *His* sovereignty.

"My liege," a small demon said.

"You interrupt my solitude?" Garnoc asked. "What news do you believe is worth risking your existence in this realm?"

The small demon shuttered and dared not look into Garnoc's eyes. Cowardice, which limited him to a scout for their forces, preserved his existence. The demon seemed to hyperventilate as it attempted to clear its fragile little throat.

"Speak!" Garnoc roared. "Do you risk yourself for nothing at all?"

"Yes, my liege." The demon's eyes grew large as saucers, even as he heard himself say the words. "I mean, no, my liege." He coughed. "There are two outsiders searching Independence—for a young girl."

Garnoc sighed. The matters that the minor demons deemed worthy. Some days, it pleased him greatly that he had not created such insolent creatures. "Are these outsiders from the heavenly host?"

"No, my liege," the demon answered. His speed of response demonstrated a lessening fear. "They are demonic. It is said that they come from Arrow Springs."

Garnoc grabbed the demon by the throat. "What makes you think a couple of demons, from a neighboring principality, would be enough to break my solitude, without me breaking your neck?" He lifted the demon to eye-level.

The demon's throat crackled as its voice screeched. "Commander Adwur, my liege."

He tossed the demon aside. It made sense. Adwur knew better than approach Garnoc with the information, so he sent this expendable flee to do it. "And why would Adwur believe I would care?"

The demon shook his head and then glanced up at Garnoc, as if squeezing his neck had brought the waters of recollection to the surface. "He said you would know them, my liege. Ophois and Anput?" How could those names mean nothing to this scout?

Garnoc unfurled his mighty wings and roared at the demon. "You tell Adwur to take several of his best. Bind the intruders and bring them to me at the viaduct." He reached down, grabbed the demon by the wing, and sent him whirling into the sky, wingtip over wingtip.

~~~~~~~~~~

CHAPTER SEVEN

Thursday, May 14, 2020

Three o'clock in the morning and Ophois had tired of the wise-crack responses of the lesser demons throughout town. If one more sniveling snout laughed at him for losing track of a twelve-year-old girl, he would pull his scimitar and cut them down in their tracks—regardless of who controlled the principality.

They turned down an alley. Three demons toyed with a couple of strung-out teens. The demons looked up and fled like their feet were on fire.

"Wow," Anput said. "That has to be the quickest you have driven off potential information, yet." Her golden wings rippled with laughter.

The metallic sound of swords being unsheathed stopped her mid-laugh. Her golden feathers ruffled back into place.

They both spun to see their attackers.

The flight of the three demons now made perfect sense.

Four of the largest and orneriest demons Ophois had seen since entering town stood at the opening of the alleyway. They circled Ophois and Anput, leaving them one option—turn and flee.

But, before they could turn, a voice filled the alley behind them. "Hello, Ophois."

They spun again. A demon commander stood ten feet away, flanked by another large demon.

Unlike most run-of-the-bar demons, these six demons bore battle shields, swords or mace, and were clad head to toe in armor. These were warriors. Servants of Prince Garnoc, no doubt.

"We are on mission for Prince Mael," Ophois said. He mostly succeeded in keeping the quiver from his voice. "Who dares interfere with our quest?"

The commander laughed. "I am Adwur, commander of the forces of *this* principality and servant to Prince Garnoc." He pointed a boney finger in the air and swept a small circle with a curled claw.

Instantly, arms of steel locked onto Ophois.

"Hey. Let me go," Anput said, indignant.

Ophois squirmed for a few seconds. These were not demons with whom he could contend. They would require a different approach.

"Prince Garnoc, you say?" Ophois asked. "That is excellent. I have news that your prince will find most interesting. I command you, take us to him at once."

Adwur laughed and smacked Ophois across the nose with the back of his gnarled hand. "You command no one."

Green snot dripped from his burning snout.

"You will see the Prince," Adwur said, "because he commanded it to be so."

The beast next to Adwur slammed a fist into Ophois' stomach. "You would do well to remember your station, slave."

Adwur smirked and turned his back to Ophois. Wide bat-like wings spread across the alley. He arose into the damp night air. "Bring them!"

Ophois' feet left the ground. He despised the sensation of flying without spreading his wings. Steely arms held him like a vice.

"Get your hands off me," Anput ordered. She held more authority in her principality and it showed in her protest. "You will regret this." Still, in this region, they were both, as Adwur had put it, slaves.

Soon, Ophois saw their destination approaching. He struggled with renewed vigor against the unyielding arms around him. Clearly, Garnoc remembered their past interactions. Fear crept from Ophois' knobby knees to his tightening throat. He elbowed the creature holding him. The grip only tightened.

"Hold still," the demon growled. His voice was low and gravelly. "I would hate to drop you in the river."

Somewhere to his right, two other demons began to chuckle.

They soared over the Missouri River.

Moments later, they veered left and he opened his eyes. They were now only a couple dozen feet above the Kansas River. His eyes snapped back shut.

The behemoth released his grip and tossed Ophois downward.

He popped his eyes open, expecting to plunge into the water. Instead, a steel structure approached at breakneck speed. Ophois reached out and grabbed the structure to slow his speed, spun around it, and alighted on the viaduct. Relief swept over him.

Soon, Anput joined him.

"Stay put until Garnoc shows up to deal with you," his captor said. "If you choose otherwise, I will hold you at the bottom of the river until he arrives."

They waited for Garnoc.

~~~~~~~~~~~

Patricia rocked with eyes closed, praying one-by-one for each person ministering at her church. She prayed for her two sons and one remaining daughter. She prayed for her eight grandchildren, and twenty-three great-grandchildren.

"Lord," she whispered. "Thank you for allowing Sylvia to see Charles this way." As was the case during nearly every morning prayer, her eyes moistened. Charles had always possessed a special relationship with Julia, Sylvia's mother. Then when the Lord saw fit to take Julia from them, it tore him up inside. If not for Sylvia, their then infant granddaughter, Patricia wasn't sure Charles would have survived the grief. Now, as Sylvia approached the age of her mother when she passed, the resemblance was unmistakable. Watching her and Charles laugh together, and even Ima entering the fray, was the most precious thing in years.

Patricia went on to pray for friends, and even people she didn't know who needed the Good Lord's protection.

Suddenly, she stopped. Someone or something was watching her. She hated the sensation, but she knew it well. Her eyes snapped open and looked at Charles. His chest rose and fell in a blissful sleep. Oh well, it wouldn't be the first time she'd had that feeling when no one was present.

"What are you doing?"

In a single triple-speed heartbeat, she nearly leapt out of her chair.

"Ima, dear child." She took a deep breath to steady herself. "Are you trying to give an old woman a heart attack?" Her hands shook.

The corners of the girl's mouth drooped. "I didn't mean to scare you." She turned to leave the open doorway.

"No, no. It's okay, child." The blood pounding through her head began to recede. "What did you ask?"

"I—" Ima glanced at Charles. "What were you doing?" she asked, this time in a whisper. "Your mouth was moving." The girl tilted her head sideways. "But Papa is sleeping. Were you talking to yourself?"

Patricia laughed. "No. I was praying. You know, like we do at meals." She motioned for Ima to come join her.

Ima walked over to the chair and sat next to her on the deep window sill. "So you talk to—God?" The girl's eyes squished closer together. "Does He—talk back?"

Patricia paused. How to answer such a simple, yet profound question? "In a sense, yes. Though some people have heard Him in an audible voice, I never have. But I hear Him here." She tapped the center of Ima's chest.

"You mean in your heart?"

90

"Yes, but not the physical heart, the spiritual heart. Your heart is the center of your being. Some people call it your soul." She paused. How much had the young girl ever heard? Did any of this make sense? "I don't know how to explain it, other than to say, you just feel it. You feel Him. And you know He is speaking to you."

"So it's kind of like my conscience?"

"Sometimes. But sometimes, when we listen to ourselves or even that inner voice, it can mislead us. When God speaks to you, it is always truth."

Ima sat silent for a couple minutes. She seemed to have had enough of this strange topic. But then she added, "So how do you know?"

"Know what?"

"If it's Him?"

Patricia smiled and nodded. "That is a great question and I'll admit, sometimes I can't really be sure." She reached over and picked up her Bible from the nightstand next to her. "Do you know what this is?"

"A Bible."

"Right, and it contains God's story." She tapped the Bible. "If what I think God is telling me doesn't conflict with what this says, then at least I know it could be from Him. The more you pray and listen, the more you start to know when He is speaking to you."

"Hey," Charles said, "you two monkeys ready to go to the zoo today?"

Ima giggled and jumped up and down.

"You better go get dressed for the day," Patricia said. "We can talk more about this later."

Though Patricia drove to church each week, nerves began to wrestle with her gut, as she thought about taking the highway into Kansas City.

~~~~~~~~~~

Adiya stepped aside as Ima bounded from the Sherwoods' bedroom. The girl could have passed through her without the slightest awareness, but most angels chose not to intersect with people when unnecessary.

Ima skipped down the hallway and into her room.

Eldwyn winked at Adiya. "Today, you will have an energetic charge, I feel."

Adiya laughed. "Do you think she is excited about the zoo?"

"A smidge, perhaps."

Moments later, Ima bounced down the stairs.

Adiya floated down behind her. The pure joy emanating from Ima filled Adiya's wings like wind in a sail.

Ima leapt up to the kitchen table and poured herself a bowl of crispy rice cereal. She giggled at the popping sound rising from her bowl.

By the time Patricia and Charles made their way down the stairs, Ima was drinking the sugar-sweetened milk from her bowl.

More sugar, just what the girl needed. Adiya grinned and followed her as she bobbed out of the kitchen and to the entryway.

"When are we going to leave?" Ima asked.

Patricia shook her head.

Charles rubbed his eyes. "I just woke up, child."

Goldie seemed to pick up the excitement of Ima and began to chase her ball across the dining room.

"I'll tell you what," Charles said. "Why don't you take Goldie for a walk and we'll plan on leaving in about a half hour."

The door swung open. Both dog and girl jumped through the doorway.

"How long do you think that will buy us?" Charles asked Patricia.

"Not long, I'm afraid. I think we've created a monster." They both chuckled and headed to the kitchen for some toast and coffee.

"The prayers of Patricia will be much needed today, I fear," Eldwyn said. His face bore a seriousness that indicated he did not refer to the ball of energy that just departed the house.

"Whatever the enemy's interest in her," Adiya said, "today will be the most exposed she has been since leaving the facility."

Minutes later, Ima returned with Goldie. The retriever panted heavily. Apparently, the walk had been quick paced. Ima did not seem the least bit winded.

After twenty minutes of the girl ricocheting off the walls, Adiya and Eldwyn sat in the back seat of the Sherwoods' Impala. Ima sat between them leaning on the seats in front of her, chattering to Charles and Patricia.

~~~~~~~~~~~

Ophois shivered as the eastern sunrise reflected off the shimmering water of the Kansas River. With the recent influx of rain, the waters rushed to join the larger Missouri River.

Knowing that water rushed beneath him proved difficult enough when the darkness of night hid all but the splashing rush of the river. Now, in the morning light, the flow of water worked to drive him insane.

Anput sat perched on the viaduct, calm and regal. Her smooth golden appearance rivaled the morning sun's intensity.

The demons that brought them to the viaduct had backed off to the shores. Never any farther.

"Remain calm," Anput had said. "They are only testing you. They want us to attempt an escape so they can attack without repercussion from their prince."

Her presence, more than that of their captors, had kept him there through the early morning hours. He trusted no demon. Since the rebellion, their nature was to scratch and claw, often literally, to advance their rank and position. However, he and Anput always seemed to find their objectives in alignment. She was the closest thing a demon could have to a friend.

A sudden chill flowed through his being. A presence approached. Ophois spun his head to the right. Anput also turned to identify the approaching being.

The rush of the water faded from Ophois' awareness. Black darkness emanated from the approaching being. His head appeared as a massive lizard with the teeth of a tyrannosaurus. A line of spikes ran the full length of his neck and back like a horned tree lizard, yet he possessed the arms and torso of a gorilla. His legs were as powerful as a rhino.

Garnoc approached.

Ophois glanced to the shore. Their captors lay prostrate on their faces in the presence of their prince.

"Submission," Anput whispered.

Garnoc landed between Ophois and Anput. He stood half again the height of Mael. He drew his dragon-like wings back against the row of spikes on his back.

Ophois knelt low. "My liege."

"I am not *your* liege." Garnoc's voice hissed deep and unsettling. "Your principality is to the east. Is it not?"

Ophois swallowed deep. "Yes, my li—" Uncertainty about how to address the demon prince struck him silent. He only dared stare at the demon's talon-clad feet. He observed the remaining extent of Garnoc's form through peripheral vision.

Garnoc's upper lip pulled into a pleased grin, revealing razor sharp fangs.

"What would bring a farm-rat like yourself into my principality?" Garnoc asked.

Ophois looked up to answer the question.

The prince growled when their eyes connected.

Ophois' eyes snapped back to the ground. "We are looking for a young girl, my li—" Ophois growled under his breath. It would be better to be banished than to cower like a beaten puppy.

"You may refer to me as *your majesty*," Garnoc said. His voice bore amusement with the sniveling of Ophois. "Why should I care about some human that Mael seeks?" He waited not for an answer. "Mael is a minor prince in a tumbleweed principality. I do not care about any of his petty efforts."

"You are correct, your majesty," Anput said. "Certainly Lucifer's assignments for one such as you, in such an impressive city, far exceed those he has given Mael."

Garnoc turned and studied Anput. "It is clear you are not of Mael's principality. You speak as one who is accustomed to working with meaningful princes. Might I enquire of your principality?"

Anput rose to a knee, but did not look up to the eyes of Garnoc. "Your majesty may inquire of anything he likes," she said. "I am from the principality of Las Vegas. I have been assigned the operations of one of the casinos."

Garnoc turned his attention back to Ophois. "You could learn much from this one."

"Yes, your majesty."

The powerful right arm of Garnoc reached to the shoulder of Ophois. "And what could Mael possibly be up to, that Lucifer himself would have any awareness?" He tightened his grip. The message need not be spoken. He was not to be trifled with and he demanded the truth.

Anput's words had hit their mark.

"The girl we seek—she is not human. At least, she is not of the Creator."

Garnoc released his shoulder and, with strong fingers, raised Ophois' head until he stared directly into the smoldering eyes of the enormous prince. "What do you mean, not of the Creator?" He spit green sulfurous spittle to the side of Ophois. "All is created by *Him*." He growled deep in his throat.

"We have succeeded in cloning humans to create what we call mims."

"Mims?"

"Yes, for Manufactured Images of Man." Ophois paused to let this sink in. If Ima was in Kansas City, or had been, they needed Garnoc's help to find her. "These mims are unlike any human you have ever met. They offer no opposition, no will to override, just pure control."

Garnoc pulled away from Ophois, clearly considering what he heard. "This girl you seek, she is one of these mims?"

"Yes, your majesty," Anput said. "If you help us find her, you can observe for yourself."

Ophois feared the next question, the one he himself did not understand.

"You believe she is in Kansas City?" Garnoc asked.

Whew. Not the question Ophois feared. "Perhaps. She appeared to follow one of the railroads into Kansas City." A stretch, but not an outright lie. At one point she was following the rail toward his town. "But we have been unable to locate her. This is why we asked to speak with you."

"If these mims are soulless creatures, as you say, then how is it that this one has escaped your charge?"

That question. "Umm, this one seems different," said Ophois.

"Or perhaps," Garnoc said. "It is due to your incompetence as a caretaker."

Garnoc stayed for what seemed like an hour. He did not speak, but paced the viaduct. Finally, he spread his reptilian wings and began to float away from the viaduct. He turned his head. "I will see what I can discover." With another flap of his scaled wings, he moved much quicker. "If I find you are telling me the truth, perhaps, I will not bury you beneath the river." He banked toward the east.

Garnoc barked out orders to their captors. "Ensure they remain, until I return."

"Yes, my liege," one of the demons said.

~~~~~~~~~~~

Ima watched a black and white sign turn into a blur, as it passed the side window of the car. The sign contained the outline of the state of Missouri and the number twenty in the middle. "What does that sign mean?" she asked.

"It means Mama Patty is taking the long way to the zoo." Papa held out the word *long* for a couple extra beats.

"You just never mind how I get there," Mama scolded Papa. "Church and the grocery store are about all the driving I do these days. Interstate seventy scares me. People drive way too fast."

Papa pursed his lips together and nodded at Ima.

"Hey, you two behave yourselves." Mama shook her head and then went back to staring out the front window over two clenched hands.

"I told you I would drive," Papa said.

"You don't have a license." Mama sounded perturbed, yet she smiled.

"Well, I haven't forgotten how to drive," Papa said. His tone was defensive.

"That may be true now, but a week ago you didn't even know my name. There's no way I am going to let you drive." Mama's eyes glistened in the rearview mirror. The memory of Papa's former state must have caught Mama off guard. "Besides, you never would have passed the test." She slowed to a stop and cranked her neck to check for cars. The angle of the merging road made it difficult to see cars that would approach from nearly behind them.

Ima looked out the back window. There were no cars to be seen on the road. "I don't see any cars," she said.

"That road is right in my blind-spot," Mama said. "I'll take your word for it." She accelerated onto the road, glancing multiple times in the mirrors for any approaching cars.

"That's why you have to look before you get to the intersection," Papa said.

"Believe me," Mama said, "I'd let you drive if I could."

They chit-chatted for several minutes until a sign announced that they were approaching Lexington.

"Have you ever played the Alphabet Game?" Papa asked.

Ima shook her head. At the facility games were rare, and she often found herself on the wrong end of the fun.

"It's really easy," Papa said. "You know your alphabet, don't you?"

She grinned and nodded.

"Well then, you just look for words outside the car containing an A. Then you work your way up through the alphabet. When you see one, like that sign there for Waverly, you say, A – Waverly."

The green road sign flew past the car.

"Then we all start looking for the next letter," Papa said.

"B – Business." Ima giggled when she spotted a green sign with the word business over another map of Missouri. This time the map contained the number thirteen.

Mama laughed. "I think she's got it."

The game progressed quickly as they picked letters off signs, car license plates, and semi-trucks. They reached the letter J and fell silent for several minutes.

Just as Ima began to grow tired of looking, she spotted a sign for McDonald's—just five minutes ahead. "J – Just!" She yelled it into the ears of Mama and Papa.

Mama jumped. "Easy child. I 'bout had a heart attack."

Ima giggled and then lowered her head to evade the eyes peering through the mirror right in front of her. "Sorry."

Again, they soared through many common letters until they hit W. Minutes later, she saw a sign for the Blue Pkwy. She wasn't sure how to pronounce the word. That didn't stop her. "W – Pickwee."

Mama and Papa both roared with laughter. After he regained his breath, Papa said, "That's an abbreviation for Parkway. But that was a good find." He barely got the words out when he continued. "X – Exit." He'd apparently been waiting for that one.

Ima had to squint to even see the exit sign. "Y – Parkway!"

"Aww. I should have seen that one," Papa said.

They rode for a few more minutes, stuck on Z.

Mama smacked Papa on the shoulder and nodded toward something. He nodded back, but said nothing.

Soon, a giant sign with a monkey and a zebra came into view. Excitement surged through Ima. "We're almost there!"

"Almost where?" Papa asked.

Ima furled her eyebrows. Was it not the right zoo? She didn't understand. "Isn't that the zoo we are going to?"

"Yes."

Then the giant Z jumped out and swatted her. "Oh, Z – Zoo!"

Papa clapped his hands together. "We did it. Great job, Ima."

The weather was perfect for spending a day at the zoo. Nothing could ruin this day.

~~~~~~~~~~

Garnoc stood atop his skyscraper surveying the city below. Since his arrival in the principality, the greater Kansas City region had developed as planned. He successfully established the city as one of the nation's most affluent cities, feeding humanity's natural bend toward materialism and achievement. At the same time, he succeeded in segregating the city, so that this affluence only fueled the city's rank among the most dangerous in the nation. Those who had more than they needed lived in fear of losing it and strove to build their little kingdoms, while those who had less than they needed resorted to violence and theft to meet those needs. A perfectly balanced ecosystem to keep the focus off the one true solution.

Yet Garnoc remained unsettled by what the sniveling demon from the east had communicated. Was it possible that Mael had succeeded in creating the perfect non-human—in the likeness of humans? If so what would this mean? How would the glacial movement of power among the demonic hordes shift? If Mael's troops were able to seamlessly command these mims, as he called them, in mere decades Mael could cause power shifts among both humanity and demons—shifts to power structures, which took millennia to establish.

Had this single mim-on-the-run come to Garnoc's city? If so she needed to be found. What was her purpose? There were too many questions. Garnoc let out a frustrated roar, which reverberated across the city. Though he hoped this scheme of Mael's would leave his city untouched, he also desired to see this young mim—to study her and if need be, to kill her.

~~~~~~~~~~

CHAPTER EIGHT

A diya emerged first from the metallic-brown Impala. People wandered under the gaze of a giant wooden lion, marking the entrance to the zoo. Eldwyn exited the car next.

The car's back door popped opened and an energetic Ima bounded out. She slammed the door, a bit harder than intended. Finally, the front doors swayed open. Charles and Patricia climbed out.

"Come on," Ima said. She already stood half way between the large blue letters, highlighting the zoo's entrance, and a small handicapped parking sign where the Impala sat.

"Slow down, child," Patricia said. "Our legs are not as young as yours. You keep up this pace and you'll run us both to death."

Ima lowered her gaze to the concrete and the bouncing ceased. Adiya could only guess what memories flashed through her impressionable young mind.

"I'm sorry, Ima," Patricia said. "I wasn't thinking." The perceptive woman had also noticed the dejected posture of the child.

"Don't you worry," Charles said. His voice remained upbeat and even brought a smile to Adiya's face. "We have all day. The zoo isn't *that* big. You'll see everything there is to see."

Adiya glanced around the courtyard beyond the admission gates. "What a blessing that she will not see it all," Adiya said to Eldwyn. As with most public spaces, many other angels milled about the courtyard, ever vigilant. Above them, along the walls, and in the darker corridors glowered dozens of

100

demons. They dared not challenge the angels directly, without the advantage of significant numbers. Still, they hissed and cursed at the heavenly warriors.

If she were to guess, Adiya would put their numbers at about two-to-one. Not enough of an advantage to venture an attack. So they held their distance, much like the animals behind the defined perimeters of the zoo. A few demons, being granted stronghold by their human charges, maintained a close escort.

The scene rang all too familiar—one she had observed for thousands of years. Most of the demons kept watch to prevent interference with their humans.

Perched atop an octagon gazebo, a small raven-like demon had not diverted its stare from Ima since she entered the courtyard.

Ima walked toward an exhibit of river otters. She giggled and pointed to two otters sitting on a rock nuzzling noses. "They're kissing."

"It sure looks like it, doesn't it?" Patricia joined Ima. Behind a thick wall of glass, an otter performed graceful under-water acrobatics.

"Hey, Ima," called Charles. "You think that's neat, wait until you see the giant polar bears swimming under water."

"Where?" Ima asked.

Charles pointed across the courtyard, beyond the gazebo.

The raven no longer sat atop the building. Adiya scanned the area—no sign of the demon. Was she being a touch over-protective?

Eldwyn stood beside her. "Moments ago, it departed. North, in a big hurry."

~~~~~~~~~~~

Ima scampered toward the polar bear exhibit. A large white bear walked along manmade rocks next to a large pool. She had seen pictures of the bears in her study books. In their natural habitat the bears were an intense white. But this bear was more of a dirty-white. Its fur streaked together as water poured from it.

Many people gathered to watch the bear. They laughed and applauded as the bear pounced from the rocks onto a giant rubber ball floating in the water. In an instant, both the bear and the ball disappeared under the water. Through a small window, Ima caught a glimpse of the bear swimming under water. With several adults crowding the edge of the exhibit, she couldn't get close enough to really watch the large animal.

A hand rested on her shoulder. "Let's go inside and watch it from there," Papa said. "You'll be able to see much better."

She hadn't even noticed the opening to her right. They walked toward it. Ima felt a cool breeze rush from the room.

"It feels so good in here," Mama said. "I could stay in here for a while."

"Me too," Ima said. She watched the grace of the giant creature underwater. It almost seemed to walk on the bottom of the pool. Soon, it swam across the glass within arm's reach of her. She placed her hand on the glass.

The bear circled to the surface of the water. Then it came back down and floated at eye-level with Ima. The large animal seemed to look her straight in the eyes. She glanced at the children to her sides. Many of them had their hands on the glass. But it seemed focused on her. Such a vast and powerful presence, yet it seemed so peaceful.

"It seems to like you," Papa said.

The bear treaded water for a couple minutes, surfaced, took a breath of air, and returned to her. Why had it locked onto her? Could it even see her through the glass?

Ima stepped back and a couple other children stepped up to the glass. She walked to the other end of the room where there was another opening. She approached the window. Within moments, the bear once again floated right in front of her.

"Well I'll be," Mama said. "Have you ever seen anything like that?"

Papa just chuckled.

Ima felt as though the creature understood her. Two strangers, out of place among the people who surrounded them. What if these people knew she was a mim? Would they put her in a cage to stare and laugh at? As nice as Mama and Papa were to her, she doubted even they would understand. Surely, their kindness came with conditions.

Only Uncle M knew the truth and continued to care for her. One person among billions showed her unconditional kindness—and they killed him.

Her nose burned and her eyes grew damp.

Knowing eyes stared at her through the glass. It became too much, so she ran from the room.

By the time Mama and Papa caught up with her, Ima sat on a bench watching a black swan nuzzled in the grass.

"Whoot-whoot!"

Ima swung her head to the left. A shiny silver-and-black train approached. A white cloud of steam rose from a funnel-shaped smoke stack atop the scaled-down engine.

A college-aged conductor smiled and waved at Ima. He pulled down on a rope.

"Whoot-whoot!"

Ima jolted and giggled. She jumped up. "Can we ride on that?" She turned rounded eyes toward Papa. "Please?"

"Of course we can," Mama said. "Sounds like a great way to save these old knees."

By the time they reached the train station, the train had pulled away. A sign indicated that a train left every five minutes. They wouldn't have to wait long.

"Look," Papa said, "they also have a tram to the African safari." The tram was pulling into the station as he spoke. "Maybe we should go walk through the safari and catch the train later, when we're tired."

"Africa—like lions, giraffes, and zebras?" Her favorite studies at CeSiR involved animals and their habitats. The white-and-black striped tram looked like a train, but it ran on roads instead of tracks.

"Come on, Ima," Mama said. "We don't want the tram to leave before we get on."

They climbed into one of the striped cars. Ima sat between Mama and Papa, so she could see out both sides of the tram.

They waited a few minutes as more people climbed aboard. Slowly, the tram started to roll forward.

Ima giggled and pointed at half-a-dozen pink birds. "What kind of birds are those?" She pointed at one bird. "That one only has one leg."

Papa chuckled. "No, it has two legs. They often stand on one leg and tuck the other one under their belly. They're called flamingos."

The flamingos disappeared from sight as the tram rolled on. The tram passed through an area of trees. When it emerged, Ima gasped. "An elephant!" Several elephants, actually. They lumbered alongside the tram, opposite a fence.

The largest elephant raised its massive trunk and blew out a trumpeting roar. It seemed to be saying "hello" to her. The gigantic animal kept pace with the tram. It purred out a loud rumbling sound as it walked. Moments later, several other elephants seemed to purr in response.

"This is so awesome," Ima said. "Thank you for bringing me to the zoo." Was it possible? Had she found herself a real live family?

~~~~~~~~~~~

Garnoc watched a small, black dot approach his lair from the southeast. The deep tinted windows of the penthouse suite kept much of the day's sunlight from entering. Still he would prefer a stormy cloud-ruled sky.

"My liege?" A demon of lust stood next to Garnoc, eager to give an update on the prior night's achievements.

Garnoc inhaled a growl through clenched teeth. Could the update possibly warrant interrupting his thoughts?

His swift backhand sent the demon flailing. "I will send for you if I desire further update."

The demon did not argue. He just let himself sink through the floor. The demon's work in the city was important, but at the moment, Garnoc anticipated a much awaited message.

A raven-like demon soared above the window. He would wait on the roof as long as Garnoc desired. A lowly messenger knew better than enter the lair without invitation.

Garnoc unfurled his wings and ascended to the ceiling. He took a deep breath to remove any indication of his anticipation. Composed, he passed through the roof.

"Aahh, my liege," the raven said. Even his voice screeched like a bird. "I bring word."

Garnoc stepped toward the bird-brained demon. "Then I suggest you bring it," he growled.

The raven hopped twice backwards along the railing of the building. "Aahh, it is the girl. The one called Ima."

"Yes, what about her?"

"She is in town. At the zoo." The demon bobbed his head.

"You are sure it is her?" Garnoc took another step toward the demon. "If you are wrong—"

"No, my liege, not wrong." The demon took a step back and slipped from the building. "It is her. He called her Ima." He started to fall, extended his wings, and paused mid-air. "Aahh, even the animals can tell she is different. It is most definitely her." Without waiting for a response, the demon streaked away.

This would have angered Garnoc, if not for the valued message the raven had delivered.

~~~~~~~~~~

Adiya sat atop the tram watching the enormous animal follow Ima like a faithful puppy. "Have you ever seen an elephant behave that way?" she asked Eldwyn.

"In all my years, I have not." The sage angel perched next to her. "Something very special, that child."

The tram crossed a small bridge and then decelerated into the station.

"Welcome to Africa," said a voice, in the tram speakers.

"It has cooled significantly since I was last in Africa," Adiya said. "Not too many days with a high of sixty-five in the Serengeti."

Eldwyn did not comment. He stared at the skies to the west. Even when Ima led Charles and Patricia away from the station, Eldwyn remained motionless.

Adiya stayed close to Ima, but called back to Eldwyn.

He did not answer.

Only when the tram exited the station and swept toward the front of the zoo did Eldwyn snap out of his trance and leap from the tram.

Patricia headed into the Ladies room, while Charles and Ima walked to a drinking fountain.

"What is it?" Adiya asked. "Is something wrong?"

"I know not," Eldwyn said. "Perhaps, it is only the wariness of an old angel." He grinned at Adiya.

She marveled at the variety with which the Creator endowed His angels. Then again, why would the infinitely creative instill such beauty and uniqueness in all of creation, and not His messengers?

Yet it was this very distinctiveness that led Lucifer, arguably the most beautiful of God's creation, into pride and rebellion. The beauty and freedom that made all of His creation "good," came with choice, and the risk of arrogance.

"Are you ready to go see more animals?" Patricia asked.

Adiya and Eldwyn—the perpetually old, yet never older—joined their charges as they crossed a bridge to a small island.

A couple minutes later, they crossed a second bridge.

"Let's go see the baboons," Charles said. "Then we can visit the African wild-dogs."

"Yeah, baboons!" Ima said.

Adiya loved the adventurous spirit of this girl.

In the background, the wild-dogs barked and yipped at one another.

"Do you feel that?" Eldwyn asked.

~~~~~~~~~~~

Tudur sat with his charge, Mayor Trenton Richards, at his desk in the Mayor's office. Sergeant Chris Davis continued to piece together the puzzle against CeSiR Tech. Mael's house-of-cards would not survive the brewing storm. Something needed to be done to divert the storm.

Mael's efforts centered on the young Sarah McIntyre. A reasonable approach, but the more danger and attack she came under, the more Chris Davis resolved to bring down CeSiR.

No. A direct attack would not succeed. The only remaining option would be to bring down the detective before he found support from other law enforcement.

Tudur guided the mayor to pick up the phone. He dialed the number from a sticky-note in front of him.

A captivating voice answered.

"Yes, hello," the mayor said, as directed by Tudur. "Is this Leilah Bahar?"

The woman seemed hesitant, yet confirmed her identity.

"Well, Miss Bahar, I am not sure exactly how to say this—" His informants told him she harbored a toxic bitterness for her former flame. "We have a mutual friend, Chris Davis?"

The cursing that burst from the phone confirmed his intel.

"Miss Bahar, I can understand your disdain. Anytime a friend betrays us, it is painful. But for him to assault you like that, well, it is truly a crime." He waited for her to correct him. To offer that no such attack happened. She did not. "You should also know that he crashed his squad car racing back to Arrow Springs after the attack."

She remained silent. Not even a concern for the detective's well-being. The seventeenth-century playwright, William Congreve, clearly understood a "woman scorned." This could prove just what Tudur needed.

"Miss Bahar, before I arrest Sergeant Davis for this egregious assault, I need to confirm that you would be willing to sign a statement, describing Chris' heavy drinking that evening, and outlining the details of the attack."

Only a moment passed before she agreed.

"Excellent. I will fax a copy of your statement this evening. If you agree to sign it, I will ensure *civilian* Chris Davis never bothers you again." Tudur's skin tingled. Deception proved so much more effective than aggression. "Thank you, Miss Bahar. I will speak with you soon."

Perhaps, with Leilah's cooperation, he would have no need to collect the young propitiation offering from the elderly couple.

~~~~~~~~~~

Ima walked into a small shelter. It was a manmade structure, crafted to look like a rock-walled cave. Unlike a real cave, the structure offered little protection from the growing warmth of the day.

On the other side of a tall glass wall, a brown ball of fur rolled across a dirt floor.

A blur of darkness shot from a tree branch and landed next to the brown ball. The ball sprang to its feet and shrieked an ear-splitting yelp. The blur slowed and transformed into a second baboon, nearly twice the size of the first.

The first baboon sprang into the air, spun, and landed behind the larger animal. It picked at the back of the larger one and brought its hand to its lips.

"Eww, what is it eating?" Ima asked.

"Probably bugs from the other one's fur," Papa said.

The large baboon grumped and swiped a long arm at the smaller one. The little guy was long gone before the hand arrived. It landed next to the glass wall.

Ima reached a hand toward the animal. The glass felt warm. As if knowing it had an audience, the smaller baboon raised one of his legs over his head and then rolled to the dirt.

Ima giggled at the strange creature.

The small baboon came back to the glass and sat on a small ledge. It looked at Ima, opened its mouth, and bobbed its head. Was it laughing at her?

The zoo animals seemed so happy—even being confined to small, fake habitats. They conveyed a joy that proved

108

contagious to those watching. The large baboon charged its companion. Before it could pancake the smaller animal into the glass, the little one flipped into the air. The big one crashed into the glass and the little guy landed on top of it. Children laughed.

Her thoughts drifted back to her time at CeSiR. Was she really any different than these animals? The freedom she had thought she possessed was a mere illusion—concrete rocks, fake trees, and a cage to sleep in, even if her room didn't have bars. She started to understand why Uncle M had been so insistent on getting her out. Even the animals in their fake ecosystems possessed something she didn't—joy.

What she once barely perceived missing now glared like the sun off the water in the baboon exhibit. She'd had no joy, because she had no companionship, no friends. No other otters to snuggle with in the sun. No baboon buddies to chase around the yard. The mim children mocked or ignored her. Even Uncle M's friendship was clinical. He created the mims. He had to care for them.

Papa and Mama on the other hand, they were the first people to extend kindness without condition. She watched their interactions with Sylvia. They understood family. And they treated Ima like one of their family. She hadn't understood what she was running from. Perhaps, she still didn't. But she now understood what she was running to.

One exhibit over, the wild dogs, once yipping playfully, now barked and growled like junkyard watchdogs.

Chills slithered up her vertebrae.

Even the playful baboons bared their nasty fangs and looked around their exhibit as if looking for an intruder. Had the dogs upset them too?

Soon, both baboons stared straight at—*her*. Fangs bared, they swept a large arc about her, keeping her in the center of their gaze.

The larger baboon let out a guttural roar. His piercing eyes, those ferocious teeth, and that unsettling roar forced her to back away from the glass. Any second, they would charge the transparent wall. Why had they turned on her?

They all turned on her.

How long would it be before Mama and Papa turned on her?

~~~~~~~~~~~

Adiya turned a wide-eyed expression to Eldwyn. "Now I feel it." The dark chill of approaching evil crashed through her being. Decades, perhaps even centuries, had passed since she last felt such evil.

Adiya and Eldwyn ascended through the roof of the shelter. The western sky dimmed under a spiritual darkness. Movement on the horizon, confirmed her fear. The arrival of such evil was not coincidental to their presence.

Eldwyn motioned toward Ima. "For her, they come." He stroked his beard. "She is not even one of His. To be assigned to one such as her is most unusual." He glanced at Adiya. "What are your specific orders?"

The thoughts had run through Adiya's mind many times, but it concerned her to hear them stated aloud. "I am to protect her. To keep her from harm. Yet I am not to interfere with her decisions, about Him or the enemy." Adiya looked into the bluish-grey eyes of her friend and fellow guardian. "I fear I will lack the ability to distinguish the difference."

Eldwyn said nothing. He simply closed his eyes and nodded.

Like a fighter-jet formation, five black dots appeared at the center of the darkness to the west. From this distance it was impossible to gauge the size of the demons, but the one in the center was four times the size of the others. Only such an immense beast could account for the torrent of evil assaulting her being.

"Garnoc," Eldwyn said. "Many years it has been since a prince took personal interest in one of my charges." He spun his staff to a vertical position and rested his chin on it.

"My charge, you mean."

"One so special, as to be assigned a guardian, though not a follower but one of these mims?" Eldwyn shook his head. "When Patricia and Charles took her under their roof, she became my charge, likewise."

Adiya's heart soared with kindred affirmation.

Behind her, the African-wild-dogs had begun to growl at the approaching beings.

Garnoc and his four compatriots grew ever larger and more ominous.

Each of the four demons possessed a two-horned head, like that of a rhino-beetle. One horn protruded from the forehead—the reason for the rhino name. Except, the horn curved down between the eyes. The second horn protruded up from the chin. The pair of horns formed pincers when the demons spoke. The remainder of the body bore the spiked appearance of an armadillo-lizard, without the tail. They were demons-of-war and not the first she had faced. Yet they seemed like mere cockroaches in the presence of Garnoc.

The light and warmth of the sun retreated as the five demons arrived overhead. Emboldened at the presence of their prince, demons from throughout the zoo encircled Adiya and Eldwyn. A wall of isolation to discourage the intervention of any well-meaning members of the heavenly host.

Adiya unsheathed her flaming sword and tapped its hilt against her shield to ensure it was secure on her right arm.

Eldwyn still rested his chin on his staff. In the palpable darkness, his white robe seemed to fluoresce. The cross on his robe blazed red.

"You are free to depart," Garnoc said. The deep words hissed through razor sharp teeth.

"You know I cannot do that," Adiya said.

Garnoc grinned. "Ah, yes. Your charge." He descended into the structure next to Ima.

Adiya and Eldwyn both dropped into the makeshift cave.

The demons-of-war separated Adiya and Eldwyn from Garnoc. They left just enough space for her to see Ima's look of concern at the baboons' violent reaction.

111

The baboons roared fiercely in Ima's direction—yet past her, and toward Garnoc.

Garnoc turned and roared back at the animals.

Though unable to see him, they felt his presence and fear overwhelmed them. They sprang toward their shelter.

"Where are they going?" Ima asked.

Charles walked toward the exit of the cave. "Something seems to have spooked them. Let's go see the painted-dogs."

"Not so fast, little one." Garnoc reached out a massive arm and grabbed Ima by the neck.

Adiya let out a war cry and leapt toward the nearest demon-of-war. Her sword swept down toward the demon's head.

Fire erupted from the sword when it struck the demon's mace. He had raised it to block the sword.

Laughter rumbled from behind the four demons. Garnoc surrounded Ima with his dragon-like wings. She was cut off from the other people in the cave, including Patricia and Charles.

Adiya pressed down against the mace. The demon used both hands to keep it above his head. His arms shook and his eyes grew large, surprised by the strength of the smaller angel.

With a brief surge she pushed down hard and then whipped her sword back. As she had hoped, the demon pushed upward with his mace. She used the momentum to propel her arms and upper body backwards while pressing forward with her left foot. As her body spun in a head-over-heals circle, she let her right foot walk up the demon's chest, as her left connected with the bottom of his chin. With a sickening crunch the two horns smacked together.

The demon staggered back toward Ima.

Garnoc, intent that no one but himself bring the girl harm, let go of her throat and swatted the staggering demon away.

The demon fell face-first toward Adiya, now planted firmly on both feet.

She grunted and swept a fierce arc with her sword. It connected with the neck of the falling demon. Its beetle-like head fell to the ground before the entire being vanished in a puff.

The three remaining demons-of-war stood their ground. Their eyes betrayed an uncertainty that moments before could not be seen.

"Enough!" Garnoc regained his grip on Ima. "It is not my intention to hurt this one." He enveloped her with his right wing. "Unless you force my hand."

"Then what do you want?" Adiya asked.

"Just call me curious," Garnoc said. "I have heard some very interesting things about this one."

His eyes locked onto Adiya's.

His gaze repulsed her. It was as if she was caught in his icy embrace. She felt violated.

"The real question," Garnoc said, "is why you are so protective of this insignificant one? Oh, I understand. You are doing what you were told. But why does *He* care about her. She is not even *His* creation." He drilled Adiya with his gaze for several moments and then grinned. "You know not. You wonder the same thing." He laughed and nodded. "Let me be. And perhaps, you both shall live through the day."

~~~~~~~~~~

Ima's throat constricted. Her lungs burned with the need to exhale. She tried to run to Papa, but her feet wouldn't move. "Papa," she whispered. The sound didn't even reach her own ears.

What was happening?

Time slowed as Papa motioned for her to follow him. His lips moved but she heard no sound.

Why had the baboons screamed at her and then run away?

Everyone left her. They always did. Why wouldn't they? She was a mim. Not a person. Not human. Even Uncle M abandoned her.

Pain moved from her throat to her head. Pressure wedged into her skull like an icicle falling from the roof. Thoughts wound their way through her brain—memories of other mims

113

taunting her for being different. She hated them. Spite, unlike anything she had ever felt, flowed through her like venom. At the top of her malice sat Maiya Mirinova. The woman that controlled her life at CeSiR Tech.

Ima had never experienced love. Most didn't even like her, let alone love her. *But Mama and Papa.* No, they would turn their backs on her. If they knew what she was, they would abandon her at the side of the road like a stray cat. She would never know true love. It wasn't possible.

She lifted her eyes to find Mama. The elderly woman sat on a concrete bench with her head in her hands. Papa stood next to her with a hand on her shoulder. His eyes were locked on Ima. Did he want to come to her?

Like Ima, Papa seemed incapable of closing the gap between them.

Despair flooded from her chest to her mouth like water in a leaky rowboat. Again, she struggled to breathe. The suffocating despair progressed to her nose and then to her eyes. She closed her eyes and tried to focus. She had nothing to fear. Nothing to lose.

The flip-side of being unloved was that she didn't need to love, to hurt, to care. Alone meant independent. Nowhere to call home meant freedom.

Mama looked up at Ima, tears streaming down her cheeks. Her lips moved, but she said nothing.

Mama and Papa, they said their house was now her home.

Who was she kidding? She was an orphan, no, worse. An orphan had parents at some point in her life. Ima had a DNA concoction and a surrogate carrier. No parents—no orphan.

Science. In her studies, Ima loved science. Then, she learned the bitter truth. She was the product of science. CeSiR had no right. No right to play god with her life. To create her and then treat her like a possession.

But she was. She had no rights.

No, *they* had no right. She wished instead of fleeing CeSiR, she had burnt it to the ground—everything, everyone. She could have destroyed it all.

How could she think such a thing? She had no desire to hurt anyone. What about Uncle M? He was responsible for the science. An image of him bleeding into the river flashed through her mind. Then an image of him trapped in his office with flames raging everywhere. Guilt swept through her. Tears welled into her eyes and then streamed down her cheeks.

What was happening to her?

She needed air.

Ima focused on her feet, willing them to move. Even one step toward the exit of the cave. Nothing. No motion. The silence of the world around her screamed in her ears.

Why did everything bad happen to her? Other mims were so successful. Judges, mayors, politicians, even a firefighter. What about her? Uncle M said they would make her a surrogate. She would be sentenced to a life, and a shortened one at that, of birthing other mims that would go on to be— what? President?

And what now? With Uncle M dead, would they even tolerate her? They would probably just kill her when they caught her. There was nothing special about her. She'd heard it for twelve years.

They were right.

~~~~~~~~~~

Garnoc's hands burned as he squeezed his leathery fingers deeper into the child's head. The heat paled in comparison to his fury with Ophois. The demon had told him the mims were soulless—that he should be able to take control of this, Ima, like an exoskeleton.

He pressed deeper.

Her opposition scalded his fingers. He finally pulled his hands out with a roar.

"What is this?" He turned to face the angel called Adiya. "Why is she so special?"

The child coughed and started toward the exit.

"What does *He* want with her?" He roared at Adiya and grabbed the child by the throat. "I will crush her!"

115

Adiya thrust toward him. "No!" But, before she could reach him, one of his minions hit her in the head with his fist.

She staggered to a knee.

Garnoc's free hand curled in expectation.

The demon-of-war lifted his mace high with both hands and slammed it down toward her neck.

Even as the exhilarating crack echoed off the cave walls, the angel's eyes bore through Garnoc in defiance.

The elderly angel had intercepted the blow with his staff, right above her neck. The other end of the staff connected with the back of the demon's knees. The demon fell to its back as a torrent of curses flowed from its mouth.

The one called Eldwyn spun the staff above his head faster and faster. Soon the walking stick burst into bright flames at each end. His white robe, with its hideous cross, shone so bright that Garnoc shielded his eyes with his clenched fist.

The angel brought the staff down on the midsection of Garnoc's warrior. Thunder clapped and the staff blazed clean through the demon. Garnoc's protection detail dwindled to two. Not that he needed protection.

Garnoc snapped his thick fingers together and pointed at the two angels. They had pestered him long enough. The remaining demons-of-war sprang into action. The previous two were passive, at his direction. It had proved their demise. With the reins released, the measly angelic warriors would find these two a different story.

Adiya staggered back to her feet just in time for Garnoc's guard to send her sprawling. The demon had feigned an attack with his battle-axe. When the angel raised her shield to block the blow, the demon countered with his own shield. With a crack, the two shields collided and the angel was tossed into the concrete wall.

Before she could emerge from the wall, the elderly angel stepped toward her assailant. His mistake. While he focused on her attacker, a spiked elbow slammed into his jaw.

"Not this time old man," the second demon-of-war said. "You are mine."

116

Garnoc smiled for the first time since arriving at the zoo. He possessed no fear of two measly angels, but now he could focus on the task at hand—no interruptions.

The battle moved beyond the walls of the fake cave. Metal clashed outside as the two demons exchanged strikes and parries with the two angels. Finally, he was alone with the girl and the decrepit couple.

Garnoc returned his focus to the one called Ima. With a typical human, full control required at least some consent on behalf of the person. A process that often took weeks, months, even years. Assuming of course that at least some desire existed to keep the human alive.

But this was no ordinary human. In fact, if Ophois were to be believed, she was not human at all, but a scientific experiment. A clone. At least in principle what Ophois had communicated made sense. If no soul existed, no will of opposition, then there should be no need for delay, manipulation, or coercion. Perhaps that believability is why Garnoc had been gullible enough to trust the one demon who had never given him reason.

Truthful or not, he would soon prove Ophois correct—or deceitful. Either way, he cared not about the fate of the girl. He would take control, or she would die in her opposition.

Garnoc wrapped both wings tight around the girl. With both hands, he reached into the center of the girl's being.

~~~~~~~~~~

Adiya stepped back and ducked. A curse-filled swing of a giant black battle-axe glanced off her helmet. Her shield lay in splinters on the walking path. Only the embossed cross seemed unscathed by the axe.

She rolled to her left and leapt into the trees. Existing only as physical realm objects, the trees would do nothing to stop the weapon of the enemy. But they did provide some obstruction to his view.

In the distance she could hear thunder-claps as Eldwyn's staff connected with the enemy. Most likely with his spiked shield, but she prayed to the Creator that one would connect with the demon's head. She had her hands full with her own sparring partner and could use the help of her friend. Every moment wasted in this battle brought Ima closer to the destructive influence of evil, or death.

She considered sheathing her sword and furling her wings in an attempt to go stealth. Perhaps even changing her appearance to blend in as one of the many passersby visiting the zoo. It would be a risky move. Her captain, Eitan, had recently pulled off such a feat when he infiltrated the enemy stronghold at CeSiR Tech. But he was an expert. Without perfect control, she would be revealed to the enemy, and completely vulnerable to attack. No, she could not risk it.

She needed rest. Her entire being ached from the rampant attacks of the demon-of-war.

Where was he now?

She stood with her back to a large oak tree. A swing of his axe from behind the tree would lop her in half without hesitation. The challenge of hiding—you also lose track of the enemy.

Shadows moved on the ground beneath her feet. The wind rustled through the upper boughs of the trees.

Neither angels nor demons cast sun-blocked shadows, unless by intention. Another disadvantage when hiding. Reflections on the other hand—sparkles of light danced with the shadows. The light of the sun bounding off her silver, and now dented, helmet. She loved the sun, the blinding brilliance of His creation. But, at this moment, it risked revealing her location.

She glanced up to determine how best to move to avoid the wonderful brilliance. She saw not the sun, but a hideous black grin trailing a razor-edged battle-axe.

He had taken to the sky. Scouted her out from above. Surely drawn by the starburst of sun off her armor—in the physical realm invisible, but not in the spiritual.

Thankfully, she had not sheathed her sword.

She rolled to her right and bent at the knees to drive strength to her core. She spun her sword in her left hand until it pointed to the place she had just stood. As her right hand wrapped around the ball at the end of the sword's hilt, she thrust the sword backward across her hip.

The sword missed the axe.

The demon continued his descent, axe firmly fixed in both hands. His weight drove the axe to the ground where she had stood.

The axe had not been her target.

As the axe slammed harmlessly to the ground, she steadied her grip on the sword. Pushing the hilt down to her extended knee for support, she braced the blade with her dominant left hand. The cantilevered blade of the sword met the full weight of the demon.

Her arms, tired from relentless parries, shook as she struggled to lock them in place. The initial resistance of demonic armor gave way and the sword sliced smooth.

A horrific cry echoed through the zoo's African safari.

Her heart sank.

The cry had not come from the demon-of-war. Her sword had split him in half, quick and without report.

No, the cry was not demonic.

~~~~~~~~~~~

Eldwyn and the demon-of-war proved evenly matched. Strike-parry-dodge. Adiya paired up against the demon with the axe. That worked to Eldwyn's advantage. His staff worked much better against his foe's mace than an axe.

Strike-parry-dodge.

Fear for Adiya's safety flooded his mind. The demon's axe had glanced off her helmet before she disappeared in the woods. Was she wounded? Had the demon finished her off?

Strike-parry-parry-dodge.

The youthful wail emanated from the cave across the open walkway. Behind Eldwyn, African-wild-dogs whimpered.

From the wooded area, Adiya emerged. She paused and looked at Eldwyn.

Parry-strike-strike-parry.

She turned toward the cave, where the cry had originated.

No.

She ran toward the cave.

No. Not alone. She should have helped him finish the last demon before returning to the prince.

As if sensing Eldwyn's thoughts, the demon sneered. "Like a lamb to the slaughter."

Eldwyn needed to finish this. Strike-parry-strike-dodge.

His current approach proved effective for survival, but not for winning. Drastic events called for drastic measures.

Strike-no parry.

Pain flooded Eldwyn's left bicep as the spikes on the mace sunk into his flesh. Blood rushed from the wound.

The demon grinned for a moment. Then he saw the staff swirling in Eldwyn's right hand. The flaming staff smashed into the side of the demon.

Eldwyn grasped desperately with his left hand onto the shaft of the mace, holding on for survival. His arm screamed, as pain reverberated up into his shoulder and neck.

The demon-of-war buckled under the thundering attack to his side. Eldwyn held the demon up by his mace. The other end of his staff swung back in an arc, over his head, and then crashed into the side of the demon's head. One more thunder clap and the demon disappeared to the Abyss.

Another piercing scream echoed from the cave.

~~~~~~~~~~

When Adiya arrived in the cave, she pulled up in horror at the sight.

Ima hung like a rag doll in the grip of the prince. Fire raged in his eyes. "That is quite close enough." He proceeded to curse her femininity.

Fury coursed through her. She raised her sword.

Garnoc responded by raising Ima like a shield. "I am about done with her anyway." He bared rows of razor sharp teeth. "You are just in time to watch her die—something to think about when I return you to the throne of your precious Creator."

Behind Garnoc, Charles watched the child, now so precious to him, floating in the room. His greying eyes refused to blink despite the glossy sheen covering them. Fear shook his body.

Beside him, Patricia sat with eyes closed and lips moving.

Garnoc's eyes followed Adiya's to the old couple. He snorted a laugh. "Pathetic. Would you not agree?"

"There is only one pathetic creature in this room." The words bit from Adiya's mouth.

"Just because you have bested my guards, do not presume you are of any concern to me. I have swatted larger flies than you back to the throne by the dozens."

Likely the first truth spoken by the demonic prince in many days. Still, she could not leave the girl without trying. Her mission was to not interfere, *except* to preserve her life. She feared she had already failed.

~~~~~~~~~~

Charles watched in horror. For a couple minutes Ima had stood staring at the baboons not speaking, not moving, yet gasping to breathe. He had tried to run to her. He sensed danger. Everyone had left the manmade cave. Yet he could not approach her.

Something evil was at work. Patricia had immediately sensed it. She sat on the bench praying. Her lips moved, but the words were between her and The Heavenly Father.

His inability to approach the wheezing child made him feel more helpless than he had during the early onset of his dementia. Helplessness and fear were feelings with which he was all too familiar.

The brilliant color of Ima's skin, lips, and crystal-blue eyes, began to fade. They were losing her. Something drained the life from her body. Still, his feet were frozen to the floor. He was helpless to help her.

In just a few short days, this child had brought Technicolor life to an old grey corpse. Now the gemstone of his recovery slowly turned slate-grey.

He had to act. He couldn't move toward her. Somehow, he knew that reaching her wouldn't help. He dove into memories long hidden beneath the ice of Alzheimer's. When he emerged the words from Ephesians chapter six were crystal clear in his mind.

Charles declared aloud, *"For we are not fighting against flesh-and-blood enemies, but against evil rulers and authorities of the unseen world."*

Ima gasped a breath of air.

"I know you are here," Charles said. "Leave her be."

The response came immediate.

Ima squeaked as air seemed to press from her lungs through a restricted throat. Her body lifted inches off the floor.

Pale cheeks, glistening with tears, turned to face him. Her eyes screamed with terror.

Her floating body verified his suspicions. He'd grown up a conservative evangelical in America. This kind of thing didn't happen in his world. And yet there was no denying what he saw.

Or was there?

Beads of sweat seeped from his brow. Perhaps, there was no girl. No one called Ima. No zoo. No healing of his dementia. Maybe he still sat dozing in his chair in front of the television.

His heart sank to his stomach with the realization. The sweet child he'd grown to love in such a short period of time was just one last torment of his mind.

His knees buckled. He dropped to the floor. The concrete smacking his kneecaps certainly felt real. Had he ever experience this realistic a hallucination?

Shaking fingers grasped his hand as it rested on the concrete bench. Warmth flowed from Patricia's fingers.

She still sat on the bench with her eyes closed and her lips moving. Yet, in his moment of desperation and despair, she reached out and rescued him—pulling him back to the lifeboat of awareness.

No. This wasn't a relapse. It was an attack. The work of the enemy. The words of James flowed into his mind and out his mouth. *"Resist the devil, and he will flee from you."*

~~~~~~~~~~~

Garnoc roared at the old man. The fossil had no idea the fire with which he played. "What do you think Adiya, do you think he has humbled himself?" Humans seemed to think the words were some kind of magic incantation to make all things better. "So do it old man. Resist!"

Eldwyn stepped into the cave next to the elderly man.

Garnoc smiled at the blood and flesh gaping wide on Eldwyn's arm. Bruises already lined the angel's face. "Good, we are all here," Garnoc said. "We would not want you to miss the child's demise." He pointed his sword at the elderly man. But first, this one has a lesson to learn in what it means to resist. *"Let there be tears for what you have done. Let there be sorrow and deep grief."*

He kept his sword pointed at the old man, but turned toward Adiya. "Is that not what the passage goes on to say?" He ran his tongue across razor sharp teeth until green ooze seeped from it. *"Sadness instead of laughter, gloom instead of joy?"* He turned and yelled at the old man. "Is that what you want old man? Sadness and gloom—that I can give you." Ima coughed as his gorilla-like hand tightened around her throat.

"Humble yourself before the Lord and He will lift you up in honor," Adiya said. But she was not looking at Garnoc. Her eyes were fixed on the old man.

The man rose from his knees to his feet. In a confident voice he cried out, *"Jesus replied, this kind can be cast out only by prayer."*

Garnoc shuddered. He remembered the first time those words were proclaimed. The time the pesky disciples had attempted to command him to leave the young child he controlled. They were demoralized when they could not. But then the Creator, the Word become flesh, intervened, He commanded Garnoc to leave the child.

Though Garnoc tried his best to destroy the child before leaving, Jesus simply reached out and lifted the boy to his feet—perfect and unscathed.

That night Jesus had taught his disciples that they needed to pray and fast and they too would be able to remove such spirits.

Garnoc turned his gaze to the elderly woman. Since the encounter had begun, she did nothing but sit on the bench moving her lips. It hit him like a maul across his lizard head. She was praying.

He turned a glare to Adiya. "What is so special about this child? Why would He send you to protect her? She is not even *His* creation."

Adiya shook her head and returned a look of pity. "You pathetic, blind creature. Look around you." She pointed to the baboons cowering by the gate that would not let them into their shelter. "They are His creation. *We* are His creation. There is nothing that you see around you that is not His creation!" She dared lecture a prince. Who did she think she was? "Tell me?" she asked. "Who spoke the mims into existence? Was it ex nihilo?"

Rhetorical or not, Garnoc would not stoop to speaking the only true answer. Only the One, the true Creator could speak something into existence from nothing. If Mael truly had succeeded in creating these so called mims without souls, it was only because the Creator chose not to endow them with souls. Not because Mael had become a creator.

And yet he had to question the truthfulness of Ophois and his assessment of the mims. This child had a will. Though not committed to following the Christ, she definitely exhibited a will to make such a choice and thus a soul.

A soul he would soon extinguish. He lowered the child back to the floor, wrapped his wings back around her, and began to squeeze.

~~~~~~~~~~

Ima couldn't breathe. The past several minutes were a blur. She felt as though she had been floating. Railroad spikes rattled around in her head. Her lungs burned for oxygen. Was she being punished for the evil thoughts she had earlier? She wouldn't really hurt anyone. Where had such thoughts come from? It felt like they weren't even her thoughts.

She locked eyes with Mama. Mama's lips still moved—the pantomime of a monologue.

Papa had said something. Something about resisting and fleeing. There was no one to resist and she had tried to flee, but she couldn't move. Not even to breathe. It seemed as if her body were encased in crystalline molasses.

She was helpless. And as much as Mama and Papa seemed to like her, they weren't helping her either. Even the animals, so friendly only minutes earlier, had turned on her.

Her world began to fade to darkness. Would she get to see Uncle M? Was there anything beyond this cruel world? She would soon find out.

Through faded sight she watched as Mama finally stood to her feet. Was she leaving? Did she know that Ima's time in this world had come to an end?

Mama's mouth stopped moving. She took a deep breath. Something Ima longed to do.

"Leave her!" commanded Mama. Her voice cut through the fading darkness, resonating off the cave walls. She'd never heard such authority in Mama's voice—or anyone else for that matter. "In the name of Jesus, the Messiah, and by the power of His blood, which he shed on the cross, I command you—leave her!"

Ima sucked in a long-overdue breathe. Who was Mama yelling at? Ima didn't understand. She said something about

Jesus. Ima had heard that name at prayer time before going to bed. What was a Messiah?

Ima didn't understand what Mama was saying, but she knew the crystalline molasses dissolved like the morning fog. Her legs—they now worked. She ran to Mama and jumped into her embrace. As little as she understood of what had happened, somehow she knew Mama had just saved her life.

~~~~~~~~~~~

Adiya and Eldwyn had both drawn their weapons for one last assault on Garnoc, once he made it clear he was bent on destroying Ima.

That was when Patricia Sherwood, the mighty prayer warrior, had interceded for the child.

Garnoc screamed in pain as a mighty shockwave ripped and tore at his wings until Ima emerged from his grasp. The wind of the Spirit blew him backward, through the glass, and into the baboon exhibit.

He extended his wings and rose into the sky. He tried to push back toward Ima, cursed his Creator, and then allowed himself to be carried off by the surging current.

Adiya looked to Eldwyn. "Are you okay?" He had taken a more severe beating from his opponent than she had.

"I will be fine." The cross on his robe still shone bright red, which it had done since Patricia called on the power of the blood, shed on the cross.

"Are you ready to go home?" Charles asked. The shake in his voice betrayed the emotional ledge on which he found himself.

Ima turned and smiled. "No, but I think I want to see something other than baboons."

He nodded and lay his hand on the girl's shoulder. The battle-wearied make-shift family walked out of the cave.

Eldwyn and Adiya followed them.

Garnoc hovered in the distance, high overhead watching them.

~~~~~~~~~~~

CHAPTER NINE

Ima sat at a table with Mama and Papa. She pulled another fry from a basket and dipped it in her ketchup. She loved the tangy-sweet taste. She'd had fries once at the facility. That alone was an extreme treat, but to taste them bathed in tomatoey goodness, nearly made up for the weirdness she had recently experienced. Nearly.

"Mama?"

"Yes, hon?"

She didn't wait to swallow the ketchup-fry mixture before continuing. "In the baboon cave, you just sat there with your lips moving. Who were you talking to?"

An overweight blackbird bobbed between the tables picking up dropped pieces of French fries.

"I was praying for you, sweetie." Mama looked older and more exhausted than Ima recalled seeing her. The morning's drive must have taken a lot out of her. "At first, I thought you were sick. But, when I couldn't move to come get you, I knew it was a battle."

Ima stopped mid-bite and set her hamburger down. What did Mama mean? What battle? Papa had said something about a battle. What was it? He said to battle, no to flee. "Papa, I tried to flee, but I couldn't."

"I know, child," Papa said. "I don't know what evils you've seen in your past, but I've never seen anything like that before."

Mama sipped her water. "Do you remember this morning, when you asked me if God spoke back to me when I prayed?"

Ima nodded.

"He did," Mama said. "I heard him in the cave. He simply said to pray—that you were in trouble. So I did."

Ima looked at Papa. "The words you said—was that from the Bible?"

"Yes."

Another blackbird floated past their table, plucked a potato chip from the ground, and then headed up to the trees.

"Why?" Ima asked.

Papa wiped a hand through his thin silver hair. "I didn't know what to do. God promised that the truth would set us free. I've never seen anything like what happened to you today. It was clearly spiritual bondage, so I could only think to speak the truth from Scripture and hope for God to set you free."

Mama picked up a tray full of burger wraps, baskets, and napkins. She headed toward the trash can. "We can talk more about this later. Anyone up for seeing some more animals? I hear they have a sky safari that sounds like a lot of fun."

Ima jumped up and ran between the tables sending three blackbirds fluttering into the sky.

They walked past the hippo exhibit, but the hippos all ducked under the water as they passed. Though the early-afternoon sun shone brightly, it still felt as if a dark cloud hovered over her, always staying just out of sight.

Ahead a strange looking bird practically barked at her. The bird looked like some kind of prehistoric raptor. Three-foot tall, the bird had a pointed beak and another point of feathers sticking out the back of its head. The bird's fanned tail feathers and unfurled wings made it appear three times its actual size.

Ima jumped when the white throat of the bird puffed like a rubber balloon. The bird released a low guttural growl. Even the zoo animals seemed to reject her presence. In the mere hours since arriving at the zoo, it seemed the animals had gone from understanding compatriots to fearful strangers. How long before Mama and Papa did the same?

"Now that is one funny looking bird," Papa said.

Funny? There was nothing funny about the growling menace. Maybe she should pretend to be sick. She couldn't shake the feeling at the base of her vertebrae—danger lurked in the shadows, like a lion in the deep grasses of the African plains.

"That's a bird with an attitude," Mama said.

The concrete path turned into a boardwalk, shortly before they crossed a small creek. From the bridge over the creek, Ima saw round eyes staring at her from the surface of the lake, just beyond the creek. The hippos cautiously watched her. How could such a giant animal be fearful of her?

Soon they crossed another boardwalk-bridge to an open court. A line of people waited to ride the sky safari.

"Wow, where did all these people come from?" Mama asked.

The wrinkles in Mama's face seemed to have deepened, like the air within her was slowly seeping out. Was it from walking all morning? She did complain about her knees once in a while.

"Mama, do you feel okay?"

The dear woman smiled. "Don't you worry, sweetie. I'm just a bit tired from the encounter."

Encounter? Ima still didn't grasp what Mama and Papa thought had happened. Was there more to the world than what she could see? They seemed to think so.

The line in front of them moved steadily. They already seemed twice as close as when they started. Two little boys with red hair and freckles swung on the ropes which guided people to the sky safari. They looked almost identical and acted out just as equally. She guessed they were twins.

One of the twins swung back on the rope, a mite too far. Thump. He landed on his back with saucer-like eyes.

She fought not to laugh.

The twin's brother didn't show such restraint. His chest heaved as he laughed at the misfortune of his sibling. As if fated by his connection to his twin, the laughter caused him to lose his balance and down he went. A mirror image of the breathless twin on the ground.

Ima no longer possessed the necessary self-control. Laughter erupted from her.

Mama, who had obviously seen the twin-flippings, scolded Ima. "It's not nice to laugh at others' pain." Then, a wide grin spread across her face.

Amazing how a mere grin could make the woman appear ten years younger.

Soon the twins were seated on a green and white chairlift, screeching with delight as their feet lifted off the ground. Ima wondered if the fear of falling would be enough to keep the two seated on the open seat until the end of their ride.

Minutes later, Ima stood between Mama and Papa, her feet on top of yellow outlines painted on the ground.

"On the count of three, I'm gonna ask all three of you to sit down." The attendant in her drab brown uniform was kind but no-nonsense. "Okay, and one, two, three, sit back."

The seat swayed beneath them, like the rocking chair in Uncle M's office.

"Great. Heads back, hands in your lap. Here we go." The attendant latched a small bar across the front of them. "Enjoy your ride."

As the seat swept Ima's feet off the ground, the attendant repeated instructions that Ima had heard a half dozen times waiting in line.

A giggle rose from Ima's swaying feet, to her ribs, and out her mouth. "This is so much fun." She turned to Mama. But Mama stared at the ground retreating beneath them. Her knuckles whitened around the steel bar.

"It'll be okay, Mama. Lots-a people ride on this every day."

Mama turned and nodded. A mechanical grin forced its way onto her cheeks, but the blood still didn't flow to her knuckles.

Wind caught Ima's golden locks, sending a chill winding down her spine. Instinctively, she lifted her legs to avoid a wooden deck several feet below. A young brunette with a toddler sat at a table on the deck. The toddler pointed at Ima and the mother looked up and waved. Ima waved back at the mother and then flicked her fingers up and down in a childish wave to the toddler.

He giggled and then tucked his head under his mom's armpit.

Soon, their chariot floated out across the boardwalk that they'd used to walk to the sky safari. Next to the boardwalk, a cattle-style fence surrounded a large field. Though it was hard to tell from the air, it looked to be at least eight feet tall.

She looked around for the animals. Based on the fence, she expected to see giraffes.

"Over there," Papa said. He pointed toward the far corner of the field, where some zebras and giraffes huddled.

Like the other animals, they seemed fearful of her. Why? When she arrived at the zoo, they seemed so friendly. It's like they discovered her true identity. She read once that animals had more astute senses than humans. They knew. Eventually, Mama and Papa would find out. They would abandon her like the zebras and giraffes, and baboons, and Uncle M.

~~~~~~~~~~

Adiya sat cross-legged on a flimsy roof which covered the carrier in which Ima rode. Garnoc floated at the top of the trees watching Ima. His wings rippled every time he looked in the direction of Patricia. Had the precious prayer warrior not interceded, he would have killed the young girl. Likely, after dispatching both Adiya and Eldwyn. Though they would have fought to their end, she doubted they could have proved worthy opponents of the prince, apart from the Creator's intervention.

"Why is she special?" Garnoc asked. He remained a safe distance from the elderly couple. Still his booming voice cut across the open savanna. "She is clearly not one of His. Yet you protect her like she is."

"All that exists is His," said Adiya. "He is the Creator ex nihilo."

Garnoc swore and spat at a couple passing by in another carrier. "You know what I mean. She is a mim, created by Mael. Or are you unaware of what transpires in your own region."

131

She was aware. The white dove-like feathers on her wings stood on end at the thought. The audacity of attempting to usurp the Creator. Mael knew better. He was present the day Lucifer attempted to claim equality with *Him*. They all were. A droplet of paint on a canvas claiming equality with the artist. "Even if Mael had succeeded in creating a human from nothing, which he clearly did not, he would still have been copying the Master."

Garnoc snarled and stared at her with disdain. "How do you reckon?"

"The first act of creation is the conception of an idea. At best, Mael has only replicated what the Creator first conceived." Thoughts of other mims she had met washed through Adiya's mind. Soulless creations no better than animals. "And mostly cheap imitations at that. Like a child's sidewalk portrait of a sunset compared to the orange sky at dusk."

"And yet you protect this cheap imitation." Garnoc swept his wings back and roared at her. "WHY?"

The carrier on which Adiya sat slowly moved away from Garnoc, who seemed content to watch them leave his presence. "The Creator cares about all his creations, Garnoc. Even you."

He turned and began to rise higher into the sky. "No, He rejected us, *for them*. You too, if you were not too blind to see it."

Moments later, he disappeared into the Kansas City skyline.

Adiya struggled with the Creator's patience. That He allowed the defiant demons to exist, to prowl unpunished, and now to create these abominations. With a mere word, He could bring them to judgment. Yet He did not.

"Look," a young black girl, seated next to her mother, said. She bounced excitedly in the chairlift behind Ima and the Sherwoods. "Where are they going?" She pointed toward the ground in front of them.

Adiya turned and a memory from millennia ago washed over her like a flood.

A pair of zebras walked side by side along the fence—followed by a pair of giraffes, and four ostriches. Even a pair of hyraxes bounded along behind the other animals. On the opposite side of the divide, three lions walked in line not much more than a neck's distance away from the giraffes, yet seemingly oblivious to the smorgasbord of animals parading opposite the divide.

Not since the days of Noah, had Adiya seen such an unusual sight. To her left, the black rhinos looked ready to leap from their exhibit to join the gathering animals. Adiya swung her helmeted head to the right to see a family of hippos emerging from the bottom of the lake to join the other animals in the procession line—a line gathered just in front of a very special little twelve-year-old mim.

The animals, so fearful and aloof in the presence of Garnoc, now sensed his departure and made their way to the vicinity of the safari, apparently to be near the child floating awestruck above them.

Adiya dropped through the roof and stared at Eldwyn. "Have you ever—"

His head simply swung from side to side.

Oryx, kudu, and elands all approached their natural predators in a display of solidarity-laden honor of the young girl, for whom God clearly had a special purpose—though yet undiscovered.

"They are all so beautiful," Ima said. "I wish I was walking down there with them."

Adiya had no doubt that the child could have, and no harm would have come to her.

"The calf and the yearling will be safe with the lion, and a little child will lead them all," Eldwyn said, his voice barely above a whisper.

The passage in Isaiah clearly referred to a day yet to come, and still, she could think of no more appropriate sentiment.

Adiya blinked a single tear from her eye and it ran down her cheek.

~~~~~~~~~~

Ophois sat atop the viaduct snarling at the sun, still perky in the sky. In a couple hours, the freeway bridge would cast a shadow of relief from the wretched orb.

Nearly a dozen hours had passed and still Garnoc's cronies stood guard. He considered making a run for it. Surely, he could outrun these behemoths. Or even better, he could outsmart them. These demons were warriors, not strategists.

Anput now sat within speaking distance. The guards seemed less concerned with their actions as the day progressed. They had to be as disenfranchised with their assignment as Ophois was with their presence. "What do you think?" he asked Anput. "Can we make a run for it?"

Anput looked from guard to guard. Three remained within sight. The closest sat on the edge of the freeway bridge. The other two flanked them on each end of the viaduct. "The odds of a successful flight could be as high as two-to-one." Ever the odds maker. Gambling ran in her blood. Something unsaid flickered behind her red-diamond eyes.

"What are you not saying?"

"There is only one direction in which to flee." She gazed east along the rippling river. "Pure, unhindered speed is our only hope for escape. That means soaring low and fast along the river. Not just for a bit, but until we exit the principality."

"I hope you are attempting humor." Surely, there were other options. Soar upwards—half the demons in Kansas City would spot them. Lose the less agile guardians winding through city streets—make a wrong turn and run smack into one of Garnoc's minions. No. Anput understood the odds. She had processed the options. Which left him with none.

His upper lip quivered. "I—I cannot."

Anput simply nodded. No mocking. No lectures on reason. Just resigned understanding.

Whack!

Something hit him traveling at breakneck speed.

Before he could identify the assailant, they plummeted into the cool waters of the Kansas River.

The heavy rains of the past weekend stirred the river basin to a thick murky brown. Ophois could not see his own hands, let alone his attacker. Panic flowed through his being, more rapid than the rushing waters of the river.

Walls of water crashed in on him. The pharaoh's chariot heaved and flipped in the torrent of frothy water. Ophois found himself facedown at the bottom of the Red Sea.

Unrealistic fears of drowning in the dirty waters of the Kansas River pounded inside his head. Unrealistic not only because, as a spirit being, he need not breathe, but because of the thick hands wrapped around his neck. He could not inhale the water, even if he so desired.

When he gathered his wits and lifted himself from the floor of the sea, Egyptian soldiers littered the seabed. Already, they had ceased trying to struggle to surface.

"You deceived me for the last time," Garnoc said. The voice was crystal clear, not echoed and muffled as humans supposedly heard sound under water. "I have seen your mim."

Of course, Garnoc did not take half a day to locate Ima. He went to see her for himself. Had he not told Garnoc she was different from the other mims?

Garnoc pinned Ophois to the silty river bottom.

Lifeless eyes stared up from Egyptian corpses. In a single act of the Creator, Ophois' entire contingent of worshipers were turned to fish-food.

Garnoc spun Ophois around to face him. Gone was the horde of soldiers, though bulgy-eyed fish did swim all around them. "Mael's mims are a joke," Garnoc said. "I cannot wait to discuss this failure with Lucifer. Soon, my territory will increase."

Ophois kicked franticly, clawing at Garnoc's thick leathery chest, but the vice around his neck squeezed tighter.

One of the massive hands released his neck. It curled into a rock-hard fist and slammed against his snout.

The murky water-world flickered and started to fade to blackness.

"Ahhh!" The scream from Garnoc snapped Ophois out of his stupor.

The other hand released his neck and he scrambled backward.

Through the murky water, a bright blue line arced across Garnoc's scale covered neck. Though the blade barely scratched his neck, green fluid oozed from the back of Garnoc's knees. He fell back on his hind end still dazed by the attack.

"Time to go!" Anput said. "Remember what I said about our escape route. It is the only way." She shot past Ophois, angling toward the surface.

If Garnoc regained his composure, they were both dead. As much as Ophois disdained the idea of soaring across the surface of the river, it held much more appeal than being destroyed beneath the surface.

The two demons shot from the water—wings swept back and weapons pointed forward. They could worry about Ima's whereabouts later. First, they needed to get out of Garnoc's principality, intact.

~~~~~~~~~~

Tudur left Mayor Trenton Richards sitting in his black BMW outside the Arrow Springs police station. His meeting with Listh would not take long. The mim should behave until he returned. Though, he sometimes proved unpredictable.

"It is good to see you again, my friend," Listh said. He looked like some sort of three-dimensional stick figure, with glasses and a goatee.

"I can only assume," said Tudur, "that your presence in Arrow Springs means word of the mims has made it to Washington?" He had worked with Listh on several governmental projects over the years. He was unsure of Listh's current assignment, but he assumed it was some government official.

"Indeed," Listh said. "I am assigned to Vivian Laren, director of Homeland Security." They walked to the front bumper of the BMW and Listh pointed at the occupant. "Is that one of them?"

"Yes it is," said Tudur. "This is Trenton Richards—mim, mayor, and my personal playground."

Listh shook his bald head. "When the call came through, I could hardly believe Mael had succeeded." He removed his round, wire-rimmed glasses. "Such a pity that Mael was too inept to keep the operations under wraps for just a few more years." He stuck his head through the car's window and stared at Trenton. "From what I hear, we could have wielded some real power around the world with these creations."

Tudur felt no need to reveal that his own superior had lit the fuse, igniting the cascading events, which led Sergeant Davis to uncover CeSiR's activities. Leon was a buffoon, ever since his encounter with the Messiah. No demon, whose claim to fame was driving a heard of pigs to commit suicide, belonged on this mission. Lucifer should never have put him in such an influential role.

"Is Vivian in the station?" Tudur asked.

"Yes, along with several other government agency reps." Listh donned his glasses and shot a knowing look at Tudur— one that said he knew of the chess match between Sergeant Davis and Trenton. "CeSiR is going down, Tudur. It is too late to prevent it."

Tudur paced in front of the car. "I feared as much. Chris Davis has been a bane in my tenure here in Arrow Springs. He is pathetically committed to the Creator and constantly receives the protection of the host. If both Sergeant Davis and Mael survive the coming showdown, I fear I will not. Mael will blame me for his own failure. I need your help, Listh."

His friend rubbed the goatee hanging down from his perfectly circular head. "Perhaps, I can get the team to invite Sergeant Davis to the raid on CeSiR. Then it will be Mael's responsibility to take him down. The focus would be off of you."

Tudur grinned. This was perfect. If Chris Davis survived, Mael would own the failure. If not, Mael would be content. Much better than arresting Chris on some trumped up assault charge. "I should not be at CeSiR when the team shows up,"

Tudur said. Mael may dispatch him on the spot for leading Chris to their operation.

"What do you propose?" Listh asked.

Tudur returned to the driver's door of the BMW and stood next to the Mayor. "Perhaps, I can make use of the governmental presence here to explain my absence during the attack." He went on to lay out a plan.

Listh nodded. It almost looked as if his face slid up and down his perfectly spherical head. "That would give you a believable excuse for absence." Listh pointed a thumb over his skinny shoulder. "I need to get back in there. The angelic presence at the meeting is quite intense." Listh walked toward the building. "See you soon."

~~~~~~~~~~~

He sat in his car spying on Mayor Trenton Richards. He could sense the evil powers swirling around the mayor's car. In the reflection of the review mirror and through a pane of glass, he studied the mayor. Trenton fidgeted and turned from side to side. He too sensed the presence of the dark powers around him.

How long had he watched the mayor, powerless to stop his atrocious actions?

The mayor stiffened as evil returned to the car. A smile crept onto the mayor's face as he started the car. He only pulled the car around to the back of the station. What was he up to now?

~~~~~~~~~~~

Ophois soared beside Anput only feet above the Kansas River. They banked right, as the Kansas joined the Missouri. Ophois pointed upward with his left thumb.

Anput shook her head. "We need to stay low. Not a matter of staying out of sight." She pointed to a boat ahead and they split up. She went around to the left, while he went to the right.

The boat flashed past.

"Down here," Anput continued, "we do not risk running into other demons, angels, or people."

As much as he disliked being this close to the water, he understood. Even with his scimitar pointed straight before

138

him, running into another spiritual being could be fatal. An angel, he might rip right through, so much the better. Another demon, he would prefer to not destroy a fellow being. A person, now that concerned him. Smashing full-speed into a human's spirit—especially that of a follower of Christ—was like flying an airplane into the side of a mountain.

Within seconds, they reached the Broadway Bridge. They weaved around the supports. Not because an impact was a concern, the bridge was purely a physical object. Best to remain where they could see what approached.

Somewhere behind them, Garnoc roared and barked at his guards. Only two had even pursued the fleeing duo.

Their speed now exceeded three-hundred-fifty meters per second. In the physical realm, water would have been rising on a sonic wave behind them.

Swoosh.

He passed through a rail-bridge support. Thankfully, he was not in the physical realm.

He glanced back and saw that the guards were already fading.

Within a minute, they passed multiple road and rail bridges. Finally, on the north-east side of the city, they darted under a railroad that marked a departure from the city and the official dominion of Garnoc. Neither considered slowing. Mere principality borders would provide no protection from Garnoc and his forces.

After just a few minutes of slaloming through the course of the winding river, they arrived at Lexington.

They slowed and Ophois breathed a huge relief as they veered off the river. They settled in the small town.

"Thanks for intervening," Ophois said. "I thought Garnoc was going to rip me to shreds."

"Glad I could help," Anput said. "What was that all about?"

"Great question. He said he had seen Ima."

"So she *is* in Kansas City," Anput said.

Ophois paced in a circle atop the pea-stone roof of a local factory. Garnoc had never been touted for his rationality. He knew Ima was different from other mims. What did he expect? "Animals."

Anput nodded. "Most of the princes I have encountered are brutes."

Ophois cocked his canine head to the side and stared at Anput. *What?*

Anput noticed the look. "Were you not referring to Garnoc?"

"No." Ophois wagged his head. "Something he said. A messenger said the *animals* reacted to her."

"That makes no sense. Why is that a reason to attack you?"

A grin erupted from deep within him. He realized something the intelligent Anput did not.

"What?" She glared at Ophois.

"I care not about Garnoc's psychotic reasoning. I care about Ima's location."

Now it was her time to cock her head to the side—still not following his logic.

"Where would you find 'the animals' in the city?"

A smile crept onto her face. "The zoo!"

He so wanted to rip the girl to shreds. She had caused him more grief than he would have believed possible for a twelve-year-old mim who had spent almost no time in the real world.

Her smile disappeared. "How does this help? We dare not risk returning to the city."

His throat still throbbed from Garnoc's maniacal grip. "Oh, I surely agree with that. But I would not expect a twelve-year-old on the run to stop to enjoy the animals at the zoo."

Anput knelt down and picked at the small stones with her claws. After a few minutes of thought, she looked up with her brilliant red eyes. "Someone took her—someone who cares enough to take her to the zoo."

"See," Ophois said, "this is why we make such a good team. If we backtrack to where we lost her scent, and then, look for a godly couple or family that may have taken her in."

"Wait. Why a godly couple?"

"Garnoc's irritation made no sense," said Ophois. "There was only one reason he would have been so irate with his encounter."

Anput hopped up with a hand full of gravel. "He got his butt kicked." She kicked the gravel into the air.

Ophois clapped and rubbed his hands together. "Shall we go find us a little rabbit?"

~~~~~~~~~~

After some bantering with Chris Davis in the police station, Mayor Trenton Richards, controlled by Tudur, followed a burly FBI agent into the briefing room.

Tudur winked at Listh. His friend stood next to a woman who must have been Vivian from Homeland Security.

Alex, Chris' new guard-dog angel, stood behind a table glaring at Tudur.

"Evening, Alex," Tudur said. The rumor among the demons of Eran's demise appeared accurate. "Where is Eran? Is he not Chris' protector?"

Alex' hand moved to the hilt of his sword.

"Come, come. You should be joyous. Are you not preparing the demise of the operations at CeSiR?"

Chris had finished introducing the mayor to the various members of the crack team of government agents destined to lead Chris to his demise.

After a skirmish with Vivian, who tried to take the mayor into custody, Tudur ran Trenton out of the room, through the front door, around the building, and to his BMW, which he strategically parked on the street behind the station.

Now to go get the sacrificial lamb, whom the Sherwoods had been so kind to look after for him—his propitiation for Mael, as the prince's kingdom began to crumble.

~~~~~~~~~~

Ima's eyes drooped heavy in the back seat of the Impala. She sat in the middle, as she had on the way to the zoo. Except this time she sat back against the seat in a near comatose state, reflecting on her day.

After the sky safari, the animals remained friendly to her. Birds chirped and hopped along beside her. Lemurs and meerkats chittered as they bounced around one another playing games.

Her eyes closed as gorillas, elephants, bobcats, and warthogs played leapfrog. The smile, a permanent feature of her face since lunch, widened from ear to ear. Contented slumber washed over her, as the red glow of headlights flickered through her eyelids.

"What in the—" Mama's voice chiseled its way into Ima's awareness.

She opened her eyes just in time to see tail lights merge into their lane, only inches in front of the Impala's bumper. The left light flashed, as if claiming a right to that space of the road.

The red LEDs at the top of the car's window continued to flash.

"Why on earth?" Before Mama could even finish the question, the taillights doubled in brightness, setting in motion a series of slow-motion events.

A screech erupted from somewhere beneath her seat. The seatbelt across her chest tried to slice her in half. Her ribs already out-screamed the car tires, but that was preferable to greeting the windshield with her head.

Papa yelled some words at the driver of the offending car that she often heard at the facility, though never from Uncle M. The highly descriptive language though out-of-place on the lips of Papa, seemed somehow fitting.

A blaring noise erupted from the front of the Impala, as if the prancing beast of prey had become a roaring predator. Mama's hand pulled back from the center of the steering wheel and the roar subsided. She slammed the heal of her hand back into the wheel and the car screamed once again.

The strange sensation of sideways motion rocked Ima's chin from her chest to her shoulder. If the wheels that steered the car where in the front, then why was the back of the car moving sideways—even as the front of the car appeared to stop in time to avoid crushing the small hatchback in front of them.

As if sensing the danger behind, the hatchback scooted across two oncoming lanes, intent on escaping unscathed. It jetted onto a small side street, barely visible in the waning light of dusk.

Ima released a breath she had been unaware she was holding. The threat was gone. They would not rear-end the little car.

Another horn blared somewhere. This time it came from an oncoming pickup. The mischievous hatchback had barely cleared the oncoming lanes when the truck flew by. An odd dissonance formed as the two horns danced with one another.

The screeching of the tires beneath Ima continued—this time from their sideways slide.

Mama spun the steering wheel.

Soon, Ima saw a tree trunk approaching out her side window. What was a tree doing in the middle of the road? But they were no longer heading down the road. They were heading across the road—sideways.

The tree skimmed the back bumper of the Impala, as the car skidded to a stop on the gravel shoulder with a duet of pops and hisses.

The blue stench of burning rubber filled the cabin of the car. Ima coughed. "Mama? Papa?"

"We're okay, sweetie," Mama said. "The good Lord protected us from that attack at the zoo, this was nothing." Mama reached up and pushed a black button with a small red triangle inside a larger triangle.

Click-click, click-click. Two green arrows on the dash began flashing.

Papa opened his door and took a walk around the car. He returned and explained that the nasty smell was the result of two shredded tires.

"Can you fix the tires, Papa?" The remaining twilight, now blood-red, crept through the windshield of the car. Behind her, the darkness of night overtook the light.

"We only have one spare," Papa said.

Could a car run on three tires? Until a week ago, she had only seen cars in the books at the facility, or the few sneak-peeks she got of vehicles driving from the gate to the parking garage. Still, within the past few days she saw many cars and all drove on four wheels. No, she didn't think three would do.

Mama patted Ima's hand as it sat on Papa's seat-back. "Don't you worry, hon. We'll just call roadside assistance and they'll have us back on the road in an hour or two."

Two hours in the car—in the dark. Visions of the train baring down on the car parked at the intersection only days earlier barreled through her thoughts. "What if a semi-truck comes? What if they don't see us? What if it hits us?"

Mama squeezed her hand in assurance. "Child, you can't live your life afraid of the what-ifs. The Bible tells us that God is sovereign. You can trust him."

"What is sobrin?" Ima asked.

A deep laugh shook Papa's seat. He turned and smiled at Ima. "It's sovereign, with a *v*. It means He's in charge. He has the power to ensure that exactly what He wants to happen does happen."

Ima sat silently for several seconds staring at the fading purple sky. Tears warmed the creases of her eyes. She looked to Papa. "So God wanted Uncle M to die?"

"Oh, dear child," Mama said. "We cannot begin to understand the thoughts of God. His knowledge is just as perfect as His power. And His love is just as perfect as His knowledge." Mama unfastened her seatbelt and turned herself farther around in her seat. "Often when we talk of wanting something, we are referring to wishing that something to be true. But God, He knows every option, every possibility, and every outcome of every decision."

Mama opened her door, stepped out of the car, and climbed in the back seat with Ima. "As much as I love you, I would never wish you loss, just so that I could meet you. But maybe that is precisely why He chose that option out of the millions of possibilities. Perhaps He has a purpose for you that is so incredible, that if we could see it, we might begin to understand." Mama pulled Ima into a warm embrace. "*Maybes* never provide a satisfying answer, but that's all we've got. Only God can escape the dissatisfaction of *maybes*."

Shadows of Ima and Mama danced across the back of the front seats. A deep rumble rattled the windows of the Impala. Their shadows split in two making four heads on the seat backs.

The roar of an engine and the wine of a dozen tires rose in both volume and pitch. The shadows and lights vanished when the sound reached its max.

Ima trembled as the semi rumbled past.

Mama placed her hands on Ima's shoulders. "You know what God also offers in perfection?"

Ima wagged her head from side to side.

"His perfect peace. In the midst of all the unknown, the pain and sorrow, you can have what the Bible calls God's peace, which exceeds anything we can understand."

Ima couldn't fathom such an incredible peace, but she wanted to.

~~~~~~~~~~

Mayor Trenton Richards pulled his BMW into the gravel driveway. The farmhouse sat in complete darkness except the glow of a single metal-halide light over the large double barn doors out back. Was it possible the elderly couple and their little blond guest had already retired for the night? Certainly feasible.

Tudur led the mim out of the car. Gravel crunched under his feet. He swung the door shut, careful not to make more noise than necessary. Though, he really cared not if the household awoke. He *would* leave with his prize. No opposition, from inside or above, would deter him from taking her. One question remained. *In what condition?* And, perhaps, *what would remain of the others?*

He approached the large porch at the side of the home. The first step squeaked as wood slid on old rusted nails. Trenton's steps lightened as he ascended the remaining steps. One small squeak proved enough.

"Rarf!" The deep growl-laden bark shook a knee-high window to Tudur's left. The curtain swished aside to reveal the same golden retriever he had seen with Ima, earlier in the week.

The house remained dark.

Trenton reached out and tried the door handle.

Locked.

"Rarf-arf!"

Tudur separated himself from the mim and passed through the door. He closed his eyes and focused on the physical realm. Manifestation was not his strong suit. He felt out of practice. With such a malleable host for two decades, the need seldom presented itself. He felt the air cool around him as his transition pulled energy from the room.

"Grrrr."

He could not get distracted by the mongrel. He would deal with it soon enough. Tiny ice crystals fell at his bat-like feet. With the process complete, he stretched his sinewy wings across the room.

He turned bared white fangs to the dog. "You want a piece of me now!" Tudur let a wail rise from deep within his chest and flew toward the mutt.

The dog ran in place as it sought a hastened retreat. In a golden flash, she vanished from the room.

The house remained dark. The trace aromas of toast and coffee hung in the darkness.

Tudur walked back to the door and unlatched the lock. He opened the door to find Trenton wandering aimlessly around the porch. Pathetic.

Again, Tudur closed his eyes. The return trip always proved simpler. Light flashed as energy returned to the physical realm. Tudur wasted no time joining with Trenton. He needed to get the mim off the porch, before someone drove by and recognized him as the mayor of Arrow Springs.

He reentered the home and closed the door behind him. Though the mim could see no better in the dark than a normal human, Tudur saw perfectly. No need for a light. In fact, no desire for light. Ever.

Even the soundest sleeper could not have slept through the infernal canine. Still, those who slept in the house were the least of his concerns. He needed to assure himself that no angelic warriors awaited him.

A sweep of the first floor revealed no activity—angelic or otherwise. He proceeded to the second floor. He sneered as he entered the first room. A flowery bedspread sat in a disheveled heap and a young girl's nightgown hung over the back of a chair.

Ima's room.

So kind of the couple to provide care and keep for his little prize. How would they take the removal of the girl from their home? Would they give him trouble? Hardly. A room full of government officials might have proved a challenge, but two old people and a mim—not a chance.

Did they know? Surely, they would be much less accommodating if they knew exactly *what* they were protecting.

He swept the remainder of the home. No, presence. Too bad. He so wanted to collect Mael's sacrificial offering. At least he knew she was still staying with the couple. He would need to retrieve her another time.

Tudur led Trenton back through the house and out the door. Disappointed, they started the BMW and the gravel began to crunch under the wheels.

~~~~~~~~~~

Once the hatchback was long gone and the Sherwoods' Impala rested safely beside the road, albeit minus a couple tires, Adiya joined Ima and Patricia in the back seat. She wrapped a wing around the shaking girl. Ima's tension, from the passing semi-truck, began to subside.

Patricia went on to talk about what it meant for Jesus to be the Prince-of-Peace. That it was the only way to find relief from all the voices in their heads that accuse. "Those voices are right," Patricia said. She went on to explain how nothing

Ima could do would allow God to forgive her, but that perfect peace for imperfect people required a perfect replacement. The girl shook with sobs as she realized that Jesus loved even her enough to die for her. The horror in Ima's eyes told Adiya that the child appreciated and believed in Jesus' sacrifice for humanity. But she was not humanity. She was a mim.

Sorrow rippled from wingtip to wingtip, as Adiya watched a precious creation doubt the Savior's perfect love. Not that it existed, but that it existed *for her.*

Ima was not the enemy. Mims were not the enemy. Adiya's fallen comrades' hatred for His chosen creations and their evil opposition to His purposes—that was the true enemy.

~~~~~~~~~~~

Ophois and Anput backtracked their path from Lexington toward Arrow Springs. After much deliberation and trying to pick up the now non-existent scent of their prey, they decided the most likely place for the young mim to have given them the slip was at the rail intersections of Marshall.

They had deduced from the girl's fear and past decisions that she would have stayed with the tracks. The problem was, the tracks split into a Y. He and Anput had functioned on the premise that the girl had a familiarity with the tracks—that they ended when heading west from the Y.

A faulty premise.

One that nearly destroyed him in Kansas City. Yet one that provided important information about the present accommodations of the girl. She had a makeshift family. It would not take much canvasing of the town of Marshall to find a demon that had seen something. Something that would lead them to the girl.

Ophois licked his lips in anticipation of the renewed hunt.

~~~~~~~~~~~

The wrecker pulled alongside the Impala.

Ima watched the yellow flashing lights strobe off the chrome trim on the the car's dash.

"Are they going to tow the car?" Mama asked.

148

Ima's neck was still sore from the accident. She couldn't imagine sitting in her seat as they pulled the car down the road. Could she even stay in her seat? Wouldn't she fall forward into the flickering dash? She glanced back at the truck behind them.

"No," Papa said. "They said they had a couple tires that would work for us. They'll just replace the shredded mess we have over there and we'll be on our way." He opened the door and hopped out. His face pulsed a fiendish yellow as he walked past her window.

True to his word, after ten minutes of the car bumping up and down, he waved goodbye to the repairman. "Thanks again!"

Mama was back in the driver's seat. She checked her mirrors and pulled a big *U* in the middle of the road.

"We'll be home in just a few minutes." Papa rubbed his hands together. "I think there's still some of that pudding and cream-cheese dessert at the house."

~~~~~~~~~~~

CHAPTER TEN

Ima awoke to the silence of the Impala's engine. Now what? Did the car break down? She glanced left then right. She exhaled a breath of relief. The familiar sight of the farmhouse welcomed her home.

She fumbled for her buckle. On her third try, she heard it click, releasing her from the seat. She scooted her bottom across the seat to the door. She yanked on the silver handle. An uneventful conclusion to a much too eventful ride home.

Home. The thought wrapped her up like a blanket, fresh from the dryer. Was it possible? Had she finally found a real home—better yet, a family? How many nights, had she sat on her cot in her nondescript room at CeSiR Tech longing for such a miracle? Had Mama's God—her God, if she accepted what Mama told her after the accident—really provided such a wonderful thing? And for her?

She stepped from the car and swung the door shut with a thud.

On the porch something felt—off.

Mama fumbled through her purse for the house key. "Oh, for goodness sake, I just had the darn thing. How could it get lost in there that quickly?"

The house awaited them in silence.

"It's a wonder you can find anything in that duffle-bag-of-a-purse you carry," Papa said. He laughed. "I think you have half the house in that thing."

Silence—inside.

That was it. Goldie, she always met them at the door. She should be barking her head off, while they fumbled around on the porch. Especially after waiting all day to go out. "Where's Goldie? She's not barking." Ima's voice broke.

"Don't you worry," Mama said. "She's getting old, like the rest of us." She's probably asleep in our room. I'm sure she didn't even hear us drive up."

Yeah. Of course. Asleep, just like Ima didn't hear them pull in until they shut off the car. That had to be it.

"There it is." Mama slid the key into the door and swung it open.

They were all tired from a long and stranger-than-usual day. They walked through the door and Papa closed it behind them.

Ima turned and flipped the light switch on the wall.

As light illuminated the dining room, Mama's scream echoed off the walls.

~~~~~~~~~~

Adiya stood beside Ima, as the lights came to life. But she already knew. The Father had given advanced insight to her and Eldwyn, along with a renewed command not to interfere.

What did the Creator intend to accomplish? So many times she had wondered that. Obedience always led to enlightenment, beyond anything she could imagine. Yet not always without cost.

Adiya spread her wings and pulled her flaming sword.

Even as Patricia's scream hung in the room, she reached out and drew Ima to her side.

"What is it, Mama?" Innocent eyes gazed up at Patricia.

Charles took a step forward, shielding them from the sight.

Eldwyn flanked the elderly man, eyes and staff ablaze. He would not defy the commands of the Maker. If such defiance had been in him, he would have fallen millennia ago, when a third of their ranks followed Lucifer in his arrogant rebellion.

No, he would not act.

His love for the old man rolled into a tear that ran down his taught face. Not a tear of pain, loss, or bitterness, like those that will one day be banished from the earth, as in Heaven. Rather, a tear of love, which even God himself often sheds.

Eldwyn spread his wings. With his right wing, he wrapped Charles in a hedge of peace, and shielded the women from the evil before them.

~~~~~~~~~~

Ima wanted to turn, needed to turn, to face a horror of the proportion necessary to bring such a piercing exclamation from the strongest woman she had ever met.

A familiar stench attacked her nose, a mixture of sulfur and iron. And something else, something she recalled from her time at the facility.

By the sheer power of her will, she forced her head toward the presence, which she felt at the far edge of the room.

No. Not that.

Not him.

Ima pressed into Mama's waist.

A shaking hand patted her shoulder—a waffling expression of *it will be okay.*

Ima's voice cut through the now silent room. "What do you want, Trenton?" As if she didn't know. As if she expected CeSiR to let her walk—floating, splashing, screaming, crying— away.

Visions sprang to her mind. Blood splattering from Uncle M. The sound of his gurgling voice, as he said goodbye. She had no idea who fired the shot from the building, but it could have been Trenton. He and Leon were the meanest mims she'd ever encountered. Mean to others, but especially to her. Everyone singled her out. She was the brunt of their jokes— never funny.

Monstrous trees flashed through her thoughts. Terror pursued her through the fog of her memories. She stood on a bridge, wondering if a train would force her to jump to the icy waters below. But she had found rest, comfort, and peace in the wonderful woman now trembling next to her. The woman who had first pointed that same shotgun at her.

Now viciousness incarnate controlled that steel barrel. The overpowering scent of sweet musk fought with the reek of sulfur.

"You know what I want," Trenton said. "Time for you to go home, Ima."

Home—never. CeSiR was a lot to her. Her birthplace, her school, her boarding house, even her torment, but never a home. She now understood the real meaning of home. So much more than wood and plaster. And definitely not concrete and cotton pants. "This is my home. Leave us alone."

Delight curled Trenton's lip upward in a crooked grin. "The lamb has found a backbone. So much more fun."

"You get out of my house. I don't know who you are or were to her, and I don't care." Papa took another small step toward the intruder.

The gun barrel leveled to Papa's head.

Ima buried her head in Mama's soft chest. She couldn't bear to see another man she loved shot.

Mama started to pray out loud. "Dear Jesus, we—"

"Another word and I blow her head off her shoulders." Trenton's voice shook with hatred.

He could only be referring to her, but Ima didn't look to see if the barrel now pointed at her. *At Mama.* If he shot Ima in the head, which she had no doubt he would, the bullet wouldn't just kill her. It would take Mama with her.

She had to move away.

She pushed to get away from Mama's chest, but strong arms held her in place. A willing embrace of self-sacrifice.

She couldn't allow another person to die on her behalf. First, Uncle M. And many years before, as she learned from Mama in the car, this Jesus, who she didn't even know. Mama held her tight.

Ima turned her head away from the woman's blouse. "Take me, Trenton. It's me you want. Just don't kill them."

"Ima, no." Mama's voice quaked.

"Smart girl," Trenton said. "If she comes with me, you all live. If not, I will use your handy shotgun here to paint the three of you onto that wall." He took a step to his left. "So, old woman, how about you make yourself useful for something other than spouting words. I am quite sure you have some duct tape in the house. Be a dear and go get it for me."

"That's never going to happen," Mama said. The shaking had ceased and she glared at Trenton.

~~~~~~~~~~~

Through a glass window, he watched the events unfolding in the farmhouse. He wanted to intervene, to stop the maniacal rampage of Trenton Richards, once and for all.

But he was powerless to interfere.

The elderly woman straightened and barked out her defiance.

Trenton aimed and pulled the trigger.

~~~~~~~~~~~

Ophois and Anput walked into a neon nightclub in Marshall. Ophois soaked in the lustful atmosphere. After a day of water-world frenzies in Kansas City, this dark gyrating environment greeted him like heaven on earth. Actually, better. Very few holier-than-thou angels walked into this place. Even those who did moved with caution and less confidence than normal.

The pair split up and Anput headed to the patrons of inebriation to see if any of the demons had noticed any locals who recently acquired a young child.

Ophois moved toward the stage where a young woman danced. Here, the patrons sat in a state of hypnotic excitement. Places like this were the Promised Land for demons. In a state of near absence from self-control, the humans willingly relinquished control to their handlers. Control that, once given, was seldom returned.

He too sought out information on local residents who had recently given harbor to a young runaway—a blond haired girl age twelve. Several informed him of men they had seen, even some sitting near them in the club, who would enjoy such company.

154

If Ima visited the zoo with someone from this area, the situation would not be as deliciously evil as those he heard described. Perhaps this crowd of demons had life a little too good to possess the information they needed.

What were they looking for? A couple, a family, a parent-wanna-be? The zoo—it seemed like a trip someone without children at home would take. Grandparents? Possibly. Either way, where would someone without kids, now with a child age twelve, be seen in town? Not the nightclub.

Ophois waved to Anput and pointed to the door.

As he walked, he glanced back over the crowd that watched the young woman dancing. He licked his lips. Oh, for such a posh assignment.

Anput shook her golden head, as she approached.

"We were not thinking," Ophois said. "I know just the place to ask around. If she is in the area, we will find her."

~~~~~~~~~~~

A loud bang rattled the windows in the old farmhouse. Shotgun pellets hit the window that looked out on the porch.

Screaming, yelling, and swearing joined the echoes of the blast.

The grey smell of gunpowder soon gave way to the sickly sweet smell of iron. The smell of blood.

When the gun went off, Ima had turned her head back into Mama's chest. Mama crumpled out of her grasp. Without the woman's maternal protection, Ima saw blood spattered on the beige wallpaper. A crack had snaked its way up the window.

Ima didn't feel any pain. She didn't believe she had been shot. But the blood. *Mama.*

She turned and saw the source of the blood.

She puked up cotton candy when she saw a chunk of Papa's leg was missing.

Mama lay next to him on the ground, holding his blood soaked pant-leg and begging Jesus to let him live.

"I think we now understand that I *am* serious," Trenton said. His voice dripped with ice. "Unless I am mistaken, and I

155

seldom am about such things, he will die in roughly twenty-five minutes. That is just enough time for the paramedics to save him. So I suggest you get me that tape. Stop wasting your time begging your unsympathetic Creator for a miracle."

Three successive clicks startled Ima. It appeared Trenton had reloaded the shotgun faster than she could turn her head. "Either of you move," Trenton said, staring to Ima's right, "And they will all be dead before you can stop me." He paused, as if to see if some unseen foe would comply. His steely gaze turned to Mama, kneeling in a growing puddle of blood. "Move now. Or, do not. I am content to stand here and watch him bleed out before you. Your choice."

Mama staggered to her feet and rushed to the kitchen as fast as her wobbly knees would carry her.

Papa lay on the floor with grimacing pain chiseled deep into his already wrinkled face. "Im-ma," he said, "we—love you. Don't forget."

"Oh, how sweet." Trenton stepped aside, as Mama returned from the kitchen with the duct tape. "What do you think, Ima dearest? Should we see just how unconditional their love is?"

She wanted to scream. No, to run at him and scratch his eyes out. Inflict even a portion of the pain he'd caused her. Her feet wouldn't listen, or was it her brain that refused to issue the command?

Trenton waved the gun toward Ima. "Well, little miss mim. Please sit on the floor with your arms and feet in front of you."

A groan gurgled from Papa's throat.

"If you want to see your husband tomorrow, I suggest you hurry and tape her hands and feet together. Several times around should do nicely."

Mama knelt frozen between the bleeding love-of-her-life and a child she knew so little about.

Ima nodded, as tears trickled down her face. She would not come between the couple who had shown her such incredible kindness. No more death. Not on her account.

Ima pushed her hands forward balled into fists, wrist-to-wrist.

Mama's lips motioned the words, "I'm so sorry." But no sound escaped her mouth. Her shock seemed to exceed Papa's.

Ima lifted her feet, ankle-to-ankle, to make it easier for Mama to wrap them in the paste-scented tape.

"Good, very good." Trenton's voice grated across the room. "Now, tape them together. Just like a roped calf. Tie her up like the animal she is."

Mama's eyes closed briefly, as she pulled a length of tape away from the cardboard roll.

Ima spread her knees and reached her hands to her ankles. Mama finished tying her up.

"Now, a couple strips for those fiery little lips."

The deed was done. Mama turned a severely aged face to Trenton. "Please, let me get him help."

Trenton approached Mama. "Sure." He smacked her across the face with the butt of the gun and then dropped the cordless phone next to her. "The number is 9-1-1." He chuckled and bent to pick up the duct tape.

He approached the paling body of Papa.

No. Leave him alone! Ima tried to scream, but the tape kept the words tangled in her vocal cords.

"Relax," Trenton said. "I only intend to help him survive until the arrival of the paramedics." He pulled a long stretch of tape and began winding it around Papa's thigh.

Deep guttural screams filled the room.

Trenton didn't stop. For once, Ima believed that to be a good thing. He seemed to be saving Papa from dying, at least for the moment.

Mama was already talking frantically into the phone. She told them that a madman had shot her husband and he needed an ambulance, now.

"How rude," Trenton said. "I try to save his life and you insult me." He stood and walked toward Ima. On his way, he swatted the phone out of Mama's hand, as she attempted to remember her address for the woman on the phone.

Mama scrambled across the floor and retrieved the phone.

Relief swept through Ima when she still heard the woman's voice coming through the receiver. It hadn't broken.

Trenton barely slowed on his way to the door. With a single hand, he whisked Ima off the floor by her bound hands and feet.

Her knees came together and tried to pull her shoulders out of their sockets. Pain flooded her joints.

Trenton stopped at the door and pointed at an invisible adversary. "If I catch a glimpse of you following me, she will be dead before you can intervene."

He carried Ima around the corner of the house, where his car sat hidden from the road and driveway. The trunk popped open and he tossed her in with the ease of someone tossing their jacket into the car.

What little light the night offered soon vanished as the trunk slammed shut. A metal bar pushed into her already numbing shoulder.

~~~~~~~~~~

Adiya sheathed her sword and rushed to Eldwyn's side. He knelt beside Charles Sherwood's limp body and stroked the man's grey hair. Eldwyn whispered encouragement to hang on.

Tears streamed down the wise angel's face. He had spent most of this man's life watching over him.

Adiya felt his pain. She had heard humans say that angels do not cry, because in Heaven there are no tears. How far could that be from the truth? This certainly was not Heaven. And unlike Heaven, where the absence of pain results only in tears of joy, the earth was filled with pain and sorrow. Sorrow, such as seeing a godly man maimed or a child treated like cattle, could only produce tears.

She longed to follow Tudur. To rip him apart for the harm he had caused this unusual family. But the Father's instructions rang clear, *wait. Trust.* That she did unconditionally. The time would come to find Ima. For now, this dear couple needed her assistance.

She knelt next to Patricia and wrapped her wings around the sweet woman. Patricia shook with sobs of fear and loss. Loss for the second time. She had made peace with his absence when the Alzheimer's fully took him. Yet the presence of Ima had somehow given them a renewed life together. Would it prove to be a mere handful of days?

Adiya's pleas joined Patricia's, begging the Father to sustain the fragile body lying on the floor next to them.

"Weakness besets him," Eldwyn said. His voice was low and somber, absent his usual charm.

Sirens rang in the distance.

"It shall be close," Adiya said.

"No, in His hands, it shall be." Eldwyn extended his wings over the body. "He grows colder." He closed his eyes and energy flowed from the wings to the man.

How much pain could these mims cause in the hands of the enemy? Ima intended no harm, yet by her very presence she threatened the life of this dear man. No. The enemy was Tudur and his puppet, Trenton Richards.

Ima had brought healing and renewed life to the Sherwoods, even if only for a brief time.

What did the Creator intend for this child? What purpose could make her so special, and yet so normal.

A stiff rap on the door shook Adiya out of her reflections. "Paramedics! We're coming in." The door slammed open and two EMTs entered the room.

A brunette woman flowed through Adiya and directly to Charles' leg. Compassion and urgency remained with Adiya in her wake. "Sir, can you hear me?"

Charles' eyes remained shut. After a few long moments, his head bobbed like a leaf on a near-breezeless pond.

"Good," the paramedic said. "Ma'am, what happened?"

"Rate of one-thirty. Pressure's seventy over palp," called out a male EMT, on the other side of Charles.

"There's a lot of blood over here," the brunette said. "Likely hemorrhagic shock."

The male EMT nodded, as he intubated Charles and hooked the breathing tube to oxygen.

The brunette unwound the duct tape. "This likely prevented full exsanguination." Another loop of bloody tape. "We don't have time to clean the wound." She removed the remaining tape. "Severed the femoral artery. We need to get him to Fitz, as soon as we can stabilize." The woman turned to Patricia. "Did you do this?"

Patricia turned a colorless face to the woman. "He, he was sh—shot. My shotgun. May—"

The brunette EMT nodded. "That came in from 9-1-1. Did you wrap his leg?"

Patricia just stared at her beloved's bloody leg.

The brunette glanced to her counterpart. "Appears to have taken most of the muscle. Doesn't look like it got bone."

Adiya pulled the fragile Patricia tighter into her wings.

"Mayor wrapped leg." Patricia's body shook. "After I wrapped up Ima. He took her." A revitalized stream of tears wound their way through the wrinkle-troughs in her face. "He took Ima."

"Beginning hemostatic wrap," the female EMT said. "Proceed with saline."

The man nodded and worked on getting a port installed.

"Did you say there was someone else?" the brunette asked. "Was she also injured?"

Patricia simply shook her head.

The EMT raised her eyes to the fluid flowing into Charles' arm. "Get the cart." After the man exited the house. She pulled her radio from her belt. "Dispatch. We have a gunshot wound and an apparent kidnapping. Please activate the alert."

Minutes later, they had Charles loaded on a gurney and wheeled him out the front door.

Adiya turned to Eldwyn who had not left Charles' side since the gunshot. "You go with them. I feel I need to stay here and seek the Father's will regarding Ima."

Eldwyn nodded and placed his hand on Patricia's shoulder. With shaky legs, she followed her life's love. "God be with you, Adiya."

"Thank you, my friend. Likewise."

~~~~~~~~~~~

A devilish-red glow filled Ima's vision. The car jerked to a stop and Ima's heels smacked into what she assumed was the back of the rear seat.

The chamber clicked to blackness and her head bounced off something metal. Where was this lunatic taking her? Were they headed back to CeSiR? If so, her life—the truly-living-life of the past handful of days—would end with their arrival.

Could she escape? Surely a car's trunk was designed to be opened from the inside. Did anyone ever accidentally get shut in a trunk? Didn't seem likely. Besides, her hands were securely taped to her ankles.

Her shoulders screamed from the sickening trip to the trunk. He had treated her like a bag of trash. Did she deserve any better? Mama tried to convince her she had meaning. That God cared about her. But Mama didn't know. She was a mim not a human. Did Jesus really offer His sacrifice for a mim?

Even the other mims rejected her. Defective. Trash. That truly described her.

"Ya are the perfect mim."

"I don't feel perfect."

"In a strange way, that's precisely what makes ya different from the others."

The conversation with Uncle M—only nine seemingly-a-lifetime days earlier—brought warmth to her cheeks, even as she rested them against the raw metal of the trunk.

She missed him, missed the warmth of his eyes, the way they lit up in her presence.

He was the first in a long line of those hurt on her behalf. The sweet-copper smell of blood, pooling in the dining room at the farmhouse, haunted her mind. Could there be any hope of Papa surviving the wound? Trenton had said so. He claimed

161

his actions may have saved the man's life. Would he lie about it? Of course he would. He had probably told more lies in his life than truths.

If only she could get her hands free. She knew there was sharp metal somewhere at the top of her portable prison. A sharp sting in her leg told her it was there, somewhere. The car had hit a bump and something pierced her leg. But where? And could she get her wrists to the slicing metal while they were attached to her feet.

The flicker of hope, the drive to fight for her freedom, stood no chance against a flood of helplessness. Her brain replayed the sound of shotgun pellets ripping through Papa's leg, or was it the bullet slamming into the back of Uncle M?

The car pulled a sharp right turn without slowing.

Ima slid across the trunk. Her tailbone smacked the carpeted wheel well.

A grunt slid through her duct taped mouth. Not from pain, but frustration with her situation and the unknown condition of Papa.

If she were the young sleuth in the television show Papa had watched, she could figure out exactly where they were headed. Little sounds trickled in, mixing with the whine of the vehicle's tires on the road. Traffic seemed to pass right under them. She could count the turns, time the distances.

She was no sleuth.

The hot-coal glow of red returned to her tiny prison cell. Near her head the light flickered, no, pulsed. She extended her feet to the seat back, bracing against the deceleration. Were they at CeSiR? Soon, she should hear the voices of the guards. Perhaps the one who had shot Uncle M. Though she didn't know who to blame for that, except for Maiya. Not true. She knew exactly who to blame.

The car bounced and lurched.

Ima released a muffled scream.

"Almost there, darling," Trenton said. His voice rose from beyond the renewed darkness.

The carpeted bottom of the trunk kept disappearing from beneath her. She floated momentarily in midair, then the metal framing would slap her back down. One particular bump rammed her head into the right wheel well. A sickening thud slammed her teeth together.

Her world faded to a blacker black.

~~~~~~~~~~

Ophois led Anput into the brightly lit building. She looked at him and grinned. Her golden head, with a topaz stripe rimming her ears, bobbed up and down.

"Of course," she said.

Someone with a newly acquired child would need groceries. If the couple were elderly they would be quite noticeable.

The store was quiet and mostly empty. This time of night, most shoppers were putting their children to bed, not buying groceries. Shoppers were not his objective. They would be too hit-and-miss. The odds of seeing his quarry would be thin.

An upper-teen girl leaned against the cash register. Her mad-at-the-world expression said she had better places to be. Raven-black hair shone under the high-intensity vapor lighting. She practically turned and looked right at Ophois. A diamond flickered in the middle of a silver nose ring.

"You got a problem with my charge?"

Ophois spun to see a bulky demon alight atop a shelf loaded with canned goods.

His green eyes challenged Ophois. "She belongs to me. Has since her mom overdosed on ice, while she was still nursing." Veins pulsed with a faint green glow as he stared down a curled nose at Ophois.

Ophois held up his hands. "Easy, friend." Wrong word. This was a demon of isolation and hatred. He spent his days convincing humans that friendship was foolish. "I am Ophois. And this—" He motioned to Anput, who had remained unnoticed. "—is Anput." She stepped forward and nodded.

Surprise sprang to the demon's face, but the gesture of openness seemed to calm his tension.

"What do you want?" the demon of isolation asked. "I am certain you did not come to hang at a grocery store for the night."

"We are looking for a young girl," Anput said.

"A bit generic do you not think."

"We do not think she came here. However, we believe she is being provided refuge by a family or a couple," Ophois said.

"Okay."

"Have you seen anyone making purchases that seem excessive, or out of the ordinary?" Anput asked.

"I do not hang out in the store to watch customers." He crossed his muscular arms and nodded like a man caught watching children's cartoons. "I think I know for whom you are looking.

"I overheard another cashier talking with Patricia Sherwood, something about the Alzheimer's being gone since *she* showed up." The demon turned his back to Ophois.

Anput cast a grin in Ophois' direction.

He nodded. Hanging out in a grocery store *and* listening to the local gossip. What an exciting existence.

The demon snarled. "These days, when such a public miracle is performed, it is wise to take notice." No arguing with that one. "Anyway, she talked about making desserts and bought Fruit Loops for breakfast." He turned his face back to Ophois, as if resigning himself to the ridicule of his station. "Most women her age buy Fiber One, not Fruit Loops."

Anput rose softly and sat near him on the shelving unit. "Would you happen to know where Mrs. Sherwood lives?"

It was hard to tell if the demon liked the elegant presence of Anput, or if he were ready to flee to his own isolated solitude.

He swallowed. "They live about three miles west of town, near the old tracks."

They finally had Ima. She *had* followed the tracks, just as Ophois had thought. She may have given him the slip, temporarily, but he had still tracked her down. Mael would be pleased, as long as he did not know how close Ophois had come to losing her.

"Thank you," Anput said.

They headed toward the west end of the store and rose to leave through the ceiling.

"One word of caution," the demon of isolation said.

They turned to him.

"The couple is guarded by Eldwyn. He is known for both his wisdom and skill in battle.

They bowed to him in appreciation. Then they soared through the metal roofing of the store.

~~~~~~~~~~~

Bodies pushed tight to the walls as the gurney raced past. The young EMT with shoulder length hair and hazel eyes barked out information to the nursing staff. Patricia thanked the Lord for the young woman's graceful skill under pressure en route to the hospital.

The hemostatic wrap she applied at the farmhouse seemed to slow the spill of his precious blood. They'd told her that Charles' vitals had recovered slightly with the infusion. Their eyes said his condition remained touch and go.

Patricia's frail footsteps chased her love down the hallway. How could a gurney surrounded by medical personnel move so quickly down the crowded hallway? She was old, tired, and barely able to stay on her feet. That's how. She fought hard to keep the deep pain from turning to anger. Why would God allow this? In her prayers she always sought God's will—not His blessing. But this, this bordered on too much. She lost her husband to the Alzheimer's, only to have him back when Ima arrived. Now she staggered forward, at risk of losing him once again.

The clickety-click of wheels on tile slowed. They pushed the cart into an emergency treatment room.

Quick steps and a couple "Doctor" greetings announced the arrival of the ER doctor. He rounded the doorframe just in front of Patricia. No time for excuse-me in a situation such as this. "Talk to me."

A sensation of peace settled into her soul as she found a spot in the room out of the way of the frenetic bustling.

"Gunshot to the leg," the EMT said. "Suspect a femoral injury with significant blood loss. We intubated and started two IVs—two liters of normal saline. BP is now ninety over forty and heart rate one-twenty. Sats are ninety-two percent."

The doctor grimaced.

Was that bad? Had the gracious young EMT made a mistake? Was Charles in trouble?

"I need a trauma panel. Get him typed and crossed for four units of blood STAT along with FFP." The doctor dismissed the EMT with a curt nod. He continued barking out orders, even as Charles was en route to the surgical ICU.

So much had changed over her lifetime in the field of medicine. Patricia prayed these advancements could give her a little more time with the love of her life.

Some trust in technological advancements. Put your trust in the one True Healer.

Patricia sat in a chair against the wall of the ER treatment room. She buried her head in her hands. How could she not trust her Lord, whatever He chose to bring? Her hands shook despite being clasped together for strength.

A tender hand alighted on her shoulder. "Ma'am," a soft female voice said, "I can take you to the trauma waiting room. That way you'll be close when he comes out of surgery."

Patricia looked up. Soft green eyes empathized with her. The woman wore a large pink smock. Her rounded cheeks bore a soft borrow-my-joy-in-your-pain smile. Patricia accepted the woman's hand and rose from the chair.

"Thank you, dear."

~~~~~~~~~~~

CHAPTER ELEVEN
Friday, May 15, 2020

Adiya knelt in the middle of the blood stained floor at the farmhouse. Darkness enveloped the room. Angels preferred light—despised darkness. And yet, with the pain of the evening, she appreciated the lack of light.

Do not interfere, but protect her.

Her orders were simple.

Simple to understand.

Not simple to execute. Now, Ima was Tudur's captive. Tudur and his pet mim, Trenton.

She should have acted. Could she have prevented the needless harm to Charles? If she had attacked Tudur, surely he would have shot Ima. *Protect her.* Even now, she felt the compulsion to stay true to her mission. But how? Where?

In the darkness of the room, her wings swirled with a dim illumination from the Spirit. Eitan had said this would be a difficult mission. Her appearance echoed his sentiment.

Ima daily grew in a basic understanding of the true Creator, the Truth who laid down His life for all of humanity. Patricia taught Ima about the peace beyond understanding. But Patricia knew not of Ima's origin. Did it make a difference?

The Creator had chosen not to endow the mims with souls. Demons like Tudur exploited this fact daily.

What made Ima so special? She saw it in her eyes and in the love of the Sherwoods for the young girl. Even Charles'

167

miraculous recovery spoke to the unique value God placed on this child. *Protect her.* Why?

"My Lord," Adiya prayed aloud, "I will never question your wisdom or instruction. It is my inability to see the logic that concerns me, not a disbelief of that logic." Flares of light burst from the base of her wings and swirled toward the tips.

She felt her Lord's presence manifest before her.

Adiya swept her wings forward, as she prostrated herself to the floor. How long had it been since she lay in His manifest presence?

"Adiya, my faithful messenger," her Lord said. He knelt and lifted her chin with his gentle touch.

Tears burst from her eyes. "I have failed you, my Lord."

"My dear Adiya. You have failed no one. You did what was necessary to obey me. The child Ima is healthy and growing in awareness of her purpose. Have these events transpired outside my sovereignty?"

The question rang both absurd and potent. "Of course not, my Lord." A lack of understanding of the purpose never implied a lack of purpose. "Forgive me, my Lord."

"There is nothing to forgive. The compassion with which I created you has served you well in this assignment. You acted when needed to protect her from Garnoc, and proved patient when the only course of action to save her was inaction."

Her wings glowed with a brilliance she had not seen in a hundred years. Still, compared to the presence of the True Light, they were dull and unimpressive. "May I ask of her location?" Adiya asked. "I desire to return to my assignment, to protect her."

Loving kindness flooded his voice. "You will find her, soon enough. She is your assignment. I trust you, Adiya. Trust yourself. Trust Me."

The room went black.

As her eyes adjusted, she realized the room was not dark at all. The light of His presence flowed throughout her being.

Do not interfere, but protect the restoration.

~~~~~~~~~~~

168

Reddish light forced its way through Ima's closed eyelids. They'd stopped moving. How long had they driven? What happened? They hit a bump or something. No. A rough road. She hit her head. That's all she remembered.

Her hands felt looser than before. She opened her eyes. Her heart jumped to her throat. The red light turned to yellow—golden yellow, and bright. Sunshine illuminated her face.

She was no longer tied up in the trunk. Instead, she lay on a cot of some kind. Not exactly a bed, still it was softer than the trunk. She tried to roll away from the beam of sunlight, but something held her left hand. Just her left. The duct tape was gone—from her ankles too.

She cranked her head to see what held her. Her heart recoiled. A shiny pair of handcuffs ensnared her wrist. The other end connected her to the cot.

"Help! Somebody, help me!" Her screams soaked into the walls. No echo. Just a dull recognition.

The door scraped open and she turned to see Trenton Richards standing just beyond her bare feet.

"Good, you are awake." His toothy grin sent ripples up her skin. "I was concerned you had been damaged in transit." His head wagged back and forth. "That would have been most unfortunate. We want no blemishes on Mael's sacrificial lamb."

She'd overheard the name Mael on occasion at the facility. The other mims would cease talking about him the instant she appeared. Then again, they ceased just about everything when she came around. Their disdain for her was not a well-kept secret. "What do you want with me, Trenton?"

~~~~~~~~~~

He watched as Trenton entered the room. He despised the man—longed to destroy the unworthy mayor of Arrow Springs. What was Trenton thinking? The lies, manipulation, and secrecy were bad enough, but now he had resorted to violence, kidnapping, and perhaps even murder.

He could not bear to see what Trenton would do to this young girl. Nor could he look away.

~~~~~~~~~~

169

"What do I want?" Trenton walked to the window. "Nothing, really. Though, I am certain Maiya will be quite relieved to know you are well." He twisted a plastic rod and the bright sun-rays vanished from the room.

A chill slithered up Ima's legs. "We're not at CeSiR. Where are we?" She wanted the sun back.

"No, this is not CeSiR. I preferred something more secluded. Somewhere you can scream all you want and no one will care." He walked to a grey metal chair and spun it around. He straddled the back of the chair and sat facing her. "Oh, we *will* be heading to CeSiR. But, for now, I have plans for you."

The chill tightened its grip. Last night, she was wearing jeans and a top. Now, the dark-blue pants and white shirt of CeSiR were back. Had she changed? She didn't remember anything since the trunk. "Where are my clothes?"

"Mim surrogates have no need for such niceties." A sneer swept across his face. "I threw them away. Just be glad I put something back on you."

Not her clothes—they were from Uncle M. "You keep your hands off me, you, monster."

He stood up, took two steps toward her, and lunged.

She pulled her knees to her chest and grabbed them with her right arm.

Trenton pulled up short and started laughing. "Relax, Ima." He walked to the door. "Nothing like that will happen to you. It is forbidden for mims. Mael, I mean Maiya, would have my hide." He stepped into what appeared to be a hallway and shut the door.

Something scraped outside the door and then clicked.

Her heart beat against her knees. At least she wasn't at CeSiR. There had to be a way to escape. She began to examine the cuffs holding her to the cot.

~~~~~~~~~~

Ophois surveyed the small farm from high above. Whatever had disturbed Garnoc so thoroughly warranted identification before engaging.

A few cows and chickens roamed the farm. Not the glory of days past, just quaint. Old even. They saw no sign of an angelic base of operations. No flurry of activity, in fact, aside from the few animals, no activity whatsoever.

Why would the host protect the girl? She was a mim. An abominate creation. He would expect the Creator to wipe them from existence. Mael's arrogance manifested, though he credited Lucifer's guidance for the plan. It seemed consistent. They had all seen Lucifer's arrogance when he rebelled against their Creator. They followed him—like goats to the slaughter. What had they been thinking? From nothing He created them. Compared to His power, that is what they still were—nothing. Yet He chose to banish rather than erase them. A tool to refine His crowning creations. The ones He loved. The ones He forgave. The ones for whom He gave His own life.

Ophois released an ear shattering howl—half anger, half lament.

"Well," Anput said, "if there is someone down there, they know we are here now."

Ophois hung his head and nodded. "Sorry."

"No worries. Water under the bridge." She cast him a mischievous glance and pointed at the house. "Shall we?"

They entered the attic of the farmhouse. Not the rafters-insolation-and-cobwebs kind of attic, but a storage area for items long forgotten. Dressers, boxes, a mattress standing on its side, and a mirror. He caught his reflection in the mirror. Dark green bruises burrowed into his neck, reminders of his encounter with Garnoc, in that water under the bridge.

Anput tapped him on the shoulder and made a sniffing gesture. Yes, he smelled it too. The scent of Ima. She had been in the farmhouse, or still was. He walked from one side of the attic to the other. He stopped at a spot where the scent lingered strong. Making eye contact with Anput, he pointed down at the attic floor.

Anput unsheathed a jewel-studded khopesh.

Ophois preferred his scimitar with its more traditionally swept blade. "Shall we?"

171

Blades at the ready, they dropped through the floor of the attic, ceiling of a bedroom. Ophois grinned and licked his snout. Right place. The overwhelming scent of Ima hung in the room. Bright floral patterns on the bedspread and curtain screamed the presence of a young girl. In the corner, sat one of the two backpacks he had seen Ima and the doctor wearing as they fled CeSiR—before the bullet ripped away the doctor's life. He sniffed the backpack still fragrant with the twelve-year-old's fear.

Despite finding clothes, money, and trinkets, the girl was nowhere to be found.

They proceeded to the hall outside the room. This provided them a good view of the family room downstairs.

Ophois raised his hand, motioning Anput to be still. He pointed to an archway. Bright light cast shadows into the family room, a table and chairs it would seem. Not a natural light, as one would expect from the rising morning sun. No, this was a spectrally-pure white light. As if someone took a metal-halide light from a sports arena and set it in the farmhouse's dining room.

A torrent of fear washed across his wings. He knew that light. The Light. But, if He were present, the light would have permeated the walls—no shadows, nowhere to hide.

Ophois motioned to the remaining upstairs rooms and Anput quickly confirmed they were empty.

They had a choice.

Proceed downstairs and risk being banished by whomever illuminated the room, or depart and lose Ima when they had finally come so close.

He cupped his hand to Anput's ear. "Based on the layout, there should be a bathroom alongside that dining room. You stay out of site and be prepared to jump into the fray, should it come to that. He likely knows of my presence, but if he thinks there is only one of us, we may yet have the advantage."

It sounded good. He almost had himself convinced. But a warrior fresh from the throne room, bearing the light of the Creator, would doubtless dispatch them both without effort.

172

Regardless of the odds, Anput nodded and strode down the hall and into the upstairs bathroom, which would be directly above its downstairs counterpart. She held her khopesh in front of her and descended through the floor.

When she disappeared from sight, Ophois stepped past the upstairs railing and descended toward the archway, toward the light, and probably his demise.

~~~~~~~~~~

Despite her best efforts, Ima could not loosen the cuffs. In all her struggling, she had only managed to tighten the one attached to her wrist. Blood throbbed in her hand. She tried to peer beyond the shades, to catch a glimpse of the world in which she was now held captive.

The door handle rattled.

Ima laid down and pulled a sheet over her.

Click. The knob turned and the door opened. Footsteps approached. "I know you are not sleeping, Ima."

She pulled the sheet down to her chin. The aroma of bacon wafted across her nose. Her stomach growled at the smell. How long had it been since she'd eaten? Twelve, fourteen hours? He truly did intend to torture her.

His eyes swept to the cuffs. "Are you so intent on harming yourself?" He reached in his pocket and pulled out a small key. "If you wanted these off, you could have just asked. We do not want any blemishes on Mael's lamb, do we?"

Ima swept her head from side to side.

He leaned over and grabbed her bluish left hand. "Not good at all." He released the cuff.

It wouldn't last. She waited for the clicks that would reaffirm her captivity.

He stood back up. "Would you like some breakfast? Or are you planning to starve yourself also?"

She stared at Trenton. No curled lips. No sinister grin. Was he sincere? It really didn't matter. Hunger drove her to trust him, at least to the point of breakfast. Besides, he held control. He had no need to deceive her into action. She was helpless to resist anything he wanted. She should go along—at least until she found a way to escape.

And then what? Get someone shot with a shotgun, or maybe a rifle. She was pestilent. Everyone who got close, who cared enough to show it, ended up hurt, or worse. It might be best for everyone, if Trenton just killed her.

Trenton left the room. "I will be in the kitchen should you decide to join me."

Moments after he left, she pulled back the sheet and sat on the edge of the cot. She rubbed her left wrist and hand. Her fingers tingled.

The floor didn't have carpet and the plywood chilled her toes. In the past several days, she had grown accustomed to socks, shoes, and the comfort of home—the Sherwoods' home.

She cautiously approached the doorway. Was this a trick?

Down the hallway, at the other end of the building, Trenton sat at a small kitchen table. The house appeared to be some sort of decrepit mobile home. Peeling paint hung from the walls and the water-stained floors creaked as she walked. The pungent smell of mildew, mixed with natural gas, fought with the aroma of bacon.

She walked past a large window. Did she dare stop long enough to see where he'd taken her? She glanced left. Trees. Only trees.

A gust of wind smacked against the window. It bowed in and then out, at least a quarter inch. She hurried through the room and up to the table.

Trenton nodded toward a seat. A plate with eggs, bacon, and toast sat next to a glass of orange juice. "Glad to see you came to your senses."

Ima sat and ate in silence.

~~~~~~~~~~~

In the farmhouse, Adiya looked up at the intruder. She still knelt from her encounter with the Creator.

The demon before her edged into the room. His throat quivered. He knew the light. All demons had encountered an angel fresh from the throne room, at some point in the past millennia. More than just a reminder of their former glory, the light represented power, not angelic power, but His power—the anointing.

Adiya unfurled her Son soaked wings. "Leave now, Ophois."

His eyes closed to slits and he raised the edge of his shield to block the light. "Where is she?" His voice bore an undesired vibrato. He tried to feign control.

Adiya moved her right hand to the hilt of her sword. She rocked back until her weight shifted just behind her toes. Slow and deliberate, she drew herself up.

She grabbed the hilt of her sword with her right hand, like a dagger she began to withdraw the sword from its sheath. With only inches exposed, the sword added a flickering reddish hue to the entire room. The sword of truth—set ablaze by the Truth.

Ophois' mutt-like head turned away from the light.

Halfway to a full stance, Adiya's left hand joined her right on the hilt of the sword. She drew it the remainder of the way from its sheath. She lowered the point of the sword to the floor. Her feet were shoulder width apart and the tips of her wings reached for the corners of the room. "You have no place here, dark one."

"Just tell me where she is," Ophois said, "and I will be on my way." His voice hitched even as he issued the demand. "She is *my* charge. It is my right." The words emboldened him. He pointed his electric-blue scimitar at her.

She smiled at the meaningless gesture. "Perhaps, she *was* your charge. Now, she is mine." Adiya flexed her arms and pulled the hilt of her sword to her chest.

"That is not possible. She is our creation. She has no soul. None of the mims do. She cannot choose Him." The words came out as a whimper. "*He* chose for it to be so." As he talked,

Ophois edged to his left, content to keep the table between them, despite its inability to offer any protection.

"Are you so sure that you—one who rejected Him—know the sovereign will of *the* Creator?" She turned and drilled him with a stare. Reasoning with a demon was like giving tissue paper to a puppy. "Out of what was she created?" Adiya asked. "From whence did the materials originate that were combined to make these mims?" Demons could fool humanity into believing that these were somehow unique creations, but they knew better. They themselves were His creations.

She did not understand the Creator's decision not to endow the mims with souls. But it was *His* choice. Just as He chose to endow each human being with one.

Ophois stared at the floor next to Adiya's feet. A smirk crawled up his pointy snout.

She glanced next to her. Only inches away, a large red stain darkened the wood. Charles' blood. She drilled Ophois with a stare.

His knee bounced as he considered the meaning of the stain. "It would appear you are not much of a guardian." A sudden look of disappointment overtook his face. "Is it hers?"

He seemed intent to find her alive. What might his motives be? She would not entertain the thought. "No." But perhaps, she could use it to her advantage. "It is the work of one of your mims and your good buddy—Tudur."

Genuine concern crept onto Ophois' face. "He will take her back to CeSiR."

"Was that not your own intention?"

His smirk grew to a full on laugh. "Your sweet innocence amuses me, Adiya. No, my intention is much more sinister— and fun. I will terrorize her, then torture her. And, when I tire of that, I will tear her to shreds."

He rounded the table and took a defensive stance. His scimitar rippled with blue pulses. "Much like we are going to do to you."

Movement to her left set warning bells off in her head. His casual circling of the table left her vulnerable. Of course, he was a hound from hell, he traveled in a pack.

Before she could turn, a weapon slashed against the metacarpus of her wing. She prepared for the excruciating pain.

A feminine war-cry accompanied a loud snap.

Adiya turned to assess the damage. The intense swirls of light, once so prominent in her wing, had turned to veins, flowing to the spot where the weapon connected. An explosion of brilliant power flooded the air.

Half of a khopesh lay shattered on the blood-stained floor.

Adiya smacked the feminine demon with her wing.

A scream of horror, like someone sprayed with boiling coffee, resonated off the walls. The limp body of the demon flew through the wall and landed on the porch outside the window.

That demon would not be reentering the house. The searing of the Light against her blackened gold skin would serve as a painful reminder of her true fallen nature.

Adiya turned her attention to Ophois. "Now, what was it you were saying before we were so rudely interrupted by your friend?" She swept her wings around herself. Once again, light swirled from base to tip. "I think it is time for you to leave." She pointed her sword at the mutt. "You tell Mael, if anything happens to that child, I will destroy him—right after I, as you say, tear you to shreds."

She swept her sword toward the door.

Ophois moved faster than she would have guessed possible to join his friend on the porch.

Adiya waited a few moments for the two demons to leave the property, then she arose through the roof and followed them.

If they headed back to CeSiR, things could get very interesting.

~~~~~~~~~~

Ima still hadn't looked up from her breakfast. She couldn't trust Trenton. He'd proven that to her over the years. How many bruises came at the end of his temper? Even the other mim children shied away from his presence.

A rodent of some sort scampered across the corner of the kitchen. It disappeared into a hole in the cupboard.

She looked back to her plate. A half-eaten egg and one remaining strip of bacon, they would have come from the refrigerator. At least the rodents wouldn't have had access to them. Her gaze drifted to her toast. She'd eaten half of it. The remaining half had a hole about the size of a dime.

Her stomach churned in disgust. She looked at the counter, a fresh looking loaf of bread sat next to the toaster. There weren't any holes in the wrapper, at least that she could see. She picked up the remaining toast from her plate and examined the hole. The edges were smooth. She'd let her mind run away with her. No nibble marks, no indication the hole was anything more than an air bubble from when the bread was baked.

Her shoulders relaxed and she finished most of the food in front of her. Mouse or no mouse, Trenton couldn't be trusted. She needed to get away. She glanced out the windows, which lined the kitchen. Trenton's black BMW looked out of place against the wooded backdrop.

His gaze followed hers. "Do not bother. We are in the middle of nowhere. A place called the Ozarks, if you paid attention during your lessons." He picked bacon out of his teeth with the tip of his butter knife. The knife scraped against his yellowish teeth. "You could walk all day and night and not get back to your precious Patricia and Charles. Besides, I suspect they are still at the hospital. Charles may not even return to the farmhouse."

Blood spattered video frames played through Ima's mind. The click of the trigger, the explosion of the gun, the tearing sound as metal pellets ripped through Papa's leg, cracks spidering their way across the window.

Fury boiled in her head. Her ears burned with hatred for the man—mim—sitting across from her. "You're a monster!"

"Yes, my dear. And so are you. We are mims. Superior creations to humanity. To them, we will always be—monsters."

She wanted to call him a liar. To refute his claim. Mama and Papa loved her. But they didn't know. What were the conditions of their love? Could their love extend beyond humanity—to a monster?

"It is time for you to return to your room. I have business to attend to. Do I need to cuff you to the bed again?" His eyes drilled into hers. She could only look him in the eyes for a moment. Something sinister, even evil, lurked beyond the blackness.

She shook her head. With the cuffs she would never escape.

As if reading her mind, he wagged his finger in her face. "There are many dangerous things for you to fear. Both outside this trailer, and within. Even more than me. If you remain in your room, I can assure you they are locked out. If not . . ." He folded his hands under his chin. "Well, I would hate to see anything happen to such a sweet child." A yellowed grin told her hate was much too strong a word.

She nodded, stood, and returned to her cot in her room.

Soon the lock on her door clicked into place.

~~~~~~~~~~

He listened from his helpless prison. Trenton taunted the young girl. How long would he allow her to live? What were his plans for her?

~~~~~~~~~~

Adiya swept back her radiant wings and shot into the sky. She circled a cotton-ball cloud.

Far below, a figure black as coal, flanked by another, a dulling gold, hovered just above the treetops. She had seen Ophois' companion before, Anput, if she remembered correctly. Lush green fields swept beneath them. They were headed southeast, toward Arrow Springs, toward CeSiR Tech.

The uniformity of the spring fields made it easy to track them. If they had stuck to the ditches and wooded fence lines, she may have struggled to keep them in her sights. They seemed to actually avoid the ditches.

The heavy rains of the previous week left some of the fields shiny with standing water. The demons avoided flying over these shining patches of land.

The wind of the Spirit flowed under Adiya's wings.

Cool misty air streamed past her as she sliced through another cloud.

Soon, they approached the CeSiR Tech facility.

Adiya veered south toward the old bridge embankment. She needed a place to think.

She alighted on the embankment and sat on a large rock. She pulled her legs to her chest. *Protect her.* Was it too late? How could she protect someone she could not find?

"I hear you have had quite a week." She would recognize Eitan's voice anywhere. When she looked up, his face bore a wide grin.

Adiya rocked forward and knelt on a single knee. Not a gesture of worship, but of respect. "I have failed, sir."

The captain laughed a deep rumbling laugh. "No, Adiya, you have failed no one." He sat down on the large rock and patted the spot where she sat moments before.

She returned to her seat. "It was my mission to protect her. Now, the enemy has her, if she is still alive."

"She is alive, and well. *He* has a plan for her. I need not tell you, *His* plans always prevail." He laid a hand on her shoulder. "Tell me what happened."

She paused and listened to the river gurgling past the embankment.

Finally, she told Eitan how Ima had found a family in Charles and Patricia. She spoke of Charles' miraculous recovery from Alzheimer's and of Garnoc's interest in Ima. She went on to tell of the strange reaction of the animals and Tudur's guns-a-blazin' kidnapping. She finished with her encounter with Ophois and Anput, and that she had followed them to CeSiR.

She needed not tell him about her encounter with the Messiah. That—he could tell just looking at her.

"What did He tell you about her?" Eitan asked.

Even the memory of her time with her Creator warmed her being. "He said I would find her soon enough." Adiya placed her head back in her hands. "My orders are still to not interfere. He told me to protect the restoration."

"Her restoration?"

"Of that, I am uncertain." She looked up into his compassionate blue eyes. "I know not how to find her. How can I protect her?"

"With that," his strong hand squeezed her armor-clad shoulder, "I may be able to help you."

Eitan had infiltrated CeSiR only a couple weeks earlier, though not without cost. Eran, her friend and fellow warrior, provided an opportunity for Eitan's escape by allowing himself to be overtaken by the enemy horde. "Forces have poured into CeSiR, even as I have been here. Surely, you do not mean to infiltrate the facility once again."

The corners of his lips drew down and his eyes glanced longingly at the gate of CeSiR Tech in the distance. "No, that was a necessity to protect the life of Sergeant Davis. I only wish our Lord would have allowed me to suffer instead of Eran."

Adiya nodded, her face tight as she thought about the ways of the enemy. "Eran is before the throne, in the presence of his Creator. No regret is warranted on his behalf."

"Adiya, the compassionate advisor." Eitan stood. "Word is that Tudur and Mael are not on good terms. I suspect he chose not to take her to Mael, at least not yet. Though the enemy grows strong, they also grow divided."

"Where then would he have taken her?"

"I know not." He walked to the edge of the embankment and gazed out over the Lamine River. "I have heard that Trenton owns an old mobile home somewhere in the northern Ozarks—Morgan county, I believe. Find it and she should not be far. Time is short. If the two demons you followed here inform Mael that Trenton has Ima, he is sure to know the location of the trailer."

"Thank you, sir." Adiya knelt once more before her captain. "I will find her."

"Of that, I am certain. God's speed—may the Spirit guide your search."

~~~~~~~~~~

Ima sat on her cot. She tried to picture the layout of the trailer. The kitchen, where she ate breakfast, was at the front of the mobile home. Trenton's black BMW was parked alongside the building, right outside the doorway. The doorway was in a small hallway between the kitchen and the living room, if a room with a worn couch and a folding chair could be called a living room. The main hallway, just beyond her locked door, had four doors.

Actually, the first was just an opening, without a door. It led to a small bathroom. Though she wasn't positive if a room was actually a bathroom if it didn't contain a bathtub. A toilet and sink were crammed into a small space across from a grubby shower stall. The sink and toilet were both stained red, with what she hoped was rust. The condition of the bathroom and the lack of a door didn't really matter to Ima. The presence of a pail in the corner of her room and the locked door, the second door in the hallway, told her that the finer facilities of the home were not meant for her.

The third door at the end of the hallway was shut, but it probably led to another bedroom. If that was where Trenton slept, it might even have a real bed.

Of the four doorways, the fourth caught her attention—a heavy steel door with a deadbolt lock. Through a clouded, weather-checked window, she made out the shape of trees. This door could be her passageway to freedom.

Trenton had warned her. She was far from civilization. Nowhere to run and no one to run to, or so he claimed. Fine with her. She didn't trust anyone. And those she did—the further away she stayed, the safer they'd be. Anyone she trusted, no, anyone who trusted her, died.

She envisioned the large pool of blood on the farmhouse floor. Surely Papa was dead. Just like Uncle M. She'd been foolish to hold out hope—to believe that somehow Uncle M lived through the gunshot.

Gunshots kill. And Papa was shot.

Tears burned her eyes.

She could accept the truth. But how could she live with the pain? A peace beyond what made sense—that's what Mama had said. But that was before Papa was shot. Could Mama possibly still be at peace?

Banging on the door shook her from her peaceless reflections.

"I have to leave to take care of some things. Ima, listen to me." Trenton's voice sounded sincere. "For your own safety, do not try to escape. That room is the only place I can guarantee your safety."

The floors shook with footsteps. The door next to hers closed. She heard a padlock snap shut, but hers was already locked.

She waited.

No footsteps.

Was he waiting outside her door? Was he testing her to see if she'd run?

She couldn't. She wanted to. If not for the locked door.

The window?

She shuffled to the window and peered through the blinds. The BMW still sat in the driveway. He hadn't left.

Still, she had to know. She pried up on the window. It didn't budge. She looked for some kind of a lock. Probably on the outside. At the top of the lower half of the window, she felt a latch. She flipped the latch and it clicked.

Louder than she desired.

She pulled back her hands and the metal blinds rattled against the wall. Great. He had to have heard that. She stood frozen to the floor. A deep chill passed through her body. With it came fear, soul strangling fear. What would he do to her if he caught her trying to run?

What would he do to her if she didn't?

She returned her hands to the bottom of the window and pried once again. This time it budged. Fresh mid-day air carried the scent of pine. The smell of freedom. She pried again. It scraped open another inch. But in the process it made a horrendous scraping sound that shook the entire wall.

She froze.

What now? If she opened the window any farther, he'd know for sure. As if he didn't hear the last one.

She could leave it open. It felt good to have fresh air. But he'd find it open. He'd know she unlocked it, know she ignored his warning. She could claim she just wanted fresh air. He didn't care what she wanted. He'd probably shut it and nail it shut.

No, she only had one option. Shut the window. If it went down quieter than it went up, maybe he'd never know. If not, she could lie, say the noise was her moving the cot. Wait until he was really gone and escape through the window—freedom.

She reached up to the top of the window. Her hands shook with fear. She closed her eyes and tugged. In addition to the screech of the window sliding down, the frame let out a loud thud when it hit bottom.

She scurried back to her cot and buried herself in the sheet. What would he do to her? Would he believe her lie?

Noises from the room next door froze her heart. She stopped breathing.

The sounds seemed vaguely familiar. Not footsteps. Rattling. Like her cuffs against the cot. Not *her* cot. Another cot. In the room next door. Did he have another prisoner?

The door was shut. She'd only guessed it was Trenton's room. But he had a house in Arrow Springs. He didn't live here. So what was this place?

The cot in the next room rattled, shook, scraped, even beat against the wall. Her wall. Someone was trying to escape.

Where was Trenton? She never heard him walk back down the hall. The BMW was still in the driveway.

A low grunt came from the room next door.

Trenton hadn't left. Realization rammed her in the gut. He was in the next room.

Who was handcuffed to the cot? What would Trenton do to them?

A guttural growl.

Her heart boxed her ribs.

The wall shook.

An animalistic moan, like the baboons at the zoo, accompanied a strained rattle of the cuffs, then all went silent.

~~~~~~~~~~~

Once again, Patricia sat in the trauma waiting room. The décor of the room was designed to make her feel at home. She sat on a pleather couch. Nowhere near comfortable, but better than the chair in Charles' room.

She had spent most of the night in that small room, on that uncomfortable couch. She had tried to rest despite the fear that the door would open and bring her the bad news. Several hours after they carted him off to surgery the door had finally opened. The doctor looked as tired as she felt, but he bore a slight smile. He informed her that the surgery was successful. Charles might even regain some use of the leg. Though at his age and without intense physical therapy he would never walk again.

She had asked the doctor about the recovery time. He avoided making a commitment and cautioned her that there were still significant risks for the next few days. Charles would be watched closely. She would be allowed to stay with him the remainder of the night, but the next night she would need to leave at ten o'clock. Hospital policy prohibited overnight visitation in the ICU.

She hadn't slept after Charles was wheeled to his room. Instead, she sat in a chair beside his bed, even less comfortable than the pleather couch. She watched Charles sleep. Not real sleep. Not the peaceful snoring sleep of home, but the medicated sleep of anesthesia. She held his hand until the knots in her back forced her to sit back in the chair. Then she just watched and waited.

Somewhere around lunchtime, Charles had finally awoken. His clouded hazel eyes looked up and he smiled at Patricia.

He remembered her.

The fear that had nagged her from just beneath the surface of her thoughts retreated back into the depths of her mind. The Alzheimer's had not returned.

She had held his hand basking in the reunion.

He coughed, tried to tell her he loved her, and coughed again. The little color that had returned to his face retreated.

His eyes rolled upwards.

He wheezed and coughed again. He couldn't breathe.

She hurried into the hallway and screamed for help.

Nurses and doctors had swarmed into the room. One of them had whisked her back to the dreaded waiting room.

Now, once again, she waited.

~~~~~~~~~~

CHAPTER TWELVE

Ophois landed atop CeSiR Tech. Anput alighted next to him. They walked across to where Mael stood with his back to them. Despite the sun hanging high in the afternoon sky, the thousands of lesser demons swarming above the building cast swirling shadows on the roof.

"Given your return, I trust the girl is dead." Mael continued to stare eastward toward the river, which lay between CeSiR and the town of Arrow Springs.

"No, my Liege. We have lost her."

Mael's sword rang as he ripped it from its sheath. "*We* have not lost her. *You* have lost her." He spun to face them.

Anput's wings brushed against Ophois as she stepped up beside him. Though they had survived the encounter with Garnoc, an encounter with Mael would end only one way. No hit and run from the facility surrounded by minions. Only diplomacy could see them safely from the facility.

Ophois knelt to a knee. "I have failed you, my liege. We tracked her all the way to Kansas City. Despite a ferocious battle, we were unable to overcome Garnoc and his interference." He sensed a subtle grin by Anput. There was no love lost between Mael and Garnoc. Evasion of a twelve-year-old child would bring certain demise. On the other hand, defeat at the hands of an opposing prince might bring survival.

Mael growled and swore. "How did she reach Garnoc's territory?"

Outrun by a child to the principality a hundred miles away. That could also bring demise. "She escaped into the fog, my liege." A fog, which could only have been the work of the Creator. The fog, which prevented Mael's snipers from claiming the life of the child, when they killed the doctor. "By the time I picked up her trail after the fog lifted," *much after*, "she had found an elderly couple, prayer warriors of the enemy, to give her refuge."

Mael cracked his neck and stared at Ophois. "Where—is—the child?"

"Yes, my liege. After following her and the couple to Kansas City and battling with Garnoc to prevent his interference, we tracked them to the couple's farmhouse west of Marshall. We stormed the home and battled a mighty warrior of the enemy, who will no longer be a problem."

Mael listened intently. His breathing slowed and his wings relaxed. He was buying the exaggerated account. Time to close the lid.

"Just when we had the girl in our grasp, one of the mims, Trenton Richards, controlled by one of your warriors, snatched her out from under us."

"Tudur!" Mael roared at the sky. A circle of blue sky appeared as the demonic minions scampered from the gaze of their prince.

"By the time we finished battling the angelic warrior, Trenton and the girl were gone." Now to nail it shut. "We assumed Trenton would bring the girl back to CeSiR, which is why we have returned without her. Is she not here?"

Mael's wings were spread wide. Spittle leaked between his teeth as he spoke. "I would pursue and eliminate that traitor myself, but there is a battle brewing for the future of our work." He went on to tell them about a mobile home in the Ozarks that Trenton often used for his various exploits. He approached the pair and placed a black talon under Ophois' chin. "Can I trust you and your friend here to find Tudur and ensure he will never betray me again?"

"Yes, my liege." Success. Truth and deception. The only way to survive. A healthy mix of each and even the great prince could not tell which was which.

Now, he would fulfill both assignments from Mael.
He knew where to find both Tudur and Ima.

~~~~~~~~~~

Adiya dodged an airplane that was headed west out of Jefferson City. She weaved in and out of fluffy white clouds. How would she find one small home in the thousands of square miles of the northern Ozarks?

She spotted the small town of Versailles. Beyond the Morgan County seat, the light-greens and browns of the flatland turned to dark green rolling hills. She needed to find a single trailer nestled down there somewhere.

It seemed safe to assume that Trenton had taken Ima somewhere remote. This ruled out the small towns, main roads, and Ozark lake communities. So she would only need to check several thousand of the thirty-thousand residences in the county.

She started to sweep up and down the more remote trails, paths, and roads. If Trenton was still there, she could identify the trailer by the BMW parked next to it. How many black BMW's could there be in this conservatively rustic area?

South of Versailles, she swept systematically east, then west, then east again. The process was slow. How much time did Ima have? That depended on Tudur's motives.

Skies darkened to violet in the east. Less so in the west, but it would not take long. Eitan indicated that an attack on the facility would come in the morning. Would that lead to the demise of Ima? Or freedom? She grew queasy with the realization that the answer probably depended on her ability to perform her assignment.

She moved her search higher, trying to cover more ground before darkness forced her to go practically door-to-door.

What if the BMW was not visible? Or gone? Had she already flown right over Ima? She had to press on. She could not allow doubt to creep in. The Father loved his children, and Ima—a mim—seemed to qualify.

~~~~~~~~~~

Ophois and Anput descended toward the trailer. It took them longer to find it based on Mael's description than Ophois would have liked. The sun had just dropped beneath the western horizon. The comfort of darkness.

The BMW Trenton drove sat next to the trailer. Tudur *and* Ima. Ophois licked his lips. Tudur could prove a formidable foe. They had numbers—and the element of surprise. "We take out Tudur first," Ophois whispered.

Anput nodded.

"Then, we use his puppet to deal with our little rag doll." After all the torment the tiny mim had put him through, he would savor dispensing with her. Very slowly.

They circled around the back side of the mobile home. All the rooms sat in complete darkness. This stood to reason. Tudur had no need of light. The only reason to have light would be for the sake of his prisoner. Not likely.

Given the large bank of windows in the kitchen, they decided to begin their search for Tudur from that end.

Ophois and Anput stepped through the front windows of the trailer. Ophois walked past a table, which contained two place settings. Cold eggs, bacon, and toast sat in the center. No one had eaten since breakfast? Perhaps they were not here after all. He stayed behind an island wall which separated the kitchen from the living room. All but one of the doors from the hallway were closed.

He motioned for Anput to check around the other side of the wall, by the front door. She nodded and disappeared. Soon, she stepped into his line of sight and shook her head.

Three rooms remained. All connected to the hallway. The first, could be entered both via the doorway in the hall and through the wall from the living room. He made a rounded motion with his hands and she nodded. She would emerge through the wall, as he checked the doorway.

He peeked through the opening. Just an old bathroom. Motion caught his eye. Someone in the shower.

He reached for the hilt of his sword.

Before he could draw the sword, a golden demon stepped from the shower.

Anput shook her head. Another empty room.

~~~~~~~~~~

Patricia walked into her home—alone. The nurse practically had to push her from the ICU. Ridiculous rules. She flipped on the light to the entryway-dining room. Her heart sank to her knees. She could almost see Charles lying on the hardwood floor, next to the pool of blood now black with age. Why would they make her leave? Charles would have wanted her to stay, if he weren't in a drug induced coma.

She walked to the laundry area and retrieved a green and white brush. In the kitchen, she mixed dish detergent and water in a gallon bucket. She knelt at the blood stain and began to scrub.

She should go to bed. To get some rest—much needed rest that she'd been unable to find at the hospital. But she couldn't leave his blood on the floor. As if by some mystical connection, she could clean away the damage, not to the floor, but to her beloved.

Her tears joined the detergent on the floor. She snorted and scrubbed. Brushed and wept. She pressed down on the brush with both hands. It wasn't working.

Why hadn't she waxed the floor? She'd told herself for months, perhaps even years, that she needed to refinish the floor. She was always too busy. Feeding the dumb animals. Growing a garden. Serving at church. She always felt good about her choices. Putting others above things. Things like waxing her floor. Now, Charles was in the ICU and she couldn't even get his blood off the floor.

She wiped the floor with a towel. Then, she returned to the kitchen for baking soda and white vinegar. She sprinkled the stain with the white powdered soda. *Whiter than snow.* She brushed aside the thought. After soaking the brush in vinegar, she scrubbed at the stain once more.

It worked.

The stain began to fade. If Ima were there, Patricia would share a lesson about how Jesus' blood can wash away her stains. Ima. More tears. What did that maniac want with her? If he shot the child with Patricia's own shotgun—she couldn't bear to think the thought.

"Lord, please protect Ima. I don't know what she is running from, but we love her. Please don't allow another child we love to be taken from us." She wiped the stain on the floor with the towel. Most of the discoloration was gone. "Please, Lord, send your angels to protect her."

Fatigue overtook her. She rolled to her side and fell asleep, where twenty-four hours earlier the love of her life lay bleeding.

~~~~~~~~~~~

Ophois and Anput converged on the next room. Anput through the wall from the bathroom and Ophois through the closed door. The door contained a padlock. An entire week spent searching for the little urchin.

He emerged into the room.

To his left, Anput walked through the near empty room, a large grin on her face. "Ima, I presume."

A white cot sat in the corner of the room. On it shivered Ima. Her legs were tucked into the fetal position. She had a plain white sheet pulled up around her neck. Though no lights were on in the room, Ophois saw her eyes staring frightfully into the dark room.

She could sense their presence. Her shoulders quivered despite the warmth in the room. Her hapless gaze darted left then right, to the ceiling then the floor.

"Long, have I waited for this day," Ophois said. "Ever since the night the doctor washed up on the gravel, I have longed to complete the plot. To enact the final scourge of Mael's little game." When Mael assigned Ophois to Ima, the prince knew. He knew she was different. That Ophois would not control her like the others. That she was born with a will, a soul. Since that day, Ophois waited. Waited for vengeance. Waited to reap some satisfaction from his ruse of an assignment.

Scraping sounds emanated from the next room.

Ima flinched at the sound and pulled the sheet tighter around her neck. Her tortured face scrunched deeper into a cheap pillow.

"Perhaps, you will need to wait just a bit longer," Anput said. "We should deal with Tudur and Trenton first. Then you can enjoy your prize without interruption."

Ophois lapped at his lips with a drool covered tongue. She was right. They had the element of surprise. Tudur expected no opposition. Few things brought such joy as destroying expectations. He nodded. "You enter from here. I will enter from the hallway."

Anput agreed.

They both drew their weapons. Anput's khopesh glowed an electric blue—its restoration fueled by fear flowing from the child.

Ophois left the room and readied himself for the coming encounter. With his scimitar drawn alongside his shield, he stepped through the final door.

Another bedroom.

Another cot.

Still no lights.

Instead of a child, a grown man was handcuffed to this cot. Arrow Spring's distinguished mayor, Trenton Richards, lay on the floor, shackled to the bed.

Anput walked to the far corner of the dark room. When she returned, she simply shook her head. No sign of Tudur. He had left his charge.

Rumors had circulated around CeSiR that Mael had eliminated Legion because he left his charge unattended. This very action had brought attention to their operation, attention that Mael believed would soon lead to an attack.

Tudur took no such chance. Cuffed in place, all his charge could do was moan, growl, and gnaw at the metal cuff. In fact, the key was probably in the mim's pocket. It simply lacked the wherewithal to use it.

Ophois looked up at Anput and howled. This was too delicious. Tudur had left him the perfect tool.

He drooled as he explained to Anput exactly how he intended to use it.

~~~~~~~~~~

Tudur soared just above the treetops. The stars flickered overhead. The moon had not risen, so the ground below lay in a still blackness. Unlike the annoying cities, the area around the trailer had few house lights, even fewer streetlights, and no obnoxious neon.

His meeting with Listh went as planned. He informed Tudur of the interdepartmental plans to infiltrate CeSiR Tech in the morning. Mael had the numbers and full control of the mims. They should be able to hold the facility. Yet one thing Tudur had learned from years of miraculous defeats at the hand of the enemy—always have a backup plan.

Tudur's plan lay below, in the form of a twelve-year-old mim, waiting for him to decide his next course of action. A decision that largely depended on how the face-off at CeSiR transpired the following morning. If Mael's forces proved capable of staving off the invasion, things would return to normal. Tudur would return the girl to Mael to be used as a surrogate host for future waves of mims.

Perhaps, they could even begin their experiments with multiples using her. Small in stature, they would have to start with just twins. But, as her body broke down, maybe triplets, quads, or even quints.

On the other hand, if Mael was defeated, the project would be scrapped. Mims only proved useful if the world remained unaware. Still, in this more likely eventuality, it could prove useful to have a sacrificial offering to present to Mael. She had never behaved as a true mim. Something went wrong with the process and Mael despised her as a symbol of his imperfection.

Surely, he would find a devious way to take out the frustrations of defeat on the child. Better her than Tudur.

Ahead the trees rose and then dropped where they grew atop a ridge. He dove into the trees and swatted at a horned owl eyeing its prey. Its head snapped and it fell limp from its perch. One less member of creation to give witness to the Creator.

Tudur swept upward. Time to return to Trenton. By now, he would be quite irritable and hungry. Not that he cared. The mim was a tool. A machine with which to interface, simplifying the process of interacting physically with the world around him.

The trailer sat in darkness.

~~~~~~~~~~~

Ophois approached the mim. "Here goes nothing." His canine form merged with the body of Trenton. Exhilaration flowed through his being. He looked at his fingers. One by one he curled them into a fist. He had never felt control like this. Demonic possession or manipulation of humans almost always included a battle of wills. Here no battle existed, because no will existed.

He looked at Anput. Trenton grinned wide. "This is incredible." Trenton echoed his words. No wonder the demons in charge of the various mims treated them as their possessions. Seldom, did a demon permit another to inhabit their mim. He realized it surpassed simple control. He felt. Felt the warmth of the room. Felt the handcuff cutting into his wrist. Not just physical feelings. He felt desire, lust—the passions of a physical existence. They nearly overwhelmed him. Only now, did he fully realize the sadistic cruelty of Mael's assignment of Ima to him. Mael knew. He knew Ophois would never experience this control, this sensation with Ima.

He would control her. If not from within, then through Trenton. He flexed his arms, Trenton's arms. Power surged through them. He could snap the handcuff, but why damage his new Ferrari.

195

He searched the pockets of Trenton's clothes. First the shirt, then the blue jeans. No key. Tudur would need the key to unlock the cuffs when he returned to the mim. It had to be somewhere.

He searched inside his socks. No key.

On the floor beneath the bed. No key.

He felt everywhere under the mattress. Still, no key. He tired of this game of Tudur's, even if Tudur was non-complicit. The room reeked. No, he reeked. The smell of an animal chained for a day with no access to a bathroom assaulted his nose. It was so unique to smell the stench of the physical world as perceived by humanity, versus the bright aromas of the spiritual realm.

Time to end this game. He flexed his left arm and turned to watch the cuffs. He stopped, just as the cuff began to dig into his arm. Of course. Handcuff an animal to a bar and they may pull, bite, scratch, but they would never use the key, dangling from the cuffs. Clever simplicity.

Ophois directed Trenton's right hand to grab the key and inserted it into the hole. It clicked and he was free from the cot. He looked at Anput. She stood with a grin on her face. Probably amused by the haphazard search. "Now, to go pay our little mouse a visit."

Anput walked through the wall, back into the girl's room. Ophois followed her.

At least, he tried to follow her. Trenton's head smacked into the wall. Rainbow-stars flickered in his view. Beyond the wall, Anput howled in amusement.

He walked to the door, turned the handle, and pulled. It refused to open. Frustration and fury boiled within. It felt good. Feelings he would soon share with Ima.

He looked up. Another lock, but no key.

This was a combination lock. He cursed at Tudur. He turned the dial and listened for the clicks which would indicate the correct numbers. His keen sense of hearing would make quick work of the lock.

~~~~~~~~~~

Another chill swept through Ima's room. She lay on her bed. Her sheet wrapped tight to her neck. She simply stared at the blinds. Could she get out the squeaky window without Trenton hearing in the room next door? If she did, where would she go? She felt a presence in the room.

She could have sworn she saw a shadow, standing between her cot and the door. If she'd been asleep, she could convince herself it was a dream. Or that slushy half-awake-half-asleep state when you first wake up. But, aside from the time she spent knocked out from hitting her head in the trunk, she'd not slept since arriving. Nor did she intend to do so.

She didn't trust Trenton. The constant rattling of handcuffs, banging on the wall, groans, and other inhuman sounds stirred fear deep within her gut. Not a fear for herself. She deserved whatever happened to her. She had caused so much pain and even death. No, she feared that Trenton held someone else captive in the other room.

Now, she heard the rattling of a door handle. Not to her room. Would she be next?

"Ahh." A man's voice called out in pain, from next door.

The shadow seemed to vanish into the wall. She hated the dark. In the facility, lights were used only as a necessity. That was one of the things she so loved about Mama and Papa Sherwood's home. The rooms were bright and lights were everywhere. Mama even left a small light, called a nightlight, glowing in the bathroom next to Ima's room. Just in case she needed to get up during the night.

Jesus is the light of the world. The words of Mama came to her from the previous night's drive home. *That light shines in the darkness and the darkness can never extinguish it.* She could sure use some of that light right now. The darkness surrounding her felt thicker than mere night.

The light switch. Of course. All she needed to do was walk across the dark room and turn on the light. Her body froze to the cot. Just get up and walk through the thick darkness. Her mind knew it was that simple. Her body refused to obey.

197

"Lord, Jesus, please help me." Mama told her she could pray to Him anytime she needed. She felt a little better, slightly courageous. She pivoted on the cot and placed her feet on the floor. One after the other her feet carried her toward the switch next to the door. Her hand reached for the small lever on the wall. She had courage. She could do this. She flipped the switch.

The darkness remained. It *had* extinguished the light. She ran back to the cot and buried her face in the pillow, praying morning would come soon.

~~~~~~~~~~

When Tudur entered the bedroom, he saw Trenton standing at the door. It took him a few moments to realize what was transpiring.

Someone had his mim. They were attempting to break the combination on the lock. He wanted to strike them through the core or lop off their head. But with the intertwined state of possession of Trenton, he did not dare. He wanted no harm brought to his mim. Just to dispatch the demon.

He pulled his electric-blue saber and sliced through Trenton's leg.

The demon howled in pain and released Trenton. Out of the mim, a wolf-like creature emerged. Ophois, he should have known. Green slime oozed from the dog's leg. He failed to completely sever the foot because of its symbiotic arrangement with Trenton.

Now that Ophois was out of Trenton, severing his neck would be a different story. Tudur swung back his sword and it flashed forward.

Just before connecting with Ophois, the blade halted against the hook of a khopesh. Anput—of course. He looked to his right and a snicker spread across her face.

She had prevented the demise of her friend, at least for the moment. But in so doing, she left herself wide open. She stood only a couple feet from him both hands firmly on the khopesh. Her muscles shook as she pulled back on his sword.

He struck her across the jaw with the hilt of his saber and allowed the blade to draw across her cheek.

She spun and crumpled to the floor. Sulfur spewed into the room as a rupture between the earthly domain and the Abyss opened to receive its victim. She was not yet gone, but it would take only moments.

He raised his saber to finish the job. He swung the sword down toward her head. Two feet connected with his sternum and he flew across the room. Before he could right himself, Ophois sprang on him, now with scimitar in hand.

He rolled left just in time to avoid a slash that would have split him in half. Fury boiled through his being. How dare these two imps challenge him for his mim?

He raised his saber just in time to lock swords with Ophois, who once again swung down at him. He recognized the look of intoxication in the dog's eyes. He had control of Trenton long enough to realize the addictive power.

Mael had assigned Ophois to Ima—the broken mim. Now, Ophois realized the demeaning nature of the assignment. The taste of true control had driven him to madness. There could be only one outcome to this encounter. The mad dog must be put down.

Swords still locked, Tudur kicked the legs out from under Ophois. The demon flipped to the side and landed on all fours. To his credit, he did not drop his scimitar.

Tudur flapped his wings and rose above the trailer. As a giant fruit bat, his form gave him air superiority over the canine form of Ophois. Best to use the intoxication-dulled mind of Ophois against him.

The wolf shot from the trailer, wings swept back like a rocket, scimitar glowing like lightning in front of him. Great form for speed, but not the agility necessary for a fight.

One strong flap of his mighty bat-like wing and Tudur sidestepped the assault. As the dog soared by, Tudur raked the point of his saber down Ophois' back.

The speed of Ophois prevented significant damage. The rocket made a sweeping turn and charged at Tudur once again.

Tudur flapped his wings only slightly. He held his saber in both hands prepared to split his attacker sniveling-snout to tail.

Ophois raised his scimitar to block Tudur's saber. The weapons clashed in a small explosion.

The noise drew several demonic onlookers from their residences. Soon, dozens of spectators had gathered to watch. Unwittingly, Tudur and Ophois had become a demonic death-match. With each strike, each parry, and especially contact, cheers and jeers arose from the crowd.

Ophois proved a more worthy opponent than Tudur would have thought. Each demon bore rips from talons, gashes from teeth, and ooze still seeped from Ophois' wounded leg.

~~~~~~~~~~

Adiya swept over trees and hills still searching for a trailer accompanied by a BMW. There was simply too much ground to cover. By the time she found Ima, there was no telling what Tudur and Trenton would have done to her.

Behind her, and to the left, a crack of thunder rang out. Odd. There were no storm clouds in the sky. She studied the ground beneath her. If she abandoned her systematic search, she would need to be able to pick up where she left off.

She banked to her left and headed toward the thunder. Another peal echoed across the sky. She still could not see the source. But this time it also had the familiar ring of weapons clash. She darted toward the sound.

She broke over a hill and pulled up hard. She nearly somersaulted to avoid flying straight into a makeshift arena. The gathering of over a hundred demons was not the place for a lone angel. She had no desire to be the main event.

What was the primary attraction? Demons seldom sparred for fun anymore. There used to be a day in which this type of gathering was commonplace. Lucifer put a stop to it when Jesus mocked the practice, indicating that a house divided would surely fall.

This was no sparring match. Even from this distance, Adiya could tell the two demons meant business. They were engaged in a life-or-death battle. She was too far away to identify the tangle of wings and weapons.

She should resume her search. Whatever these two were fighting about, the match could go on for hours, even days. They seemed evenly matched.

She turned to resume her search.

~~~~~~~~~~

The pounding grew louder on the other side of the wall. Ima squeezed off the flow of blood to her feet, as she pulled her knees tighter to her chest. The rattle of cuffs and locks turned into bashing on the wall and door. She would soon have a visitor. With each thud, the sounds of cracking wood intensified.

"Jesus, I don't know if you care about us mims the way Mama said you care about humans. She said you died for them. That through you, humans could have peace beyond explanation. That your mercy was greater than anything bad I could have done. I know I've not been perfect. But I haven't been bad either. Not like the other mims. Mama said it didn't matter. All that mattered was that you loved mankind and gave your life for them."

The trailer shook with another battering of the door or wall.

"Mama didn't know I was a mim. I'm not a normal human."

Ya are special dear child. The words of Uncle M echoed in the recesses of her memories.

"You *are* special Ima!" The words came from somewhere outside herself. "All my children are special."

Tears streamed from her eyes. Could it be possible? That despite her origin, God loved her? Mama told her all she had to do was tell Him that she wanted His love, His guidance in her life, His forgiveness and mercy.

The dark of night seemed to lighten somehow. Eventually, the sunrise of morning would bring comfort. But would it? As the pounding continued, Ima felt uncertain she would survive until morning. And, if she did, Trenton had no fear of the day. She was a mim. She had no rights. No protections. He could kill her whenever he wished, or worse. He could return her to Ms. Mirinova.

With the death of Uncle M, Maiya's rule of CeSiR would be unfettered. She was queen consort become queen regnant, like when the king dies and leaves his wife to rule.

Mama had called Jesus, the Prince of Peace, but also the King of kings, and surely of queens also.

Ima had stared at Mama in confusion. "How could one man be both a prince and a king?" she had asked.

"Because He is also both man and God. He chose to become nothing so that we might become His heirs."

She missed Mama. The woman who had been so sweet and caring toward her, must now mourn the pain and possible death of the one she loved so much. All because of Ima.

No. She didn't pull the trigger. She didn't ask Trenton to hunt her down. It was his fault, not hers.

"Dear Jesus," she whispered into the darkness, "please forgive me for my sins. I need your peace, your mercy, your guidance. If you'll have a mim, please step into my life, make me a new and better creation. Your creation."

She waited for an answer. Something to affirm His response.

~~~~~~~~~~

Tudur parried a swift powerful blow from Ophois. His arms shook as he tried to hold off the scimitar pressing downward toward his nose. He bared his fangs and pressed with all his might upward. It proved too little. The mutt-of-a-demon had the upper hand. Tudur tried one last time to redirect the foe's weapon. The scimitar glanced off his shoulder.

A sucking sound emanated from the trailer below. Was Anput finally being pulled into the Abyss? What little light existed in the pre-morning hours seemed to get sucked into the middle of the trailer. Ima's room?

A shockwave of light and Spirit-filled energy exploded from the room. It slammed against both him and Ophois and tossed them a quarter of a mile from the makeshift hideout.

The unthinkable, no impossible, seemed to have occurred. How was it possible? Could the creator have really extended his grace to a mim? The very thought infuriated Tudur. Once again humanity, and not even a human, but a mim was offered grace and forgiveness. Something he only dreamed of. He had made his choice. He openly denied the Creator and followed Lucifer in his rebellion. No, no grace would ever be offered to him. His world faded as he flailed through the air.

~~~~~~~~~~~

Adiya spun back toward the demonic battle-arena. Demons lay sprawled across the countryside. There was no sign of the two combatants. She felt the power of the Spirit wash over her. Her wings glowed an iridescent-white. In the residual glow of light that permeated trees, buildings, and vehicles, she spotted a black, at least in the physical realm, BMW. The car was parked beside the epicenter of the redemptive explosion.

Was it possible? Could the newly redeemed be Ima? She was a mim—created through the evil efforts of Mael and the scientists at CeSiR.

What they meant for evil, I meant for good.

Shame washed over her. How could she underestimate the perfect forgiveness and grace of the Creator? Surely, a sweet twelve-year-old mim, like Ima, had done nothing to consciously deny the sovereignty of the Creator. Why then would He reject her? And what of the other mims?

If it was Ima, Adiya needed to get to her—now more than ever. She began to weave her way through the scattered demons. Still dazed by the shockwave, they barely noticed her. In her current energized state, the ones that did notice left her alone.

Soon, she arrived at the trailer. A residual glow, emanating from the side of the trailer, pinpointed the location of the source. Just in front of the BMW, Adiya passed through the wall of the trailer.

A ripple of laughter passed from wingtip to wingtip. In the corner of the room, lying on a cot, curled up in a ball, slept Ima. Unscathed and at peace. She even had a slight smile on her face.

Despite Ima's peaceful state, someone pounded on the opposite side of the wall.

~~~~~~~~~~~

Tudur shook his head. What—? Clarity remerged like the image in a steam covered mirror. It was not possible. He shot back toward the trailer. He needed to see for himself. To see her.

He slowed as he approached the trailer. An angelic figure stepped through the tin siding, now glowing bright with the power of the Spirit. Adiya—she had found them already. Her wings glowed with an annoying intensity. She appeared to be alone. Eldwyn must have stayed with his injured charge.

A faint swish preceded a painful blow to the back of his head. The force flipped him vertically. As he rotated, canine feet slashed at his chest.

Tudur reached for his saber.

Ophois had made a critical mistake. His entire underside soared over Tudur, fully exposed. Tudur would split him down the middle.

He grabbed the top of his sheath. The hilt was missing.

He swore. It must still be laying on the ground where the explosion had tossed him. Instead, he punched his talons into Ophois' chest. The dog's momentum ripped the claws all the way to his abdomen. Green goo gushed from the wound.

Tudur grabbed a hind leg as it flew past.

Ophois released a yelp of pain at the turn of fortunes.

The wolf-like demon orbited Tudur, clawing to get free. Though badly wounded, Ophois still wielded his scimitar.

Ophois swatted at Tudur several times. Tudur parried each attack with his shield. The gouges in the mutt's core weakened his ability to strike.

Thwack-whack.

Tudur pushed the weapon away and slashed his claws across Ophois' bicep. That would lessen the blows even more.

Ophois kicked and clawed out of Tudur's grasp. He pulled back several feet. His eyes drooped. He thrashed the air with his scimitar, now in his left hand.

"You should never have challenged me," Tudur said. "You forgot your place. You put up a good fight, but you are not strong enough to take me."

Instead of fear, Ophois face shone in defiance. "I was not the one who attacked. That choice was yours. Perhaps you are correct. I may not be strong enough to take you—" A sneer swept across his ugly snout. "Alone."

Twing—thumph.

The sounds preceded an excruciating pain that ran the length of Tudur's being. Something struck him between the rim of his helmet and his breastplate.

It took every ounce of his remaining strength to turn back toward the mobile home.

Anput sat atop the roof of the trailer. She nocked another arrow and pulled back the string.

Tudur watched, waiting for the release. He couldn't move, couldn't even raise his shield. He would soon awake in the abyss.

She held the arrow steady, sighting down the shaft. The pain surging from his neck told Tudur she was good enough to finish it.

The arrow never launched.

Ophois' scimitar blade joined the previous arrow in Tudur's neck.

His head, and then body, entered the abyss.

~~~~~~~~~~

CHAPTER THIRTEEN
Saturday, May 16, 2020

Sarah McIntyre sat in River of Life Church. All around her people prayed for the safety of Chris, Daryl, and the agents engaged in the showdown with CeSiR Tech. On her way into the church, she watched a helicopter get shot out of the sky. The situation at CeSiR was serious indeed.

Pastor Thomas encouraged them to offer prayers of spiritual protection from unseen foes. For shields of faith to thwart the fiery arrows of the enemy. And for swords of the Spirit to bring light to the darkness.

Others prayed for hedges of protection and even for the destruction of the enemies opposing the agents.

Sarah squirmed in her seat. What about the gospel of peace? She, more than anyone in the church, had been in the enemy's crosshairs. CeSiR Tech had launched personal attacks aimed at her, including burning down her house—with her in it. If Chris' belief proved correct, CeSiR had successfully created human clones and sought to do everything they could to keep their secret.

Yet didn't God care about these people?

Were there conditions on His unconditional love? Did one need to be a natural born human?

They had tried to kill her.

They probably included young children. Innocent children—are they not innocent?

Innocent children who grow up to be murderers.

Love your enemies and pray for those who persecute you.

With reluctance, Sarah raised her hand. "Pastor Thomas?"

"Yes, Sarah, please share."

"Are we not called to love our enemies?"

Even Marilyn's eyebrows furrowed at the statement. Daryl was in just as much danger as Chris.

Sarah pressed on. "And to pray for those who persecute us?" Had she overstepped? Maybe she took things too literally. After all, people weren't cloning humans when Jesus called for this extreme expression of love.

Pastor Thomas winced as if she'd punched him in the stomach. He walked to the edge of the platform and sat. "Sarah." He shook his head.

She had overstepped. Here came the rebuke.

"I still have so much to learn," he said. His eyes seemed to glisten. "Thank you for your gracious and apropos reminder. What would humanity be without the unmerited forgiveness of Christ?"

They went on to pray for the protection and redemption of the clones, especially those who were young, unaware, or coerced into action.

Lord, Sarah prayed, *Chris mentioned a young girl, Ima Fredericks, whose DNA showed up on the evidence involved in the murder of Doctor M'Gregor. If she is still alive, please send your angels to protect her, wherever she may be.*

~~~~~~~~~~

Ophois returned to the trailer. Anput sat atop the roof waiting for him. The look on her face said he looked as beat-up as he felt. Pain rippled from just below his throat to his abs. He had defeated Tudur, but at what cost? Would he heal before his wounds dragged him into the Abyss?

The Abyss—how did Anput not get sucked in? He saw the rift open. He had never known a demon so close to imprisonment to escape. If she had not, he would be there himself. They worked as a team. Only she would have stepped into a one-on-one showdown for him. A breach of etiquette that he much appreciated.

He arrived next to her and alighted. "How? How did you escape?"

She shook her head. "I remember little. Everything faded to black as I slid toward the passage between realms. My injuries must have put me right on the brink. I awoke lying next to the rift. I was not being pulled in, nor could I pull away. I was stuck for what seemed like hours. Until—" Her eyes grew wide. "Was it Ima? The shockwave—is it possible? She is a mim." She stretched her wings and looked for damage. "Pain wracked my being as the shockwave passed through me. It flung me across the room, but away from the rift. The shockwave subsided and the rift closed."

The implications of her story were both encouraging and frightening. The only demon he trusted had emerged from the threshold of the Abyss, unscathed. Yet his prey, the child he sought to destroy, might now be one of *His*? Ophois looked at Anput. "Thank you for the assistance."

"You would have done the same for me."

Perhaps, in most situations.

"We need to see," Anput said. "Verify that it was her."

Ophois bobbed his canine snout. "And deal with her once and for all." A snarl rose from his throat and out through his teeth. "Before He sends a protector." How could they even be discussing such a thing? The mims were not granted souls. The very possibility that the Creator would offer such gracious forgiveness to yet another of His creations infuriated Ophois.

They stepped off the side of the trailer and prepared to enter the hallway outside Ima's room.

Boom.

Another explosion.

This one much smaller than the sonic blast.

The sound of a shotgun.

~~~~~~~~~~~

Patricia Sherwood lay on the wood floor, submerged in the heaviness of sleep. In her dreams, a mad-scientist doctor scraped pellets from Charles' leg, the way she would scrape bone fragments off a fresh-cut roast.

Charles whimpered at the pain. How could the doctor be doing this without putting her beloved under?

Scrape-scrape.

Whimper.

Scrape.

Whimper-whimper.

Bones creaked like the hinge on a door.

Scrape-scrape. Scrape-scrape.

The doctor flicked a pellet from the leg toward a pan sitting just in front of her. Moisture slapped her in the face. She couldn't see Charles' face, but her heart pounded mercilessly on her ribs until they were sore.

Another flick.

More moisture.

Scrape-scrape.

Whimper-whimper. Bark.

She began to surface from the nightmare. Hardwood floors pounded new aches and pains into her hips, shoulders, and ribs.

A wet tongue swiped across her face. Whimper, bark.

Patricia opened her eyes. Two big brown eyes and a slimy tongue welcomed her back to the land of the living. "Hey there, Goldie. Where'd you come from?" It began to make sense. The scraping sound from the dream. It was the sound Goldie made when she got shut in the laundry room. Still half dazed, she couldn't figure how the dog managed to escape.

The dog walked a couple feet away and sniffed the floor. Another whine. "Yes girl, daddy got hurt." Memories of the dreaded night flooded her brain like white-capped waves washing over the edge of a rowboat.

Charles. She knew nothing more of his condition. After his coughing and wheezing spell. They had whisked her away to the waiting room, where she sat until visiting hours ended. The nurse had told her he was resting. That he needed his rest and even his own wife couldn't see him. Then the nurse walked her out of the ICU ward.

Based on the amount of light in the house, she slept longer than she had planned. "Lord, I hope you'll forgive me for an abbreviated prayer time this morning," she prayed, still lying on the floor. "Please, heal Charles and help him recover. You've finally given him back to me. Please don't take him now." She sat up and stopped. "And Lord, please protect Ima. Bring restoration to her circumstances."

It wasn't much of a prayer, but it was all she had time for. She needed to get back to Charles.

~~~~~~~~~~~

Ophois and Anput rushed into the hallway. Dust filled the air. Fragments of wood littered the floor. A head-sized hole had been blown through the door of Trenton's room.

Trenton's black hair filled the hole. He tried to squeeze through the hole. Stupid mim. The hole wasn't big enough to get his ears through let alone his shoulders.

Ophois chuckled. "Door not fully dilated?"

Anput struck him on the shoulder and snickered.

"Now," Ophois said, "where were we before Tudur so rudely interrupted?" He held up a finger for Anput to wait in the hall. She nodded and he entered Trenton's room.

The mim now aimed the gun at an electrical outlet. Blow a hole there and stick his head in, and the mim might succeed in electrocuting himself.

Ophois, still oozing from his wounds, stepped back into Trenton. What a glorious feeling. Not only the power of complete control, but the pain of his spiritual state began to subside. He started to feel what Trenton felt. No, punctures in the abdomen, no gash in his leg or arm—just a sliver in his ear. Stupid mim.

He pointed the shotgun at the lock and pulled the trigger.

Click.

Of course, the mim did not possess the intelligence to reload the gun.

210

He needed to find more ammo. He looked about the room and wondered where the ammo might be. Trenton's memories merged with his own. Dresser drawer, top-left.

He walked to the dresser. Pulled out the top-left drawer. Sure enough, under some pairs of underwear, he found a half dozen shells. He loaded a shell, pocketed the others, and walked back to the door.

Boom.

The lock obliterated. The door swung open with a simple turn of the handle.

At first Ophois did not see Anput. He was seeing with Trenton's eyes instead of his own. He focused and Anput appeared in the hall, with an unpleasant scowl.

"What?" Shards of wood still settled to the ground beside her. "You were at no risk of harm."

She closed her eyes and shook her head. When she opened her eyes, their red facets twinkled. She turned toward Ima's room. "Shall we?"

He loaded another shell and pointed the barrel toward the lock on Ima's door. He probably had the key. This was so much more fun.

Boom.

A scream flowed from the hole in the door.

Ophois grinned at Anput. He held up another cartridge. "We *shell*."

She rolled her eyes. "Just get in there."

He slipped the shell into the gun and opened the door. The young girl cowered before him. Her crystal-blue saucer eyes stared at the shotgun. Memories of pulling the trigger, of flesh being torn from an old man's leg, mixed with his own. Ima had seen the gun before.

"You remember this gun," Ophois said, via Trenton.

Anput stepped through the wall and joined him in the room. She drew her khopesh.

Ophois realized that once again he was seeing with Trenton's eyes. He concentrated. They were not the only beings in the room. Adiya, the angel from the farmhouse knelt over the girl. Her wings enfolded the child—wings that still swirled with streams of light. But the intense brilliance of the true Light had faded since their last encounter.

Ophois lowered the barrel at the child.

~~~~~~~~~~~

Adiya felt Ima lurch when the shot blasted through the door. Trenton emerged through the doorway. He seemed different. No, not him, his controller. Someone other than Tudur controlled Trenton.

He glanced to his left, as Anput emerged from the wall.

Anput wielded her khopesh.

"I see your khopesh is in better order than when we last met," Adiya said.

Anput pointed the khopesh at Adiya. "And you appear a bit less formidable than when we last met. Perhaps you would like another round?"

"Speaking of rounds," Trenton said, echoing the words of his controller. It had to be Ophois, though Adiya could not see him as he hid within the mim. "Depart, before I put a round through your pet project there." Trenton's finger twitched on the trigger.

Providing peace and comfort to the child would prove much easier than stopping a shotgun blast. Such a miracle was certainly feasible—if the Creator willed it. She needed His wisdom.

"You have three seconds to leave her," Ophois said.

The restoration is protected. Do not interfere.

It was not the answer she desired, but it was the right answer. The Lord's answers always were.

She withdrew her wings.

Both demons shielded their eyes from the intense light that shone from within the new believer.

Adiya stood and took a few steps away from Ima, sword at the ready. She trusted her Lord. His purposes would not fail. But she would remain vigilant.

212

Anput stepped between Ophois and Adiya. She poked at Adiya with her khopesh, secure in the knowledge that the angel would not attack while the girl's security was at stake.

Adiya backed to a corner of the room and took up a defensive stance. While it was clear that she was not to attack Ophois, she was not leaving the room.

"That a girl," Ophois said.

Anput cast her a lopsided grin. Someone had recently slashed the golden demoness' face.

Adiya nodded at the gash. "That looks painful."

"Not as painful as you will experience if you attempt to interfere." Snarling fangs emerged from the grin.

~~~~~~~~~~~

Once again Ima looked down the barrel of Mama's shotgun, with Trenton's finger on the trigger.

He was delusional. Yelling at her, barking orders to unseen beings, conversing with himself.

He always seemed unstable. But this—this was an extreme demonstration of insanity. His gaze followed something to the corner and then swung back to Ima.

She would have expected Trenton to shoot her when he was sane. Now, she had absolutely no doubt. "Just get it over with, Trenton."

He grinned and licked his lips. Then he leaned the gun against the wall. Maybe, he wouldn't shoot her after all. He reached forward, grabbed the base of her sheet and ripped it off the bed with one hand.

Ima fell forward as the sheet pulled from her grasp. She pushed back with her heels and scrunched tightly into the corner. A dark-wet circle on the cot betrayed her fear.

His eyes dilated and a toothy grin formed on his face. "Now, now, Ima, time to stop acting like a little girl and become a woman." He reached and grabbed her leg.

"You said I was safe. That you were forbidden from touching me," she pleaded.

Trenton laughed. "That was not me. I was sent to kill you. Mael cares not what I do with you first."

That name, Mael. It reviled her. Though she'd never met anyone by the name.

Trenton had clearly changed his mind about his intentions for her. Maybe, if she made him mad enough, he would just kill her. Even as he pulled on her left leg, she dug her right heel into the mattress of the cot, grabbed the frame with both hands, and shoved her back against the wall.

The cot slid away from the wall and crashed into his shins. He swore.

She dropped to the cold floor behind the cot.

With one hand, he flipped the cot into the center of the room. He clawed his way across the floor and pounced on her. With his other hand, he punched her in the face.

She struggled against the blackness that threatened to overtake her.

He growled an inhuman warning to some unseen foe in the corner of the room. He promised he *would* kill her, if it interfered. He grabbed ahold of Ima's shirt and began to pull.

She kneed him in the abdomen with what little strength she could muster and then clawed him across the throat.

Not nearly enough to stave off the madman.

At least it shouldn't have been.

Trenton screamed in pain. His hands grabbed his throat and he called her several names she didn't recognize.

~~~~~~~~~~~

He wanted to scream at Trenton—to force him to leave the child alone. But they couldn't hear him through the walls of glass. He could sense Trenton's new controller. He knew its thoughts and felt its desires. He feared for the girl. Then the courageous child scratched Trenton across the neck. Hairline cracks formed in the glass. Not enough to get to Trenton.

~~~~~~~~~~~

Adiya stepped to her left to get a clear view of the madman glaring at Ima. Something was amiss.

214

Anput seemed to sense it also. They stared without understanding at the demon possessed mim. Trenton held his neck with both hands.

Ophois growled like a dog in a fight. His wings emerged from the mim, followed by his shoulders. He took a step back from the mim. His body shook like a dog emerging from a lake.

He turned a glare to Adiya. "How is it possible?" He looked at her with fire in his eyes. "She is not human! She does not deserve His forgiveness. None of them do." He pulled his scimitar and tried to point it at Adiya.

She felt pity for the pathetic demon before her. His leg was bent at an awkward angle. His wings were tattered and sulfurous slime oozed from his chest.

"You are right," Adiya said. "She does not deserve it. He chose to give it. He is the Sovereign. We are created beings. We do not have the right to question His will." She held her sword with both hands and started to approach Ophois.

"Not so fast." Anput's khopesh flashed in front of Adiya.

She had almost forgotten about Anput.

Ophois shook his head, blinked a couple times, and leapt back into Trenton's body.

~~~~~~~~~~~

Ima's fingertips buzzed from her attack on Trenton. He'd backed off a couple steps and for a few brief moments a dazed expression crossed his face.

Ima crouched into the corner.

As quickly as it had left, the light of awareness returned. Trenton's eyes locked onto Ima. Chills slithered up her back. "You stay away from me. You psycho."

Where much is forgiven there is much love.

What? Where had that thought come from. Trenton didn't deserve forgiveness.

Then again, did she?

Could it be that she was to extend forgiveness to Trenton? He was a mim, just like her. And God had forgiven her.

No, Trenton wasn't just a mim, he had shot Papa.

What you loose on earth, shall be loosed in Heaven.

Set him loose? He was already loose. She wanted to lock him up, not set him free. Shouldn't he face the consequences of his actions?

How could she possibly show forgiveness? What would that even look like?

Trenton drew his hands away from his neck and examined them. He seemed to be looking for blood. She hadn't gotten him that good. Not nearly as bad as she would have liked. But it seemed to hurt.

Good. Maybe now he'd just shoot her and get it over with. He glanced at the shotgun resting against the wall.

His gaze returned to her. The corners of his lips curled up, as he picked up the shotgun.

~~~~~~~~~~

Run child! It didn't matter. She couldn't hear him. No one could. He'd tried on so many occasions. The glass wall always prevented interference. He couldn't control himself, even when the powerful influences were not present. He tried to scream through the tiny fissures in the glass. Tried to make himself heard.

~~~~~~~~~~

Adiya wanted to run to the girl, to sweep Ima into her wings and comfort the shivering child.

Anput was distracted by the struggle Ophois seemed to be having to maintain control of the mim. Adiya could easily overtake the half-alert demoness.

Yet her orders remained unchanged.

Trust the restoration. Do not interfere.

Across the room, Ima closed her eyes and took a deep breath. She rose to her feet.

"What are you doing," Trenton said. His voice shook. Was it fear, or anger?

The Spirit-illuminated twelve-year-old took a step toward her fellow mim.

The barrel of the shotgun bounced and Trenton's hands wavered. From inside the mim, Ophois cursed the creature.

216

He was going to shoot her.

Adiya tried to fly to Ima, to provide the much needed protection. She could not. The Creator forbade her movement.

She could only watch.

Ima's hand quaked as she pressed her chest against the end of the barrel.

She placed her hand on Trenton's chest. "I forgive you Trenton, God loves you."

~~~~~~~~~~

The hairline fractures raced across the surface of his prison. The glass wall exploded at her touch. Freedom. The freedom to exert his will. She had done the impossible. She had set him free. He felt power flowing from her hand and into his chest. Not the imitation power of the past. This was the True Power.

~~~~~~~~~~

Adiya's muscles ached with tension as Ima reached out her hand and placed it on Trenton's chest. A blinding light erupted from Trenton. Shards of light shot from the center of his being. She had never observed anything like it.

Ima said something about God's forgiveness.

Anput screamed in pain as the shards shredded her wings. She dropped her khopesh and shot through the ceiling to escape the spiritual shrapnel.

Ophois was spit out into a heap on the floor. He was barely recognizable. The fire in his eyes had dulled to embers. They begged, pleaded with her to end the pain.

How could a being go on without the approval of his Creator? She could not comprehend their betrayal of Him, but she did understand the hopelessness he must feel knowing he would never be forgiven.

Even as the Abyss began to swallow him, realization and fear flooded his expression.

He had not found relief from the torment, but would think of nothing else until the Day of Judgment.

~~~~~~~~~~

Trenton stepped back and looked at Ima.

Ever since he could remember, Trenton, the real Trenton, watched others control his life. The natural animalistic him or the evil influences he so often lived with.

Now he was free to make his own choices. Right or wrong. He looked at the young girl-becoming-woman in front of him. He could make his own choice. If he chose to assault her, it would be him choosing, not someone choosing for him.

He tossed the shotgun into the center of the room.

~~~~~~~~~~

Ima's hand burned, like she'd grabbed a beaker from the hot-plate in science class.

A tear had formed in Trenton's eye. He blinked and it fled down his rugged cheek.

For the first time since he'd entered the room she realized that he smelled of urine. Pity swelled from deep within her being. It was true, God loved him. Just like He loved Ima.

Mama had told her about Jesus' sacrifice. That He had done it for her. Mama didn't know she was a mim, and it didn't matter. Jesus loved her.

She looked at Trenton. God loved him too. "Trenton, I forgive you," she repeated. "And God forgives you."

~~~~~~~~~~

Adiya marveled at the tear, which had formed in Trenton's eye. In the center of his being flickered a faint light. The light of his will. Not the light of a believer, but not the darkness of a mim. The faint flicker of humanity.

Ima is the restoration.

~~~~~~~~~~

218

CHAPTER FOURTEEN

Ima stood against the wall in the corner of the room. Her hand throbbed. The skin on her palm was red. How could touching someone cause a burn?

Trenton sat down on the dirt-ridden floor, placed his elbows on his knees, and wept into his hands.

Last night, she had sensed a feeling of peace when she prayed to Jesus. But this response—she wasn't convinced it was peace.

"Are you okay?" she asked.

He pulled his hands down. A string of snot bridged hand to nose. He glanced at it and his cheeks turned pink. He wiped his hand on his knees and then looked up at Ima. "What?"

"Are you okay?"

He stared at her for what seemed like ten minutes, though probably only one. "I, I don't understand what just happened." That made two of them. "My whole life has been like someone else had control of me."

"I felt that way at CeSiR," Ima said. In no small part thanks to him.

He lowered his eyes to Ima's feet. "I can only imagine." Again he seemed to search for words. "I am sorry. I know we—I—tormented you mercilessly." He brushed his hand through his short black hair. "I know you have no reason to believe me, but I had no choice."

"Everyone has a choice." Ima spat the words at him.

He nodded. "I've heard that most of my life. But, until you touched me, I, it was like I was trapped. Like a puppet in a show, aware of my deeds, but helpless to—" He started sobbing again.

Ima edged along the wall to her right, until the cot sat between her and Trenton. "I'm not sure what kind of game you're playing." Not very forgiving, but what did he expect? That she was going to buy this line about not being able to control his actions?

"Ima, you have every reason to hate me and definitely to not trust me." His lips pursed and his eyes widened. "Dear God, I shot Charles, your friend."

She slammed her fist on the cot. "And I hope you burn in hell for it." She never should have told him she forgave him. She couldn't. Not now, not ever. Especially, if— She had to know. "If nothing you've done is your fault, then you should have no problem telling me the truth." Her nose burned and she wiped her hand across her face. "Did you shoot Uncle M?"

"No." He rolled forward to kneel. "That was Mael's work." His voice hung between pleading and offense at the accusation. "You have to believe me." He rolled back to his backside.

She had to do no such thing. "Mael?" That name again. Who was he? Was there someone at CeSiR Tech, higher up than Maiya, or even Uncle M? Were they just puppets? "I've heard that name before. Who is Mael?"

He laid his arms across his knees and dropped his head on top of them. "You'd never believe me if I told you."

"No!" Heat rose up her neck and burst from her head. "You don't get to decide what I'll believe." Her hands shook. "You expect me to believe—what? That you were having some sort of out-of-body-experience when you shot Papa?" She kicked the frame of the cot. "You aren't responsible, why? Because you weren't really there?"

The door to her room was open. Could she get to it without him catching her? Where would she go?

"I wasn't out of body," Trenton said. "I was trapped deep inside. Like a fish in a fishbowl, forced to watch everything they chose to do."

"Out-of-body, in-a-bowl, under-a-basket. I don't care! Because, I don't believe you." She was screaming at him, and he hadn't retaliated. "So tell me. Who—is—Mael?"

Trenton closed his eyes and nodded. "He is an invisible being, and quite evil. A captain of some sort, as I understand it. The being that controlled my body took orders from him."

She had heard enough. She walked toward the door.

He didn't stand. Didn't turn to watch her. Didn't even seem to care if she left.

She turned back to him. "An evil, invisible being. You mean like a demon?" Her mind returned to the encounter at the zoo. Something had hoisted her into the air like a ragdoll. Could he be telling the truth? This was Trenton. Had he ever told her the truth?

Mama told her there were beings that couldn't be seen. The Bible spoke of these beings warring against God's angels in a battle to destroy people. She had told Ima that God created these beings and that she had nothing to fear from them, as long as she trusted God's strength against them and not her own.

"Suppose you are telling the truth," Ima said, "what changed when I touched you?"

Trenton threw his hands in the air. "I have no idea." More tears welled up in his eyes. "All I know is that I was trapped, and you set me free."

"If you're telling the truth," Ima said, "then it wasn't me that set you free. Only Jesus could have done what you describe." She turned back to the door. "If you're free, it was His doing. Don't blame me!"

She stormed out the door.

~~~~~~~~~~

Trenton jumped when the door slammed. Ima had every right to hate him. Everybody he knew had good reason. The theater of his mind played back memories—accusations from his past. Nights at the Rivers Edge Bar, until some young woman, enamored with his political clout, agreed to leave with

221

him. Convincing Leilah Bahar to accuse Sergeant Davis of assaulting her in St. Louis. Paying that hooker in Chicago to meet up with Daryl Williams, destroying his marriage. In seconds, hundreds of memories flowed through his brain. If only, the memories of his past had vanished along with the glass barrier.

What about his controller? He feared the influence would return. Could he resist the control now that he was free? If not, it would never be over. The one who'd done the real damage through the years could still return. And if not, could he live with the memories?

Ima said that Jesus had set him free. Why wouldn't He wash away the memories? Surely, God didn't hold him accountable for all the things he couldn't control. What had he done to warrant God's discipline?

Even as the thoughts and questions flowed, he knew he wasn't without fault. He hadn't always disliked the wretched things he did. He loathed the lack of control, but not necessarily the actions themselves. Did he want control to be free from the actions, or to be the one wielding the power? He had justified himself because the actions weren't under his control. But now, what would he choose? Would he really be any different?

He returned to his bedroom and grabbed a few items he would be needing. Then he went to find the girl.

When he reached the living room, he found Ima sitting on the cracked polyester couch. He smiled. She hadn't run far. She needed him as much as he needed her.

He approached her and laid the items next to her.

~~~~~~~~~~~

Patricia Sherwood parked her car and limped toward the hospital entrance. What had she been thinking falling asleep on the floor? Her joints hurt badly enough every other day. But now, they felt like the hinges on that old gate to the cow pen. Rusted, weathered, beaten, and overused.

She sighed in relief when she reached the double-doors to the building. They slid open before her. *Welcome to our lovely abode.* The last place on earth she wanted to be right now.

No, not true. The second-to-last place. Charles had survived. She received no phone calls during the night. The nurse had assured her they would call if Charles grew worse.

After a slow walk with multiple stops to rest her aching joints, Patricia approached the desk outside the entrance to the Intensive Care Unit.

"Good morning, ma'am," an attendant said. "May I help you?"

"Yes, I'm Patricia Sherwood, here to see my husband, Charles."

"I see." The overweight gentleman glanced down. "I'm so sorry, Mrs. Sherwood."

Sorry? No! The nurse had promised to call. What happened? Fear swirled through Patricia's thoughts bringing light-headedness.

"Oh, ma'am, no. I didn't mean to imply—" The attendant removed the glasses covering his hunter-green eyes. "Mr. Sherwood is fine. He is in his room recovering from surgery." He stumbled over the words. "I just meant that I was sorry for your husband's senseless attack.

Patricia closed her eyes and inhaled a deep cleansing breath. "Son, don't scare an old woman like that. You might just end up with another patient."

"Yes, ma'am. I mean, no, ma'am. We wouldn't want you here. I mean—well you know what I mean. Let me get the door." He scanned his badge into a reader at the desk. The large wood, or at least fake wood, doors swung open.

She hurried through the door, ready to be free from the blundering attendant. The door to Charles' room was open. A curtain surrounded the bed, so she stopped and knocked on the grey metal doorframe.

A chirpy twenty-something nurse popped her blond-pony-tailed head out from behind the curtain. "You must be Mrs. Sherwood?"

Patricia nodded.

"He's been asking for you all morning." She slid the curtain back, revealing the best sight Patricia had seen in a day. "I think we're all set here. I'll leave you two alone."

A smiling Charles waved his IV-tethered hand at Patricia. "Hey there. I was beginning to think you'd left me." The oxygen tube in his nose made his voice sound nasally.

"Dream on, Romeo. You can't get rid of me that easy." She walked to his bedside, leaned over, and planted a kiss right below the plastic tube.

"Hey, what are you trying to do," he protested, "give me a heart attack or something?"

She gently slapped him on the shoulder, sat in the chair next to the bed, and took his hand in hers. "You really scared me last night."

"I wasn't exactly relaxed myself," Charles said. He glanced at his mangled leg, which now looked like a giant roll of gauze. "They said I could still lose it, if infection takes hold."

She squeezed his hand. "They're just preparing you for the worst. If I know you, you'll be up and chasing me around the house before I know it." She smiled with her lips, but he could probably see through it to her true fear. She dreaded the thought of living even a day without her beloved.

His face grew serious. "Is she?" He tried to rub his forehead with his right hand. The needle in his arm yanked his hand back down. "Is Ima—dead?"

He had misinterpreted her concern. "No, well, I don't know." It hadn't even occurred to her that the madman might have killed Ima. Why was that? "He took her. The man with the gun, he took Ima."

Charles shook his head. "What would Mayor Richards want with Ima? It doesn't make any sense."

"Charles—he shot you!" None of it made any sense.

Charles' face flushed. "If I get my hands on him, I'll wring his scrawny neck."

~~~~~~~~~~

224

Ima opened the door to her room. It felt so good to have her own clothes back. She found Trenton waiting for her in the living room. He had changed into blue jeans and a plaid shirt. Once again, he had his head buried in his hands. His shoulders shook. She couldn't pretend to understand what was going on with him.

She quietly approached a folding chair, next to the couch. She sat and waited for him to recognize her presence.

He didn't look up. "I'm so sorry." He spoke through his tear soaked hands. "I wish I could just erase these memories."

Her mind returned to when she first awoke in the powder-blue and white clothes of CeSiR Tech. Her fear receded and heat rose up the back of her neck. He could claim some kind of imprisonment that prevented him, the *true* him as he called it, from doing anything about his actions, but that didn't mean she had to believe him.

Something had changed. She knew it. She sensed a prompting to believe him. But nothing in her education, or limited experience, could support such claims.

"I know that nothing I say or do will make up for the violations you have experienced from me and from CeSiR." He raised dark damp eyes to her. "But I'm gonna do anything I can to try. I owe you—everything. Not to earn your forgiveness, but because of what you did for me."

She rose and stepped to a window, where she stood with her back to him. Outside, glimpses of light flickered through rustling leaves. Leaves only weeks old, yet proof of life in a tree that once appeared dead.

What form of *leaves* would it take for Trenton to convince her of his own *new life*?

"What can I do?" Trenton asked.

"Nothing!" She snapped through clenched teeth. His tree would always be dead to her. "Wait." She turned and glared at him. "Take me home."

His eyes bore into hers. "I'm not sure I can do that." Leaves were falling from their branches. "I want to. I have memories of driving. I know the mechanics of it. But, without the influences, I'm not sure I can actually do it."

That was the craziest excuse she'd ever heard. He couldn't take her home because he didn't know how to drive? His leaves were on the ground, burning in a pile. "Trenton, you are—" He had a phone. What was she thinking? She didn't want to get in a car with him anyway. "You have a phone, right?"

"I'll try to drive you." He reached in his pocket and pulled out the car keys. "How hard can it be? Like I said, I know the process, and my brain has memories of driving. I'm sure we'll make it."

It figured—he wouldn't want the authorities involved. Then again, neither did she. Despite the many events of the past day, she was still a mim. Best case, the authorities would return her to the facility. Worst case? She didn't want to think about it.

Trenton was her only way to get back to Mama, and Papa if he was still alive.

She would never forgive Trenton.

But she *would* use him.

~~~~~~~~~~

Adiya sat in the back seat of the BMW. The car lurched forward, nearly taking out the trailer's porch. Trenton slammed on the brakes and the tires slid to a stop.

"Sorry," Trenton said. "It'll be okay. I promise."

Gravel sprayed forward as the BMW shot from the driveway into the two-track leading to the main road.

Adiya decided she may have her work cut out for her. Her biggest challenge yet could be keeping Ima safe in this car.

Speaking of Ima's protection, Adiya had not seen the golden demoness since Ophois' demise. Would she go to Mael? Inform him of Ima's re-creation? Given how quickly Anput fled, did she even comprehend Trenton's restoration?

Adiya was not sure she completely understood it herself.

The BMW bounced down the two-track. If Adiya had a physical body, she would need to visit the chiropractor after this trip. Tree branches smacked the side of the car. Twice, Ima screamed when it sounded like her side window would shatter.

Adiya pondered the implications of a newly released soul contending with the memories of a madman. Could there truly be redemption for one with such a blemished past? Given his history, could people overcome their opinions of him? Could he overcome it himself? In truth, only one opinion mattered. Only one person offered true redemption. Over the years, she watched the love, grace, and mercy of Jesus redeem many people far worse than Trenton—and they acted fully of their own volition. Only time would reveal His will for Trenton—

Another rut.

Another scream.

—if he lived that long.

"Please, stop screaming," Trenton asked. His voice was kind, but shaken. "I'll try to take it easy. This is harder than it looked."

Minutes later, they merged onto a Missouri highway. The car sailed down the black surface with little incident.

"I'm so sorry," Trenton said. A common sentiment since the restoration. This time it came as they pulled into the driveway of the farmhouse. Surely, images of blasting a hole the size of a grapefruit in Charles' leg haunted his memories. Not to mention carrying Ima out of the house like a duct-tape-roped calf.

Ima had grown callous to his apologies. She stared out the window. "I don't see their car. Maybe they're still at the hospital." She cast a glare at Trenton.

The leg wound had been significant. To Adiya's surprise, Tudur had taken action that may have saved Charles' life, if he lived.

"I'll stay here," Trenton said. "You can go check the house."

Ima's door slammed shut before the words left his mouth. She bounded up the steps to the porch in two strides.

Adiya snuck one last glance at Trenton. True to his word, he reached for the keys and shut off the engine. She rose through the roof of the BMW and followed Ima to the house.

The door was unlocked.

Ima pushed the door open. Her exuberance seemed to have run into her memories. She paused.

A large wet tongue swept across her face.

The girl giggled and kissed the dog. "Hey, Goldie. It's good to see you, girl."

The dog pushed past Ima and sprinted to the lawn, with extreme urgency. Clearly, the dog's needs had not been Patricia's primary concern of late.

Moments later, Goldie realized Ima had not come alone. She growled, barked, and charged the driver's side of the black BMW.

"Goldie, get in here," called Ima.

The dog leapt and smashed into the driver-side window.

If Trenton had not been strapped to the seat, he would have hit his head on the ceiling.

"Goldie, come on."

The dog ignored the girl and continued barking at the car.

Boldness, or stupidity, overtook Trenton. He rolled down his window enough to extend an upturned palm to the dog.

The dog jumped onto the side of the car and bypassed the hand. Her snarling nose entered the opening. Suspiciously, she sniffed the intruder, who had invaded her world only two days prior. She cocked her head, as if confused by her senses. The growling ceased and she licked Trenton on the cheek.

Content with his presence, she left the car and joined Ima at the door.

Ima, Goldie, and Adiya entered the house.

~~~~~~~~~~~

The scents of vinegar and dish soap greeted Ima as she entered the dining area of the old farmhouse. She flicked on the light. As she turned, memories of Trenton with that cursed shotgun stood in the center of the room. She closed her eyes and inhaled a deep breath.

Reopening her eyes, she walked to a bucket sitting next to the wall by the window. A brownish water filled the bottom of the bucket. The source of the smell.

Her gaze fell to the spot on the floor where Papa had lain bleeding. The blood was gone. The floor appeared slightly duller where the pool had been. She looked back at the brownish liquid. Green soap and—blood. Papa's blood. Mama hadn't been able to leave his blood on the floor. A bottle of vinegar and a yellow box sat next to the bucket.

She glanced back to the clean wooden floor. Visions swirled through her mind of the pool of blood returning to Papa's leg, the gaping wound closing, the smoke and hot metal returning to the barrel of the shotgun, and Trenton's finger lifting off the trigger. Was it possible? Had Trenton been restored as he claimed?

The events had happened. Papa *was* shot. His blood had been spilled. Trenton had kidnapped her. The events could not be undone. But could they be cleansed—the way the stain on the floor had been removed?

Even Goldie had sensed something different about Trenton. Something on the inside. Still she didn't trust him. Couldn't.

She called out to Mama.

No response.

Not a surprise. She hadn't even picked up the cleaning supplies from the dining room. She searched the house, finishing with Mama's room.

The bed was made, everything in place. At least she'd taken the time to make her bed and pick up in her room. Maybe things weren't too dire with Papa. Mama had to be at the hospital with him. Why did she have Trenton bring her here? She should have known they wouldn't be at home. Papa's injury was serious. It wasn't something they'd slap a Band-Aid on and send him home. But how serious?

Not like Uncle M's.

Papa was strong. He'd survive. It was only his leg. He had to survive. She couldn't lose him.

But what would happen when they found out about her? She was going to lose them. Sooner or later, she lost everyone.

She walked back outside to Trenton and the BMW.

Opening the door, she leaned inside and told him they weren't there.

"Get in. I'll take you to the hospital."

Her options were limited. Walking to the hospital would take a long time, even if she knew where it was located. Trenton brought her this far. Goldie trusted him, maybe she could too.

She sat down and buckled in.

Trenton phoned Fitzgibbon Hospital and verified that Papa was there. He hung up and told her they said Papa was in the ICU.

"What is ICU?"

"It stands for Intensive Care Unit. It means he is still at risk. They want to make sure they can care for him as well as possible."

They rode the rest of the way to the hospital in silence, as she contemplated the implications of Papa being in the ICU.

~~~~~~~~~~~

Anput approached the CeSiR Tech grounds. The place was in chaos. Angels wandered the entire south-side of the property. In addition, FBI trucks, agents, and other law enforcement seemed to swarm the perimeter of the building.

A sickening chill swept from wingtip to wingtip. What could have occurred to allow the angels and their minions to so thoroughly overpower Mael and his mims? One thing was clear. The Creator had intervened. When she first heard of Mael's endeavor, she could not believe the Creator allowed them to exhibit such defiance.

Mael needed to know what happened with Ima, assuming Mael survived the angelic invasion.

Anput swept a wide berth out over the river and approached the building from the north. Though a significant demonic presence persisted, the angelic host now milled about the facility. She desired to avoid a confrontation at this point.

She found a group of demons approaching the building and merged into their numbers. She entered through the side of the building and made her way upward toward the roof. She and Ophois had met with Mael on the roof only a day earlier.

Anput arrived at the roof and found several lesser demons wandering about. They watched the angelic host spread out across the grounds below. Mael was not present.

She grabbed a sniveling demon at the edge of the roof. He had been whining about their doom at the hands of the host below. "Where is Mael?" she asked.

Before the demon could answer, an explosion rocked the building. The demon's eyes grew into miniature full-moons. He screamed in her ear. "They are coming!"

She slapped him upside the head. "Snap out, you coward." The angelic host needed no explosives to breach the walls of CeSiR. Only the unknown kept them at bay. Perhaps the agents had blasted their way in, but the explosion seemed more central to the building. "I will ask once more. Where is Mael?"

The demon's eyes stopped bouncing in their sockets and focused on Anput. "Bone room, under the building. His secret meeting place. Hiding." Fear swept across the pathetic demon's face. He had just accused his prince of cowardice. If Mael found out, well, the true coward would be no more.

Anput thanked him for his assistance, as she flung him over the side of the building. He flailed to the ground and landed beside a giant angelic warrior.

She heard his whining scream, as she entered the building.

The top floor contained an office full of dark-magic décor. It was empty.

She passed through several other floors where mims wandered aimlessly. They looked like Trenton, before Ophois took possession of him in the trailer. Where their controllers?

She entered the underground parking garage at the base of the building. Fire gnawed at a pile of debris that appeared to have been a car at one point. This must have been the source of the explosion. The scent of fear and death hung like fog in the garage. No sign of Mael.

She descended through another couple floors, before reaching the bone room, which lived up to its name. Even as she emerged, a small human skull crashed against the wall to her right. Off to one corner, Mael stood with his back to her. He flicked a small pelvic bone into the air with his sword, took a step, and batted the bone across the room. The pelvic bone crushed against the wall.

His feet passed like mist through the piles of bones on the floor. Somehow, he managed to remain in the spiritual realm while exerting direct influence on the bone he had smacked across the room. She had never witnessed such fluid interaction with the physical realm without transitioning into the realm.

"What do you want, Anput?"

He had never looked her way, yet knew of her presence. She began to see why this demon commanded such respect. "I bring news, my liege." She lowered herself to the bone-covered floor. "It pains me to say, it will only add to your consternation."

Mael snorted and turned to face her. "You believe you will bring me dismay?" Sulfurous steam puffed from his Cape-buffalo snout. "Have you not looked around? *His* divine intervention has left our forces decimated. So what? Did the Creator step in and destroy Tudur? Were you left with a mim that was of no more value than an animal? I have over a hundred such creatures here to taunt me." He kicked a pile of bones. A femur, tibia, and a handful of vertebrae sprayed into the air. He pointed his sword at the ceiling. "Surely, you saw the pile of ashes above us. That used to be my devoted worshiper and head of cloning."

It explained the explosion and incinerated car. Scorched earth. Did he already know of Ima's redemption? Was he

232

scorching the project to leave no ability to produce more mims to stand in defiance of his plan? "Yes, my liege."

Mael glanced around the room. "Where is Ophois? Has he finally dealt with that insulant Ima?"

"It pains me to report that he has not, my liege."

"And Tudur? He is no more, correct?"

He already knew. Would he be furious that Anput's arrow and Ophois' blade had diminished their numbers? No, it was at his bidding that they went to the trailer to face Tudur. "Yes, my liege. We dispatched him."

Mael grinned. "Good. At least it was not *His* doing." He drilled Anput with a stare. "And Ophois?"

"Once Tudur was no more, Ophois took possession of Trenton Richards. When we entered the room where Ima was being held, we encountered a member of the heavenly host."

Mael shook his head. "Then Ophois is no more."

"No, my liege. Well, yes, Ophois is no more. But it was not the angel."

Mael nodded in acknowledgment.

"My liege, there is more you must know. I fear it is the conditions of his demise that you will find most unsettling."

He simply snorted and eyed her. "Go on."

"Ima now belongs to *Him*."

Muscles bulged in his neck. "You are mistaken." His eyes flamed in defiance. "That—is—not—possible. She is a mim."

"Yes, my liege. But I was there. I felt the explosion. I saw the intensity of His presence within her. I cannot explain. I only know what I saw." She took a couple steps backward. "I fear *He* has chosen to use her to accomplish *His* purpose."

"What purpose!" Mael picked up a half dozen bones and whipped them at her with each word, "What purpose can she possibly serve?" The bones passed through her and smashed against the wall.

"There is more, my liege." She hoped he would not kill the messenger.

He snorted. "Of course there is. Go on."

"When Ima touched Trenton, something happened. Something horribly unexplainable." She paused for a rebuttal, but none came. "Ophois was tossed from the mim like a land mine had erupted." She spread her tattered wings and nodded toward them. "This is from the shrapnel of that explosion. I left immediately and returned here."

Mael inhaled deeply before responding. "What does it mean?"

"I know not, my liege."

He glared at the ceiling. Not at the ceiling, but through it, beyond the heavens. He raised his fist and struck the concrete. "Why do *You* torment me like this? Is there great joy in bringing me sorrow?"

Mael, like herself and every other demon, had chosen to rebel. To leave the service of their Creator in exchange for the fateful arrogance of something better—better than serving the One who possessed unlimited power and unconditional love. Foolishness for which they would all pay the ultimate price. Railing at the One on whom they had turned seemed childish. She would not say so.

"Ima must not live!" Mael cut several bones to bits with his sword. "You will lead me to her. We will gather what resources remain. The enemy will not prevent her demise."

Anput could not agree more. "I do not believe she will stay at the trailer. We should marshal our forces to the home where she has stayed this past week. She will return there."

Mael summoned a messenger and sent him to find Cadfael. "Tell Cadfael to mobilize any of his forces that remain, and lead them to—" He looked at Anput.

"A farmhouse. Just a few miles west of Marshall."

~~~~~~~~~~

CHAPTER FIFTEEN

Trenton's black BMW pulled up to the entrance of Fitzgibbon hospital. Outside Ima's window, loomed a building of brick and glass—the closest thing to CeSiR she had seen since leaving, a week ago. She turned a suspicious glance to Trenton.

"This is as far as I go," he said. "I'm a wanted man now. Rightfully so. Still, I'm not quite ready to turn myself in for actions over which I had no control." He shrugged his shoulders, as if she should just accept it.

"Are you going back to CeSiR?" she asked.

He laughed. "No, I don't think that would be prudent. For you either." He stared at his hands as they began to tremble against the steering wheel. "Ima, there are things there, well not just there, but especially there." His Adam's apple rippled as he swallowed hard. "Dark, invisible things. I haven't seen them, but I've felt them my entire life. More importantly, I have fragments of memories—its memories, the memories of the creature that controlled me. They are hideous monsters. They swarm CeSiR like honey bees to a queen."

Ima waited until she had his gaze. "Is one of these creatures named Mael?"

Trenton shivered at the name. "Yes. He's the one in charge. The mims were created under his control." He rubbed his temples. "My memories aren't like those of the real world. More like the fading images of one's nightmares." He glanced in the rearview mirror.

A car pulled around them.

"You better get going," Trenton said. "Things were unravelling at CeSiR. I'm not sure either one of us wants Mael, or his horde, to find us. Not to mention the authorities."

Ima opened her door and began to climb from the car.

"Ima, be careful. These creatures don't like you for some reason." He bent down and looked her in the eyes. His eyes, once so cold and callous, now shone with compassion. "I'm truly sorry for the way they, I, treated you."

She nodded and slammed the door.

When she was a half-dozen steps from the car, he rolled down the window and called after her. "Ima!"

She kept her shoulders facing the entrance, but turned her head back toward the car.

"You might be encouraged to know—there are others. Beings hated by those at CeSiR, especially Mael. They are glorious creatures, called angels."

Great. She walked away from the nutcase. Angels and demons? Invisible enemies? A chill swept over her as she thought about their trip to the zoo. Mama mentioned a battle. Is that what she meant? Angels and demons battling for—her? It made no sense. She was nothing special.

No. Mama said, Jesus loved her. If that was true, and she believed it was, then she was special. Uncle M had also told her that she was special.

The doors of the hospital swept open granting her entrance to the building. She felt like royalty. *Here-ye-here-ye, behold Ima. Open the gates!* A grin crept to her cheeks.

Once inside, the feeling faded. People strutted here and there. Everyone had somewhere to be. No one seemed to notice a twelve-year-old girl standing just inside the entrance.

"May I help you?"

A young man swept through the entrance, walked past Ima, and disappeared down a hallway.

"Miss, may I help you?"

Ima turned.

A stout woman seated behind a desk stared at Ima. "Oh good, I thought we were gonna need an ENT to treat you for hearing loss."

Ima cocked her head. "ENT?"

"Never mind, just a little hospital humor. Are you here to see someone?" The woman's voice had softened.

"Papa, um, Charles Sherwood?" That was dumb. "He was shot in the leg, a couple days ago." Better.

The woman tapped at a keyboard. "Ah, yes. He's in the ICU."

"That's it," Ima said, "Intensive Care Unit."

The woman squinted her eyes at Ima. "That's what I just said." She looked Ima over carefully. "Only immediate family in the ICU. You family?"

"He's my Papa, um, grandfather," she lied.

"So you said." The woman smiled. "Follow the signs to the left." She pointed toward a hallway. "Down that way. I'll call Don and let him know you are coming."

"Thank you." Ima headed off in search of the ICU, before the bipolar woman changed her mind.

Soon, she arrived at a desk with an overweight man seated in a much-too-small chair. His hair looked like it only grew out of one side of his head and was swept across to the other side. He placed his index fingers to his temples. "Let me guess." He scrunched his face. Not terribly appealing. "You are here to see, your Grandpa Charles." He lowered his fingers and smiled. "Am I right?"

"The woman at the front desk said she'd call you."

"Right." He dropped his gaze to the desk in front of him and shook his head. Without saying anything else, he scanned a white card and the large doors swung open.

Ima walked through. Only as the doors swung back shut, did she realize she didn't know Papa's room number.

With no desire to go back through the double doors, she peeked into the first room to her right. Wires and tubes were attached to what appeared to be a young woman, though with all the bruises and cuts, she might not have been that young. The woman was asleep and didn't notice the intrusion.

The hallway in the ICU wasn't very long. There couldn't be more than five rooms. As long as she didn't get thrown out for pestering the other patients, she would find Papa, sooner or later.

~~~~~~~~~~~

Eldwyn stood next to Charles' bed. Patricia, who arrived soon after visiting hours began, had left to get something for lunch in the cafeteria.

A young doctor stood before Charles, staring at his clipboard. He clearly knew the content. How to share the content—that seemed to be presenting some trepidation.

"Staring at that board isn't going to change the news," Charles said. He coughed and winced. "I'm guessing this pain in my abdomen isn't just my leg healing." He tried to smile.

Eldwyn loved this man. So strong for so many years. He took such good care of his wife, at least until the Alzheimer's set in. Eldwyn looked at Rafya, an angel of mercy.

Eitan had sent her from Columbia to be with Charles. She looked knowingly at the clipboard in the doctor's hand. "It is always hard."

"Aye, and such a life of integrity, he has lived," Eldwyn said.

"Are you sure you don't want to wait for Mrs. Sherwood?" the doctor asked.

Charles shook his head.

The doctor flipped the clipboard up against his white lab coat and wrapped his arms across it. "Okay, I'll be straight with you, Mr. Sherwood. It doesn't look good. You were put on a vasopressor when your blood pressure dropped so low. It helped prop up your BP, but pushed you into renal failure."

Charles nodded, coughed, winced, and coughed again. "The pain?"

"Yes. Your kidneys are no longer functioning. It's causing a backup of fluid and congestive heart failure." He flipped the clipboard back down and stared at it. "We've tried everything, but I'm afraid things are cascading too fast."

"Papa!" Ima's joyful voice shattered the gloom. The girl ran to the bed. Oblivious to the doctor, and the conversation she had interrupted, she laid her head on Charles' chest and gave him a big hug.

"Ima, my child." Cough. "I'm so happy to see you." Cough-cough.

The heart failure was making it hard for Charles to talk.

"How's your leg?" Ima asked.

"Now, don't you worry about me. How did you get free?"

The doctor excused himself. "I'll come back when Mrs. Sherwood returns."

"No." Charles turned fiery eyes to the doctor. "I don't want her to know."

Ima looked at Charles with wide eyed suspicion.

Eldwyn walked to Adiya, who had entered the room with Ima. "Poor child. So much pain, she has experienced."

Adiya filled Eldwyn in on the events at Trenton's trailer and Ima's acceptance of the Creator, while the doctor and Charles danced their debate around Ima.

"How is that possible?" Eldwyn asked.

"There is much I do not understand," Adiya said. "I need to find Eitan, to bring him up to speed."

"Go," Eldwyn said. "I will stay with Ima." He turned toward Rafya. "Charles is in good hands. Besides, this assignment is nearly complete."

Adiya bowed her head to Eldwyn and then left the room.

The doctor also left, having lost the debate with his patient.

~~~~~~~~~~~

Ima sat in the chair next to Papa's bed. Papa refused to elaborate on what the doctor was so worked up about. She didn't like Papa asking the doctor to keep things from Mama. Mama was the strongest woman Ima had met. What could be so dire that she couldn't handle it?

"Mama is at the cafeteria getting something to eat," Papa said. "She's gonna be so happy," cough, "to see you." He closed his eyes and took a deep breath. "Are you hungry?"

Trenton had given her a snack to munch on in the car, but she hadn't eaten a meal for over a day. "No, I'm okay. I just want to be with you." Plus, she had no desire to wander the hospital alone.

Papa glanced up at a television that hung from the wall. "Wow."

She turned to see what appeared to be the remains of a helicopter on fire. The caption read, "Firefight in Arrow Springs."

"Ima, there's a controller over here somewhere that will turn up the sound. See if you can find it."

She found the controls. Next to a red circle containing a white cross, there were a few buttons for the TV. She clicked the volume-up button. Nothing happened. She clicked it a few more times. Now she could hear a female reporter.

". . . hearing from the authorities that the firefight this morning was between F.B.I. agents and civilians at CeSiR Tech."

A man's voice came from the television. "Alison, we are hearing reports that these civilians at CeSiR may actually be *human clones?*"

"Yes, John. We've heard rumblings of that as well, but no formal statement has been released to this point." The auburn haired reporter pointed over her shoulder toward a big white building.

Ima shuddered. Horror flowed from her neck to her tailbone. Her secret would soon not be secret.

"Authorities are telling us," Alison continued, "this place is like a fortress. It has taken the agents a few hours just to make their way into the building. According to Special Agent in Charge, Earl Banks, they need to access CeSiR Tech records, to determine exactly what types of research CeSiR was involved—"

The television clicked off.

240

Ima spun to find Papa staring at her. She knew this time would come. Eventually, everyone turned on her.

"It's true isn't it?" Papa asked. "That's why you were running and didn't want us to contact the authorities."

Her eye twitched. *What could she possibly say? Oh, that? Yeah, I guess it just slipped my mind. It's no big deal.* She just nodded.

"So you're a," cough, "clone?" The word sounded so cold rolling off Papa's lips.

"I, I, um, at CeSiR they called us mims."

"Mims?"

She stared at the tile flooring of the sterile room. "Manufactured Image of Man."

He drew a quick breath, followed by several coughs. "That's terrible."

From beloved pseudo-grandchild to terrible in thirty seconds. That might actually be a record.

"You can't stay."

She sniffed and her sinuses burned. "Yes, sir."

A cool hand reached out from the bed and grabbed hers. "I'm afraid we both have to leave."

She looked at him and brushed her cheek. Was he offering to go with her?

"I wish there was some way I could protect you, Ima." He squeezed her hand. "I'm being called home."

Home? Oh. Her chest shook as the realization of Papa's mortality settled into her heart. "I'm so sorry. It's all my fault." Why had she stopped at that farm? If she weren't there, he wouldn't have been shot.

He sat forward on the bed. Pain flashed across his face. "Ima, you listen to me. You have given me more than I could have ever dreamed. You gave me a second chance at life—time with my bride. Even if it was only a week. That was a week I never would have had, even if I'd lived ten more years." He pulled her toward him.

She embraced the kindest man she had ever met.

"Ima!" Mama practically jogged to the bedside and squeezed her.

She loved this dear couple. That's why she needed to leave. Soon.

Mama took a step back and looked from Papa to Ima and back again. "What's the matter with you two? You look like you lost a puppy." Fear flashed in her eyes.

Papa quickly explained the news report. Though Mama didn't seem to understand the implications as well as Papa, he convinced her that she needed to get Ima out of town.

"I can't leave you alone in the hospital," Mama said.

Papa shushed her. "I'm fine. The doctor said the leg's healing fine." The lie surprised Ima. Why wouldn't Papa tell her? "You'll have to leave tonight anyway. You can come back tomorrow. Ima needs your help more than I do right now."

Ima swallowed the lump rising in her throat.

Mama and Ima both hugged Papa goodbye.

They walked to the doorway.

Ima turned one last time. "Goodbye, Papa. I love you."

~~~~~~~~~~~

CHAPTER SIXTEEN

Adiya approached the grounds of CeSiR Tech. A few demons still swirled above the building like vultures looking for dinner. Law enforcement agents scurried in and out of the parking-garage level of the building. Bright red lights pulsed against the white exterior as paramedics cared for wounded agents and prepared for what they might find inside.

A yellow hazmat van had driven down the large sidewalk in front of the building. Like bees around honeycomb, yellow clad units swarmed the van. They waited for the go-ahead to sweep the medical floors for biohazards. Given CeSiR's foray into medications, and their obvious disregard for ethics, the team surely entertained the suspicion of a viral threat.

In the physical realm, many signs pointed to the warfare that had occurred. Atop the supposed center for healing research, several bodies of mims lay motionless, a round scorched circle highlighted one corner of the roof, where a grenade had exploded, and smoke still rose from the downed helicopter. A war had definitely taken place.

In the spiritual realm, the sickening smell of sulfur, the sweet-iron scent of blood from the angels, and the lingering woodsy fragrance of prayers from the saints gave testimony to the destruction that had occurred.

Adiya found Eitan and several other angelic warriors standing atop the facility. Their somber demeanor, and tolerance of the circling demonic buzzards, told her many of her fellow warriors had been returned to the throne of God for a time of healing and recovery. Even the mighty Eitan's white tunic bore the telltale red and green spattering from wounded friend and foe. His golden breastplate was dented and the embossed sterling lion was missing its tail.

"Captain Eitan." Adiya alighted next to the impressive warrior. "Much has happened since we last spoke. It would appear for us both."

"Indeed. It is good to see you, Adiya. Is she well?"

"Yes, sir. She is at the hospital with Eldwyn."

She informed the captain of Ima's redemption.

"I have always believed there was something very special about her," Eitan said. "Something the other mims did not possess. It would appear that something was a free-will to choose to follow the Messiah."

"She is definitely unique," Adiya said. "Yet I am no longer convinced that it is her ability to make such a choice."

Eitan sat on a stone wall that edged the roof of the CeSiR Tech building. His blue eyes studied Adiya's face. "The Creator chose not to endow the mims with souls. How can such a choice be made?"

Adiya shook her head. "I fear we have misjudged the emptiness of the mims—that their lack of will implies an absence of what distinguishes a human." She paused to allow the captain time to process. He listened intently, but said nothing. "We have assumed the lack of His image in these created beings."

"With good reason," Eitan said. "Not only have they demonstrated no evidence of the Image of God, His light does not shine in them."

She understood his hesitation. She had seen the utter darkness in the center of their being. Where all humanity bore some reflection of His light, albeit often dim and corrupted, the mims bore only blackness. "It appears the essence of humanity in the mims is not absent, but hidden—contained."

"I do not understand."

"Nor do I," Adiya admitted. "However, I have seen the touch of restoration set this contained essence free—in Trenton."

244

"Trenton?" Eitan paced away from her.

Trenton had opposed Chris Davis, throughout his investigation of CeSiR. He attempted to kill Sarah McIntyre in a house fire. He trumped up charges against Chris, shot Charles, kidnapped Ima, and only the Creator knew what other atrocities this mim, paired with Tudur, had committed. It seemed as though Adiya had brought Eitan the most difficult news of a very troubling day.

Eitan turned and marched back to Adiya. Fire burned in his eyes. "Talk to me. Help me understand."

She carefully relayed the events at the trailer. When she mentioned that Trenton's transformation had occurred at the touch of Ima, he returned to his seat on the wall.

"You are certain this transformation of Trenton occurred with her touch and not as a result of the judgment?" he asked.

Adiya tilted her head and looked at her captain. "Judgment?"

Eitan glanced across the grounds of CeSiR. In a voice barely above a whisper, he said, "I will fill you in later." He returned his gaze to her. "It was her touch?"

Warmth flooded Adiya's being as she recalled her encounter with the Savior at the farmhouse. *Protect the Restoration.* She relayed her instructions and how she only fully understood once Ima had released Trenton.

"You are truly blessed, Adiya." Eitan's face grew serious. "We cannot allow Mael to learn of this. He will seek to destroy her. His plans are thwarted and he now despises the mims." Eitan stood and picked up his shield. "The golden demon, Anput, she is with Mael. Does she know?"

"She is aware of Ima's redemption and she was present when Trenton was released." She went on to tell him of the explosion and shards of light. "Anput left amid the shrapnel. I know not how much she understood."

Eitan's scowled and nodded. "I fear she knows enough. I saw Anput arrive, shortly after the judgment. It was not long after her arrival that most of the demons departed."

Adiya's knees weakened and her shield grew heavy. "Which direction did they go?"

"West," said Eitan. He turned and stared along the river, in the direction of Marshall. "Does Anput know where Ima is now?"

Adiya shook her head. "No, I do not believe so. But she does know where the Sherwoods live."

Eitan gave a sharp whistle and several warriors headed in their direction.

He turned back to Adiya. "This battle is won. The agents here will be fine. But at some point, Ima will return to the farmhouse. We need to protect her from Mael."

Eitan turned to the other warriors. "I fear the war is not yet finished."

~~~~~~~~~~

Mael deployed his forces to secure the Sherwoods' farm. Word from the Ozarks informed him that Trenton had left with Ima, accompanied by an angelic warrior.

It was as he feared. Ima had somehow corrupted Trenton. He was now a liability, just like the twelve-year-old menace.

Mael and Anput dove toward a scrubby little junkyard. According to Anput, there were two demons here who had an axe to grind with both Adiya and Ima.

Dogs barked somewhere in the small shack of a building.

Mael roared back. After the events at CeSiR, he would like nothing more than to grab one of the mongrels and rip them limb from limb.

The barking stopped and two demons scurried into the dirt parking lot.

They dropped to their knees when they saw Mael. Smarter than he expected of the locals.

He and Anput landed and stood before the kneeling demons.

One of the demons, a lizard-faced demon of lust, glanced up at Anput and grinned.

Mael kicked him.

246

He flipped backward, recovered, and then scrambled back to his much larger friend. "My apologies, my liege."

"I do not want your apologies." Mael grabbed the demon by the throat and hoisted him off the ground. "I want your service."

"Anything." The word squeezed through his constricted throat.

"Rise." Mael addressed the larger demon of rage. He tossed the squirming lizard next to the bull-like demon. "A young girl named Ima, Anput tells me you have encountered her." Mael leaned over the two demons. "I want her destroyed."

"It would be our pleasure." The bullish demon's voice growled deep and hot sulfur steamed from his nostrils. "We have unfinished business, her guardian and I."

Mael grinned. Nothing like being bested by a feminine warrior to stir the inner rage. "Yes, I suppose you do," said Mael. The demon's rage would be needed. The enemy would seek to protect this mim abomination. She stood as yet another meddlesome reminder of the Creator's sovereign will. A will to show mercy to everyone, except Mael and his fellow fallen ones.

The lizard demon's gaze drifted back to Anput. His tongue flicked from side to side. "Perhaps, *you* would like to lead us to her."

"Mind your ogle, gecko," Anput said, "or I will lead you to the point of my blade."

Mael grinned. Ophois for Anput, it seemed like a good trade. He ignored the lizard's insolence and addressed the demon of rage. "I have a cohort of my best warriors at the home where she is staying. However, there is a chance that she is at the hospital in Marshall. Go to the hospital and wait for her to emerge."

He drew his sword and let its point rest against the nose of the lizard. "Do not enter the hospital. You will tip off the enemy."

The demon pulled his head back and nodded.

Mael looked back to the bull-like demon. "If you would like your revenge, you will have half an hour while they drive to the farm." He sheathed his sword. "If they arrive at the house, you have failed." He and Anput rose into the sky.

"She will not reach the farm," the demon of rage said. "You have my word."

~~~~~~~~~~~

Cadfael and a small contingent of demonic warriors had retreated to a small brick hole-in-the-wall dive. The fragrance of stale alcohol soothed him. So few of his numbers had survived the battle in Excelsior Springs. They had succeeded in keeping the angelic host of the west from interfering at CeSiR.

Could success be defined by such a great reduction in numbers? They had taken down many angelic warriors, but not nearly the casualties they sustained.

At the bar, two demons squealed with delight when a life-hardened woman decked a drunken sailor with no sea to sail. From the expletives streaming from the woman, his hands had apparently wandered ashore.

Cadfael set his battle-axe on the bar counter and turned his back to the liquor lined wall. Throughout the building the revelry of the demons infuriated him. Nothing worth celebrating had happened this day. He snorted in disapproval. No one cared. They paid him no attention.

A small messenger stepped into the building and looked around. He breathed a sigh of relief when he spotted Cadfael. The non-descript demon strolled to the counter. Cadfael recalled seeing this demon at CeSiR, but he did not remember his name. Nor did he care.

"Sir." The demon's voice shook. Cadfael's minotaur-like appearance often had that effect. "Mael has a mission for your forces."

Cadfael grabbed the demon by the jaw and yelled into his face. "Look around you! Do you see forces? This is all that remains after Mael's last mission. What would he have for us now? Perhaps a hospital, or maybe a megachurch?"

The demon did not struggle against his grip or plead for mercy. He simply lowered his eyes and muffled the words, "I am sorry for your losses, sir." He showed sincerity and respect for those vanquished, more than their own comrades who had fought at their sides.

He released the demon and apologized for his mood. "It has not been a joyful day. Were we able to hold CeSiR?" he asked the messenger.

"No, sir. The enemy has displaced our forces at the facility." The demon fell silent. He appeared stunned, somehow lost in the recollection of the day's events.

"Why does Mael need our assistance?" Cadfael asked. "What of his forces? Surely, the heavenly host could not have wiped them all out?"

"No, sir. In fact, the battle proceeded as planned, until the Creator intervened." The demon closed his eyes and shuddered. "Mael calls it *the judgment*."

Cadfael staggered.

A hush spread across the joint.

Those who had not heard the messenger's words whispered inquiries to others.

Cadfael had despised his mission to Excelsior Springs. Now, it seemed Mael's assignment had saved him and probably what troops remained. "Where does he need us?" Cadfael asked. "We will do what we can."

Warriors began to pick up their shields and weapons.

The messenger told him of the farmhouse and the events surrounding Ima's redemption. "Mael wants her destroyed."

Cadfael picked up his battle-axe and snorted.

He had never liked the pathetic mim.

~~~~~~~~~~~

Ima rolled down her window on the drive back to the farmhouse. The warm afternoon breeze swirled around her. Curly blond locks whipped across her nose. She giggled and stuck her hand out the window. The air rushing past the car sucked her hand upward. She tilted the hand and it swept down behind the rearview mirror. She giggled again.

Mama's eyes stared into the road ahead of them. Her lips pursed together. Was she worried about Papa? Did she know?

The momentary joy of the mid-spring breeze fled out the window. Ima wouldn't see Papa again. She knew it. He knew it. And though she hadn't been in the room with them, Mama seemed to know it too.

Outside the car, lush green grass, fields, and the occasional tree blurred past. Evidence of new life revitalized by the same rains that washed Uncle M out of her life, only a week earlier. So much had happened in one short week. She'd lost the one person she loved like family, only to discover an even truer definition of family—of love.

A small passing lake reflected the bright blue sky. Then some houses and another small lake streaked past. The afternoon sun shone bright in her face causing her to squint.

Ever observant and caring, Mama reached across the dash and flipped down a semi-transparent visor. The visor darkened as sunlight fell on it.

Mama whipped her hand back to the steering wheel.

Ima's body lurched toward the dash, as her seatbelt dug into her shoulder. She dropped her gaze from the visor to see a pair of flashing lights suspended above the road.

"That was close," Mama said. "I don't recall the last time I had to wait for a train here."

A loud whistle announced an approaching train.

The tracks cut across the road at a wide angle. The train approached, more from in front of them than from the side. She watched the large machine in the distance and recalled hiding beside the tracks a week earlier—the smell of the breeze as the train rumbled past her. That train had saved her from the drunken man.

The engine roared closer.

Once again, her head lurched. This time instead of being thrown toward the dash, it smacked the back of her seat.

"What on earth?" Mama's eyes snapped to the rearview mirror.

The sound of tires squealing mixed with plastic and metal crinkling.

Ima spun her gaze to the back window.

A steel-grey turn-of-the-century muscle car pushed against their back bumper.

She recognized the car. The driver bore a wide grin. The car and its driver seemed to have jumped right out of her thoughts. Full circle in a week.

Mama's sedan creaked and edged toward the tracks. "No!" Mama's leg shook as she pressed down on the brake.

The train engine loomed large in front of them. Its whistle now screamed at them not to get any closer.

~~~~~~~~~~

Adiya accompanied Eitan to the farmhouse. They brought a dozen of Eitan's best warriors, some of whom had served with Adiya in Arrow Springs. They descended on the house. Had the enemy yet reached the property? They would know soon enough.

The Sherwoods' Impala was not in the drive. At least if the enemy had beat them to the house, Ima was not there. Eldwyn was a capable warrior, but Mael could have hundreds of his remaining troops with him. Too many for a lone angel to fend off. Perhaps, too many for a dozen of Eitan's best to fend off.

Eitan motioned to Yora. "Take two warriors and ensure the barn is clear, then join us at the house."

Yora nodded and the three broke formation.

"The rest of you form a hedge around the house." He looked to Adiya. "Adiya and I will check the house."

Honor swelled within Adiya. She trusted Eitan completely. There were no angels on the hemisphere with whom she would rather enter battle. But he now placed his trust in her. If the enemy laid in wait, they would have to fight back-to-back until the others intervened. She nodded her acceptance and they

251

dove toward the house. The other nine warriors would ensure nothing entered or exited the house without a fight.

"You know the house," Eitan said. "How should we proceed?"

They unsheathed their swords. Both weapons blazed like fire.

"There is an attic." It was where she had awaited Cadfael's warriors when they attacked from above. "If they are here, waiting for us, they would likely expect us to attack from above." She pointed to an old cellar door. "How about we start underground?"

He nodded and they dove for the door.

~~~~~~~~~~~

Eldwyn somersaulted from the rear seat of the Impala. With his staff he smacked the elderly woman's leg.

Her foot fell from the brake.

The car lurched forward, Ima now sat right in line with the tracks.

He jabbed the accelerator with his staff.

With no other alternative, Patricia caught on. She slammed her foot to the pedal.

The car shot forward.

The train bore down on them.

Eldwyn jump-flipped out of the car. He leapt to the back bumper and gave the car a shove.

The train's horn wailed. A collision was now unavoidable.

The powerful locomotive connected with the back corner of the Impala. Patricia screamed. The unforgiving steel of the locomotive ripped the rear bumper clean off the car.

As the train passed through Eldwyn, gut-wrenching sounds tore through him—sheering steel, shattering glass, and the snapping of plastic.

The motion of the train passing through Eldwyn proved disorienting. He stepped back and out of the train's path. To his right a ball of crumpled automotive still bounced and rolled. No way had anyone lived through that collision.

In the road three demons lay stunned at the turn of events. They had clearly been pushing the car to help it overcome Patricia's brakes. When the sedan shot forward, so too had the muscle car.

A lizard-like demon shook his head, looked at the mash of metal, and began laughing.

Eldwyn needed to check on Ima and Patricia before these three regathered their wits. He hopped over the train and breathed a sigh of relief to see the Impala nearly a quarter of a mile down the road. Aside from a missing bumper, it seemed unfazed.

~~~~~~~~~~

Adiya followed Eitan into the cellar of the farmhouse. The small room was only roughly finished, unlike the adjacent game room. The most dangerous thing present was some thoroughly aged, home-canned vegetables. The only light in the room came from sheets of light that streamed through cracks in the large wooden exterior door. Shelves lined the walls, covered with canned goods. Clearly, the couple had not been able to keep up with Patricia's zealous gardening. No doubt, there had been a day when their family had no issue consuming all the food.

"Shall we see if there is more excitement above?" Eitan asked.

"If we go up over here—" Adiya led him into the game room. "—we should find ourselves in a small hallway off the dining room." Better concealed than coming up in the middle of the dining room.

They rose into an empty hall, which led to an empty dining room, and ultimately an empty house.

They had arrived before the enemy. This would allow them the advantage of holding the ground rather than taking it. None of that mattered, if Ima did not arrive safely. What if the enemy never planned to attack here? Would they try to take her at the hospital? No. Too protected. On the road somewhere? Perhaps.

Yora appeared through a wall in the living room. He glanced around the room, until he spotted Eitan. "Sir," Yora said. "You will want to see this." He disappeared, back to his post outside the house.

Adiya followed Eitan to the side of the house, where Yora had departed.

For a time, no one said a word. They gazed across a field to the edge of the property. Hundreds of demons flowed into the field.

As the hedge of angelic warriors came into view, the demons began to flow into a much larger circle surrounding the farmhouse. The formation seemed to arise more out of fear of approaching the warriors than strategic leadership. In fact, no leadership was visible, including Mael.

Eitan held up his left hand. "Hold your positions." His sword was back in its sheath, but his hand rested on the hilt. "Wait for them to make a move."

Without trying to count the enemy, Adiya put the disparity at thirty-to-one. Not insurmountable odds, but a serious battle to be sure.

"Remember," Eitan continued, "the protection of the mim-child, Ima, is our primary objective. Hold your positions and grant entrance to no servant of evil." He motioned for Adiya to join him on the roof.

From the roof, they were able to survey the battle alignment. The demons formed a single-file circle shoulder-to-shoulder encompassing the house. Their position, nearly a hundred yards from the angels, kept them safe, for the moment.

Only feet from the house, each angelic warrior stood with sword and shield at the ready—unmoving, alert, and willing to sacrifice for the safety of their assignment.

In contrast, the circle of demons buzzed listless. They were present out of fear rather than commitment, and they lacked leadership.

To the west, Adiya spotted a small contingent of demons marching to join those already gathered. This group held a structured formation. As they approached, she recognized the lead demon. She pointed toward the group. "More approach."

Eitan turned and looked. "Cadfael. He is one of Mael's minor princes. I suspect he is the reason we saw no reinforcements this morning from Ladan."

Cadfael and his troop marched right through the outer circle of demons. They halted half way between the circle and the angelic warriors surrounding the house. "Mighty Eitan," Cadfael said, "have you stooped so low as to be protecting our creations?"

Eitan inhaled a deep breath. "This mouthy whelp is going to ignite a battle. Something I would prefer to avoid unless necessary." He walked toward the edge of the house, ready to address Cadfael.

"Captain," called Yora.

Adiya turned to the east. Two unmistakable demons approached. "Sir," Adiya said. "Mael and Anput."

Eitan turned and saw Mael, glanced back at Cadfael, and then back to Mael. He shook his head.

"I will deal with Cadfael," Adiya said.

"Thank you," Eitan said. "They must not enter the house. Attack or defend as you see fit. Stay alert for Ima." He strode to the east side of the house and dropped off the side.

Adiya did likewise, in front of Cadfael and his troop.

~~~~~~~~~~

Eitan stood between Yora and Gida. The circle of demons parted once again and allowed Mael and Anput to approach the home.

Eitan patted Yora on the shoulder. "Head to the roof and keep watch."

"Yes, sir."

"Keep an eye on Cadfael and Adiya. She will have her hands full with the demon prince." Eitan took a couple steps away from the hedge of warriors and turned back to Yora. "More than anything keep watch for the Sherwoods' sedan. The survival of Ima is our sole objective."

"Understood." Yora rose into the air and took up watch on the roof. His arrow shone bright, even in the afternoon sun.

Eitan turned his attention back to Mael. This could get ugly quick. "You have no business here. Have you not lost enough of your forces today?"

Mael held up his hand and Anput stopped, as he continued to approach Eitan. "On the contrary. It is we who have business here, not you. The old couple have aided and abetted a wanted criminal. It is all over the news. We simply seek to see her brought to justice."

Justice. It was amazing the demon prince had not gagged on the word as it proceeded from his throat. "You want revenge. Once again the true Creator has spoken and your attempt to usurp His authority is only magnified in his grace shone to this young one." Demons despised humans for the grace God showed to them. Perhaps none more than this once great leader within the angelic ranks. Mael and Eitan had once served and worshipped side-by-side. Now Mael stood before him a desperate demon grasping for some semblance of control over his destiny.

"Neither of us are leaving," Mael said. "You know that as well as I. Before the sun sets, this farm will reek of sulfur and iron." He stabbed the point of his lightning-blue sword in the dirt. "You know there will be no winner, if the two of us face off. I shall make you a deal."

A deal of deception. Humans were prone to falling for such schemes. Surely, Mael knew that no angel would trust a dealer of lies.

"Hear me out," Mael said. "We each choose a warrior to battle for our side. Perhaps Anput against Adiya. Winner takes Ima." Mael snorted and waggled his buffalo-like horns. "Why should all of us perish for one child?"

Eitan pulled his fiery sword from its sheath and swirled it in front of him. "Even if I trusted you to keep any such bargain—" He had no doubt in Adiya's skill to defeat Anput in battle. "—Ima belongs to no one. I cannot offer her as a prize for some coliseum game. Nor can you."

Mael roared at Eitan. "I created her! She is mine to do with as I will." He rushed toward Eitan and struck downward with his blade.

Eitan parried the ferocious strike. As he held the locked sword above his head, he responded, "You created nothing, Mael. You may have facilitated the creation of the mims. But you used the materials of the Creator. Have you lied to so many that you now believe your own lies?" He smacked Mael in the chest with his shield.

Mael staggered backward. "Destroy them!"

The circle of demons collapsed on the Angelic hedge.

Metal clashed on metal. Roars, curses, and prayers mixed together in a cacophonous song of battle.

~~~~~~~~~~

Cadfael's battle axe arced through the air at Adiya. She had barely drawn her weapon when the roar of attack erupted from the eastern side of the house. She twirled to the side, as the blur of an axe glanced off her shield. She continued the spin until her sword connected with the back side of Cadfael's leg.

He cursed and smacked her helmet with the butt of his axe.

Pain spiraled inside her head. Fireflies danced in her vision. How had she let herself be caught off guard? The beast before her was as dangerous as any she had ever faced.

An arrow swished past her ear. She glanced to see a demon—sword raised ready to take her head—vanish into the Abyss.

Instinctively, she dropped to a knee to avoid the sword, now just an imprint in her memory. She swung her gaze to the roof of the house, tracing the flight-vector of the arrow.

Yora nodded. His skill with the bow went unmatched.

She returned her attention to the primary threat. Minotaur eyes bore into her own. Sulfur streamed from his nostril, matching the flow from his leg.

The next attack came in a horizontal figure-eight swing of the battle axe.

She leapt into the air as the axe turned to make its return swipe. She pushed her left foot off of his powerful forearm and somersaulted over his head. As she passed, she smacked his nose with the edge of her shield.

A loud crack, like that of a tree limb, resonated from the blow. Had her shield cracked?

She landed in a crouch and a warrior from Cadfael's crew lunged at her.

She diverted the blow with her shield arm. Her shield was intact. The crack had been Cadfael's bull-like nose. She spun to see the demon prince flailing at blurred enemies. His axe connected with the demon she had just parried. The demon vanished in a putrid vapor.

The remaining demons backed away, fearful of their master's wayward strikes.

She had broken his nose. He could no longer see, either from the pain or the pressure on his eyes. The reason mattered not. This was her chance to strike.

His back to her, she swung with her full might at the gap between his breastplate and arm.

Her aim was true.

Her power was lacking.

His arm clamped down on the blade cutting into his flesh. He spun, ripping the sword from her grasp. A hapless swing of the battle axe sent her scrambling out of his range.

She was weaponless.

~~~~~~~~~~

Eitan engaged Mael. Their strength and skill evenly matched. Each swing of the sword easily parried by the other. Each lunge countered. The battle for the farmhouse unfolded like a master chess match.

Gida and Alex fought on either side of Eitan. Miguel and Teman were stationed to the west of the house. This meant they were fighting alongside Adiya. Both were valiant warriors. Eitan had little concern that the other warriors would be bested by the demon horde, despite the unfavorable odds.

Cadfael and Mael on the other hand posed a real threat. Demon princes seldom took part in their own battles. But, when they did so, it always proved reason for concern.

Between attack and counter-attack, Mael would glance from side to side. No doubt keeping tabs on the progress of his minions.

The sounds of battle rang out on all sides—the clash of weapons, warriors summoning strength, counters with fists, feet, or shields. Clangs, grunts, and thumps.

Mael scowled at a twang from the roof of the house.

Yora's white-missile arrows pierced the heavy afternoon air.

Poof. Another demon vanished in a sulfurous vapor. The arrow had found its mark.

Clang-grunt-thump.

Mael roared and charged Eitan.

Eitan kept his stance broad and balanced. He only rotated slightly as the massive cape-buffalo rushed past like a bull with a matador. A deadly bull. Eitan redirected a two-handed slash with his cross-embossed silver shield.

Twang-poof.

Mael glanced down the road, snarled, and circled several feet from Eitan. He awaited Ima's arrival.

Eitan could only hope that the numbers of the demonic army would dwindle before Ima's return to the farm. The Spirit was creating a sense of urgency around the battle. Eitan could only assume that meant the child was on her way.

Grunt-thump-thump-clang.

To Eitan's left, Alex stepped, swung, decapitated a small demon, then spun his sword one-eighty and stabbed behind him. A snarling demon, saber raised to strike, vanished.

Twang-clink. An arrow fell harmlessly, blocked by Mael's lightning-quick sword. The prince swore and rose straight into the air.

Eitan matched his ascent, keeping between Mael and Yora. The demon prince had tired of the pesky archer.

"You cannot match my power," Mael said.

The insult deflected off of Eitan, as harmless as the arrow off of Mael's sword. Eitan's strength and power were irrelevant. He knew for whom he fought.

Mael sheathed his sword and grinned at Eitan. His desolate gaze bore into Eitan, challenging him to make a move. He inhaled a deep breath, pulled back his shoulders, and raised his chin to the sky. He began muttering words barely audible. Ancient words, offensive, and long forsaken by Eitan. A chant of sorts.

Mael raised his hands, claws outstretched. At first he kneaded the air like an invisible loaf of bread. Soon a grey mist began to stream from his hands into the heavens above them.

Eitan had seen this before. In the ancient land of Uz. When Mael destroyed the family of Job with a great wind.

The sky grew darker blotting out the sunlight.

Clang-grunt—

The sounds of battle slowed as all became spectators of Mael's performance.

Clouds swirled only hundreds of feet above the farm. Lightning jumped from one side of the heavenly maelstrom to the other. Crackle. Mael's eyes turned to the rooftop of the house, where Yora stood like a Christmas-tree-angel waiting to be lit up.

Eitan caught a glimpse of motion. "Do you think we are that easily impressed?" He needed to keep Mael distracted. Buy some time. "We were present when He separated the firmament from the seas. Surely, you do not expect to strike fear with your little temper tantrum."

Mael's body shook with anger and the tempest grew. One of them would blow soon.

~~~~~~~~~~

Stale air blew in Ima's face. Since the incident at the tracks, she'd closed her window. The thought of sticking her hand outside now seemed reckless.

Mama hadn't said a word since the encounter. Yet her lips moved in wordless silence. Were they prayers for their safety or for the wellbeing of Papa? The sweetest woman Ima had ever met suffered so much and loved even more.

The car slowed and Mama's shaky hands directed them northward toward the farm. Rather than accelerating away from the corner. She rolled the car to a stop. They sat in the middle of the lane. Mama stared out the windshield.

"What is that?" Ima asked. The sky ahead roiled with flickers of lightning set against swirling clouds.

Mama's voice quivered. "I—I've never seen anything like it."

Ima forced her eyes away from the sight to look at Mama. The woman's face, normally wrinkled and a pasty pink, looked pale and mintish-green.

"It looks like it's right over the farm," Mama said.

Anger flooded Ima's brain. Her neck itched and her nose burned. How much more trouble could she possibly cause one couple? She couldn't explain what she saw. Only that she was the reason. Mama believed there were unseen powers that worked in the world, both for good and evil. The previous week had solidified this belief for Ima.

"Dear Jesus, please protect us," prayed Mama. The car began to creep toward the phenomenon.

Ima's stomach tried to implode as they crossed the railroad tracks—this time without ordeal. Soon, a line of trees gave way to a view of the farmhouse. Mama was correct. The swirl of clouds centered above the home.

"Oh, my," Mama said.

A mini tornado reached down and licked their roof.

~~~~~~~~~~

Eldwyn rode with his head sticking through the roof of the Impala. A tempest raged ahead of them. Mael had to be at the farm. While the attack at the tracks came as a bit of a surprise, a battle at the farm seemed inevitable.

At this distance, the identity of the angels and demons engaged in battle was impossible to determine, with the exception of the two colossal warriors facing off in the yard. Eitan and his band of warriors had made it to the farm.

Skirmishes flared all around the home. Yet the angels appeared to maintain a hedge around the house. The sooner Ima and Patricia made it inside the easier they would be to protect.

A twister reached down and swept the roof of the home. Mael's target never saw it coming. The miniature tornado swept up an angel and flung him across the sky.

The car approached the melee.

The angel from the roof turned out to be Yora. No doubt, Mael had tired of the marksman picking off his warriors. Yora flailed through the air like a ragdoll, until the winds dropped him in the mud next to a handful of cows. Instead of grazing in the green of the field, the spooked cows lay huddled next to the barn.

Moments after landing, Yora shook off the attack, climbed to the roof of the barn, nocked an arrow, and dropped a demon approaching the corner of the home.

The attack on Yora had drawn the attention of the horde. The sedan neared the fracas unnoticed.

Eitan's knowing gaze connected with Eldwyn, then he charged Mael and struck the demon's jagged shield with his fiery sword. He rolled left to draw the demon's attention away from the road. The selfless action left his left leg open to a counter. Mael capitalized. His sword drew blood as it swept the leg. Eitan grimaced and dropped to a defensive crouch.

Patricia and Ima had nearly passed the perimeter of demons before a nondescript minion raised awareness of their presence.

"Lord, Mael! The—"

Alex spun with his sword and removed the screaming head from the demon's body.

Eldwyn rose to a standing position atop the sedan prepared to fend off any attackers who heard the alert.

Mael switched his sword to his off hand and pointed it at the kneeling Eitan. He raised his right hand toward the sky and curled his claws into a fist.

The lightning stopped hopping across the clouds. The mass of supernatural-swirling-darkness began to glow an electric blue.

"Dear Lord, protect us." The aroma of sweet cedar rose from the car beneath him.

Mael's raised fist swung toward the sedan.

The sky exploded with a thunderous blast.

Eldwyn lifted his staff over his head. The end of the staff glowed with fire.

Blue lightning burst from the clouds. The air buzzed as electricity arced toward the car. Bluish energy flowed into the flaming staff. It began to glow a snow-pure white.

Eldwyn held on until his hands began to burn. When he could hold it no longer, he swung the staff toward Mael.

The demon prince's eyes grew large and defiant.

The end of Eldwyn's staff splintered as purified energy jumped the gap from the car to Mael. The bolt knocked Mael to the ground. White arcs of lightning traced their way across the surface of his obsidian armor. The demon prince squirmed in the heat of the blast, but his armor kept the blast from destroying him.

Several other demons, in the vicinity of the Impala, were fried like bacon, before vanishing to the Abyss.

With the energy drained from the sky, the sun began to burn through the thinning clouds. Mael's light show had only served to clear a path to the house.

Eldwyn guided Ima and Patricia into the home.

"That was weird," Ima said.

"Indeed," Eldwyn responded, unheard. He exhaled in momentary relief.

~~~~~~~~~~~

Cadfael, the Minotaur-like demon, still staggered and shook his head. Meanwhile, Adiya had to fend off several attempts by lesser demons to capitalize on her mistake. Cadfael had flung her sword hundreds of yards from the battle.

Miguel and Teman closed to her side when they realized what had happened.

Clang, swoosh, thump. She managed to ward off another attack with her shield and even landed a swift foot to the demon's rear end.

"Adiya," called Teman.

She turned her attention to the angelic warrior. He looked at her while continuing to fence with a demon. His sword skills were impressive. He held up a short-sword in his off-hand. She smiled and nodded gratefully. With a flick of his wrist, the sword flew hilt first, right to her. Though shorter than her normal weapon, she no longer felt like a cat in a dog-fight.

The mysterious clouds gone, the battle began to surge once again. Sheer numbers made the task of the angelic warriors perilous.

Around the house, car doors slammed.

Ima had arrived.

A dilemma pressed at Adiya. She longed to be with Ima—to ensure her safety from any intruders that fought their way into the house. Yet she needed to trust her fellow warriors. A wall of protection only served to protect if there were no gaps.

Only one demon presented a greater threat to Ima than Cadfael, and Eitan provided a much greater resistance than Adiya could.

She eyed the Minotaur. Though green slime continued to seep from his nose, his movements had become more intentional. His eyes began to focus, and so did his rage—directly on Adiya.

~~~~~~~~~~~

CHAPTER SEVENTEEN

The latching of the door brought a sense of peace for Patricia. The kind of peace you'd experience when the winds and waves calmed, while at sea. Was the storm over, or were they now in the eye of the hurricane?

She stretched her fingers. They ached from the death-grip she'd maintained for the last several minutes. The house was quiet. They had arrived unscathed. Well, except the bumper of the Impala.

The quiet stillness in the home screamed of an urgency she could not understand. So what if Ima was one of these mims from CeSiR Tech. She was still just a child, nearly a young woman.

Charles seemed to think the authorities would try to hunt her down—to lock her up. Or worse, to study her. She glanced down at the delft-blue eyes staring up at her. How could anyone see the child as anything but a human being? Regardless of how she came into the world.

Despite her love for Ima, she knew Charles was probably right. She had seen the depravity of humanity many times in her years. Why would this be any different?

"Well," Mama said. "I guess we got some preparation to do before we leave." How could she let this child go out on her own? So young. Too young. And she—was too old. Too old to run from a manhunt. What about Charles? *Till death do us part.* The covenant she had made to him decades ago would never be broken. Not in the throes of Alzheimer's, not ever.

"Come on, child. Let's get going." She led Ima up the stairs to her room.

Charles—her mind refused to acknowledge the truth crouching in her heart.

In Ima's room, Patricia sat on the bed and patted the space next to her.

Ima sat and put her arm around Patricia.

"Ima, I need to apologize for something."

The girl looked up at her with round rosy cheeks. Fear flickered in her narrowed eyes.

"When you first arrived," Patricia said, "I went through your backpack." The only privacy the girl had likely ever possessed, and she violated it. "I should have asked your permission. I am truly sorry."

The girl's shoulders sank a couple inches. "That's okay, Mama. I don't mind."

"Thank you, child. I still shouldn't have done it." She reached her aging arm across the girl's shoulders and gave a squeeze. "I have to admit, it created more questions than it answered. Some of the items you carried seemed, well, puzzling."

She stood, walked to the corner of the room, and retrieved the backpack. She sat back down on the bed and pulled out a box. An attractive woman with jet-black hair smiled up from the box.

She couldn't picture Ima with black hair. And thus, it made perfect sense. With the world looking for a twelve-year-old blonde, having black hair would remove attention. Patricia tapped the box. "I think this is a good idea. If you'd like, I can help you."

The girl nodded.

Patricia laid the backpack on the bed. "First, let's get this packed."

They removed Ima's clothes from the dresser and carefully packed them into the backpack. "This is beautiful," Patricia said. She held up a white dress with blue forget-me-nots scattered at the waist.

Ima turned away and stared out the window. She sniffled for a few moments, before returning her attention to the backpack. It didn't seem fair. The child had experienced such tragedy and pain in her brief life.

Mama felt as if she was pushing this little bird out of the nest and into the cruel jungle below.

"Do you have enough money?" Mama asked. She already knew the answer. The backpack contained nearly ten-thousand dollars. One more target drawn on the back of the sweet little child.

"I think so."

There were so many life lessons Mama wanted to impart to Ima. The drive to the bus station would necessitate a download of information. How do you teach a child the intricacies of surviving in a world she's never seen?

Mama picked up the box of hair color. "Well, let's see what we can do with this."

~~~~~~~~~~

Eldwyn followed Ima and Patricia to the bathroom. Patricia patiently explained the process of washing and dyeing Ima's hair. She even went to the trouble of dyeing the hair brown first before using the black dye, which Ima said Uncle M had bought her.

By the time they finished dying the girl's hair, the bathroom floor was covered with water, and spots of black and brown dye. Patricia placed a chair in the middle of the room and fetched a pair of scissors. "May as well go all the way," she said. "You will need to dye it every now and then to keep your beautiful blonde roots from showing through."

Ima sat in the chair and Patricia wrapped another towel around the child's neck.

Eldwyn decided to take a quick survey of the battle outside. When the time came for the women to leave, he needed to know what to expect.

~~~~~~~~~~

The battle raged on. Despite her best efforts and some serious blows against the much larger Cadfael, Adiya found herself backed against the white, wood siding of the old farmhouse.

With Yora and his bow serving as a bulwark atop the house, the demons had been tentative to crowd too close. But now, he launched his assault from the barn roof. This only served to drive the battle into a half-moon shape around the house, away from the barn.

A battle axe arced toward her left shoulder.

She swiveled, bringing her shield to the left to deflect the blow. The axe grazed her wing, but not enough to cause any real damage.

How much longer could they keep the demons out? Even with half the enemy destroyed, a couple hundred still remained. The longer the battle waged, more angels would find their place beside the throne of the Creator.

Cadfael spun the axe and swiped at her.

Adiya swiveled again—into the stab of a lesser demon. His saber pierced the lower left corner of her breastplate.

Blood seeped from the opening in her armor.

Before the demon could retreat to celebrate. She stabbed the pitiful wretch with Teman's short-sword and kicked him into the Abyss.

Pain emanated like a sunburst from the stab wound. It would not be fatal, but the pain slowed her mobility.

Cadfael seized the opportunity. With one hand next to the blade of his axe and the other on the handle, he crushed the shaft of the weapon into Adiya's chest.

She buckled backwards—into the house. Stars danced through her head. The shot from Cadfael had shifted her breastplate. Jagged silver, where the demon pierced her armor, ripped into her side. In decades she had not felt such pain.

Her head rested on the floor. Through flickering stars, she stared across white tile to a white porcelain sink. She was in the downstairs bathroom.

"Who do you think you are to challenge me?" The voice was nasally, but deep.

Her body twisted as a soot-black armored foot drove into her chest.

Cadfael towered over her. He pressed downward.

She tried to resist. Tried to avoid being pressed through the floor.

He gave a powerful shove and she dropped though floorboard, joists, and into a crawl space that ran under that portion of the home. A couple dead rodents rotted in the dirt. Above her, dusty spider webs laced the floor joists.

Cadfael's foot disappeared back into the bathroom. The demon prince was in the house with Ima.

A ram's horn echoed through the crawlspace. Rodent bones rattled, as the ground shuttered. Was this another of Mael's manipulations? An earthquake perhaps?

Somewhere above her, Cadfael swore.

Bad news for him meant good news for her. More importantly, for Ima.

Cadfael barked out orders. His voice now came from beyond the home's foundation. He had returned to the yard outside.

A hand reached through the floorboards, pale and elderly looking. She grabbed hold and the vice-like grip of Eldwyn lifted her back to the bathroom.

"A scuffle, I heard. So sorry not to arrive sooner." His eyes dropped to her side, as he helped her to her feet. A smear of blood swept across her armor.

"It is not as bad as it looks." She unstrapped the breastplate and pulled it over her head. Her white tunic had a large slit from the jagged metal. Unlike a human, she would heal in a few days, especially in the presence of praise and worship offered to the Creator. In the meantime, she reached down and sliced off a strip of cloth from the hem of her tunic.

Careful not to inflict more pain than necessary, she wrapped the bandage around her midsection.

Eldwyn stepped behind her and took the ends of the makeshift tourniquet.

She felt the strip tighten. He was being cautious. "Tighter," she said. She clenched her teeth. "Tighter."

Finally, she nodded.

He tied off the ends of the cloth.

She picked up her shield which had landed beside the toilet. She pointed to the wall. "Something is up out there." They both stepped through the wall.

A mighty warrior stood before her. She barely came to his shoulders. He pointed a sword at her and grinned.

~~~~~~~~~~~

Mama showed Ima her new hairdo in a hand-held mirror. A black haired bob stared back at her. Gone were the blond curls brushing her shoulders.

Mama had so much insight. Taking her hair from blonde to brown to black made her hair look so natural. She kind of liked the new look. A fresh start, a new person, a new life. An unknown life. Once again, her life led away from those she cared about, though there hadn't been many.

Mama gave her a crash course in the subtleties of applying makeup. "If they're looking for a blonde twelve-year-old then we'll give them a black haired sixteen-year-old." Mama stepped in front of Ima and took her shoulders in her hands. She looked Ima in the eyes. "You look incredible." She shook her head. "No. You are incredible."

Ima's knees bounced and warmth rose from her stomach to her chest. She'd never felt more loved. And Mama even knew she was a mim.

Mama leaned back, pursed her lips, and leaned her head left, then right. "We're not quite done." She brushed Ima's eyebrows with her finger. "They're just too light for the black to be believable." She slid out a drawer from under the sink. After pushing stuff around, she shook her head. "I'm gonna have to run downstairs to my bathroom. I have a spoolie and some cosmetic Q-Tips we can use to darken those a bit."

270

Ima grinned. "You are so sweet, Mama." Would she be able to make herself look half as good as Mama had? Mama said she shouldn't need to recolor for about a month. With everything that happened in the last week, Ima couldn't even think where she'd be in four times that long.

Mama hurried out of the bathroom.

~~~~~~~~~~

Ladan, a captain of the host from Denver, stood before Adiya. Behind him, a brilliant white horse pawed at the ground. From the blood and sulfur residue smeared across the horse's muscular legs, it had seen significant battle in recent history.

With the arrival of Ladan, and over a hundred warriors under his command, the remaining demons appeared to have clustered on the opposite side of the house. Even the beast, Cadfael, had retreated. The numbers were evened and that meant the enemy stood little chance of sustaining their assault.

Ladan explained that he and his army had engaged Cadfael's forces over the past few days and that thousands of demons had fallen in Excelsior Springs. He closed his eyes and dropped his head. When he raised it again, his eyes glistened. "We lost nearly three-quarters of our battalion as well."

The pain in Adiya's heart exceeded that in her side. The battle was the Lord's. No uncertainty existed as to the final outcome. But the enemy inflicted so much pain—on angels and humans alike.

Ladan went on to explain that they tracked Cadfael and his remaining band of misfits to the farm.

None too soon, either.

"We are glad for your support," Adiya said.

Eldwyn who had stood silently, while Ladan and Adiya talked, laid his hand on Adiya's shoulder. "The battle has now shifted. Let me join Ladan and Eitan in cleaning up the mess. You should stay with the child."

Adiya nodded. Her side screamed that she had seen enough battle for a time. As she turned to enter the house, something tapped her on the back.

Ladan held out a sword, her sword. "I believe this belongs to you?" He handed it to her. "We found it up the road a bit. You may yet find it useful."

She bowed and returned the sword to its sheath.

Her reentry into the downstairs bathroom proved much less eventful than her last venture. It even smelled pleasant now that the beast was not pressing her through the floorboards.

She made her way into the living room. Motion at the top of the stairs grabbed her attention.

Time slowed.

Patricia Sherwood walked down the open hall toward the stairway. She carried a basket full of dye-stained towels.

Awaiting her, at the top of the stairs, sat the golden demoness, Anput.

Anput snarled. "Just a few more steps, you old bat." She held her glimmering khopesh inches above the first step.

Patricia was a prayer warrior. The weapon would not inflict damage to one such as her.

Nor did it need to. If the demon succeeded in causing Patricia to lose her balance, the stairs would do the rest.

Adiya flew toward the stairs.

Anput glanced at Adiya and grinned. "Not this time, sweetie." She laid her khopesh on the top step.

Patricia stepped on the step.

Anput grabbed the handle of her weapon. "Say goodnight, biddy."

Adiya would not get there in time. She flipped Teman's short-sword from her right hand to her left. She now held the sword by the blade. With a flick of her wrist and a grunt, Adiya sent the blade soaring. "Goodnight, bi—"

The blade flew true and before she finished the expression, it made a half rotation and connected with Anput's right shoulder. The blade point pierced her golden armor. Not stopping at the armor the blade sliced through her shoulder and out the back.

Anput released a banshee scream. She buckled and rolled down the stairs.

Patricia stumbled and dropped the laundry basket. It thudded down the steps behind Anput.

Hope flickered in Anput's fiery eyes. She turned to see that only the basket greeted her at the base of the steps. The basket—and Adiya's flaming sword.

Adiya used Anput's momentum to send a deft stroke of her blade through the demon's midsection. The blow finalized the demise of Anput. A chasm opened and this time the golden demoness melted into the Abyss.

~~~~~~~~~~

Ima began to worry about Mama. The noises sounded like something, or someone, falling down the stairs.

Just when Ima was about to check on Mama, the door to the bathroom opened. Mama walked to the sink holding a small bristled brush. It reminded Ima of a smaller version of the cleaners they used in chemistry class.

Mama went to work on Ima's eyebrows. Soon, they too were dark, though naturally lighter than her hair.

Ima looked into the mirror. "I don't even recognize myself." She ran her fingers through her hair. It felt like her own hair, but shorter. A breeze wafted across the back of her neck. She tilted her head back and swept the fresh-cut locks back and forth. She giggled.

New hair, new look, new start.

They grabbed the backpack from her room and headed downstairs.

"Let's see what we can find in the kitchen to send you off with," Mama said. She dropped the backpack on the dining room table and walked to the kitchen.

Ima followed the kindest woman she'd ever known into the kitchen.

Mama pulled a soft-plastic cooler from the closet and fetched an ice pack out of the freezer. She stuffed the cooler with some sodas that she'd purchased earlier in the week. For a few moments, she stared at a row of cans still in the refrigerator. "Looks like I'm going to have a lot of these left." Her eyes glistened when she looked at Ima. "I was sure you'd be with us longer than this."

"I wish I could stay for good," Ima said. She loved Mama and Papa. If she stayed, the authorities would find her. That didn't really scare her anymore. What would happen to Mama? That scared her. Papa was shot because of her. Uncle M, too. The sooner she got away from Mama, the safer the dear woman would be.

"So do I, hon. But Papa's right, you need to get away. Somewhere they won't be looking for you."

It was only a matter of time. Soon Ima's picture and info would be plastered everywhere, along with her fellow mims.

The cooler bulged when Mama handed it to Ima. She couldn't imagine eating that much food for days. She offered Mama some money for the food.

Mama snorted a laugh and shook her head. "I don't think so." She pulled Ima into a strong hug. "And don't you dare ask to pay for anything again. You hear?" She ruffled Ima's hair and kissed her on the cheek.

They walked to the dining room, picked up the backpack and car keys, and headed out the door.

Gone were the swirling clouds, the lightning, and the winds. A beautiful sunny afternoon remained.

Mama inhaled a deep breath.

Ima sensed a peace in the air, which she had not felt for—well, ever.

~~~~~~~~~~

Adiya walked next to Ima. They approached a bus in Springfield. An elderly driver greeted Ima and asked to see her ticket. "Have a great trip young lady," the driver said.

"Thank you, sir," Ima said. She walked to a seat about halfway back.

Adiya scanned the bus for demonic occupants.

"They all got off at the last stop," the bus driver said.

Adiya turned her gaze to the grinning driver. Could it be? The eyes. She recognized those deep blue eyes. She craned her neck and studied him. "Captain?"

He laughed a deep guttural laugh.

A couple patrons, at the front of the bus, watched their driver with concerns for his sanity.

Adiya could not believe it was him. The mighty Captain Eitan driving a bus. This would be a restful trip and a great start to an uncertain journey. She walked to the empty seat next to Ima.

The child waved out the window at Patricia Sherwood. So much love, in so little time. Ima wiped at her cheeks and Patricia did the same.

The bus lurched.

Patricia waved and walked beside them.

Ima plastered her forehead to the window.

The bus picked up speed.

Ima's head rolled along the window until it pressed into her cheek. She watched Patricia fade into the distance. When she finally pulled her face from the window, she let her head drop to the seat back in front of her.

Her shoulders shook.

Adiya unfurled a wing and wrapped the child tight. The Creator chose the most precious people to provide the much needed restoration of others.

~~~~~~~~~~

EPILOGUE

Charles Sherwood awoke.

Light—beautiful light filled his eyes. Even before his eyes could adjust, he knew where he was—the throne room of God.

"Welcome, Charles, my good and faithful servant. You have done well."

He fell to the ground before the throne, out of pure reverence for the Heavenly Father. Charles felt no pain, no arthritis in his joints, and no cloudiness of his thoughts.

"Arise, my adopted child. You loved my Son and took hold of the life that He offered you." The voice of God was immense with compassion.

"But my Lord, I am just a man." He remained prostrate on the ground. "I am not worthy to stand in Your presence."

"You are my friend." This time the voice was that of the Son, the Lamb of God, seated on a second throne to the right of the Father. "Throughout our time together, you have shown mercy to others. Likewise, I will show mercy to you."

Charles rose to his knees. His gaze was drawn to the compassionate eyes of the Son.

A large book appeared before the throne and the pages turned to reveal the events of Charles' life. "In one thing you are correct," the Son said. "Your actions during life do not warrant your continued presence with your God."

Charles dropped his head and nodded his acceptance.

Another book appeared in the hands of Jesus. The Lamb opened the Book of Life. With a tear in His eye, He proclaimed, "Because you accepted my sacrifice in your stead, your name is written in the Lamb's Book of Life!"

The voice of the Father boomed with authority. "Therefore, you shall not be judged according to the works of your life." The events recorded in the first book vanished before Charles' eyes. "Because you placed your trust in the sacrifice of my Son, you shall be judged in light of His perfection and rewarded for the works you performed on His behalf."

A crown replaced the book before the throne and a rainbow composed of hundreds of identifiable colors leapt from the throne to the crown. Each color carried the proclamation of an action in Charles' life spent serving others on behalf of the Son. As each color struck the crown, gems of the clearest reds, greens, blues, purples, and yellows appeared.

With the endorsements, a roar, like that of a mighty waterfall, erupted from hundreds of thousands of the angelic host to the right and to the left of the throne.

He turned in wonder at the sound. Never had such a cheer arisen for him.

No, for God, as a result of him.

He gazed in awe at his incredible surroundings. Such beauty on earth would be unfathomable. A river of crystal flowed from the throne. A tree unlike anything he had ever seen stood on both sides of the river forming a beautiful canopy of leaves and fruit. "The tree of life," the Son said.

The Father's voice rang clear over the roar of the angels. "Soon, you shall return to the new earth and a home which I prepare for you." Silence spread across the angelic host. "That time has not yet come. For now, rest and be refreshed. There is someone very special here to show you around."

Charles turned and his heart jumped to his throat. A young woman—though here the same age as him—stood with arms open wide. He laughed and grabbed Julia into a tight embrace. He lifted his daughter and they spun, like when she was five. Her white robe swirled about them.

Laughter erupted from the throne. The Father took great joy in the reunion of two of His children.

Charles knew his time at the foot of the throne had come to an end, but he would never be separated from the presence of his Lord.

He turned and took Julia's outstretched hand. She led him along the river to a sea of crystal. They walked for what could have been days, talking and listening to a chorus of angels and believers praising and worshiping the Lord of Heaven and of Earth. The farther they walked from the throne, the larger and loftier it appeared.

"Salvation belongs to our God," Charles and Julia joined the chorus of believers from every nation, tribe, people, and tongue, "who sits on the throne, and to the Lamb."

~~~~~~~~~~~~~~~~~~~~~~

ABOUT THE AUTHOR

Robert lives in Holland, Michigan with his wife and five children. He has a B.S. in Electrical Engineering, and has taken several Master level classes in religion, including theology.

God has blessed him with the spiritual gift of teaching and a creative personality type. For over twenty years, he has brought this creativity to his professional career as a manager of software developers, and a creator of leading-edge technologies for a global high-tech electronics company in the automotive and aerospace industries.

For nearly five years, he wove creativity and a passion for teaching together as a pastor of worship, adult discipleship, and outreach. In this role, he designed and scripted several outreach events and dramas, created unique video presentations, developed discipleship curriculum, and led corporate musical worship. Since then, he has developed his public speaking skills and has had the privilege to preach at multiple churches.

Several years ago, he turned his creativity and writing toward the pursuit of teaching through story. Since then, he has refined his fiction writing craft through conference sessions, critique group involvement, online and book study, writing, and plenty of rewriting.

Robert is the founder of Hearts of Compassion Publishing (www.heartspublishing.com), a company devoted to providing readers with quality stories and the comfort of knowing that the proceeds from those stories go to support compassion-based ministries.